COLOR SONG

COLOR SONG

A Daring Tale of Intrigue and Artistic Passion in Glorious 15th Century Venice

Victoria Strauss

SKYSCAPE

SKYSCAPE

Published by Skyscape, New York

www.apub.com

Amazon, the Amazon logo, and Skyscape are trademarks of Amazon.com, Inc., or its affiliates.

ISBN-13 (hardcover): 9781477847787
ISBN-10 (hardcover): 1477847782
ISBN-13 (paperback): 9781477825044
ISBN-10 (paperback): 1477825045

Cover design by Jeanine Henderson

Library of Congress Control Number: 2014907001

Printed in the United States of America

For Ann,
who gave me Bernardo, and so much more.
I miss you, buddy.

Part I

The First Song

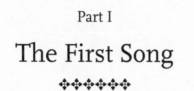

CHAPTER I

❖ Transformation ❖

Painting workshop of Maestra Humilità Moretti
Convent of Santa Marta, Padua, Italy
November, Anno Domini 1487

On the day the colors first sang to her, Giulia woke with a restless sense of anticipation, a breathless certainty that something was about to change—although within the high brick walls of the Convent of Santa Marta, change was rarer than roses in November.

The weather was raw and blustery, the sky thick with clouds. Midway through the morning, Giulia's teacher, master painter Humilità Moretti, set up her easel in the courtyard and summoned Giulia from her duties in the workshop to assist.

From among the pots of paint that crowded the small table at her side, Humilità selected one whose tight-corked throat was sealed with wax. Only a single paint was ever closed this way. Without meaning to, Giulia drew in her breath. Humilità glanced at her, and for a moment their eyes held: an acknowledgment of secrets, of a shared and painful memory.

With a knife, Humilità broke the wax and levered out the cork. The wind snatched the cork as it popped free, whirling it to the ground and tumbling it across the flagstones, the vivid gleam of the paint it had protected flashing as it rolled: the color known as Passion blue—bluer than sapphires, bluer than oceans, the most precious of all the workshop's paints. Giulia chased after it, catching it before it could fall into the drain at the courtyard's center. As she picked it up, she thought she heard the sound of bells.

Returning to Humilità's side, she watched her teacher measure Passion blue onto her palette. It glowed like a sun-struck jewel amid the duller smears of umber and bone black and verdigris, though there was no sun in the clouded sky to make it shine—a mysterious illusion of inner light that no other painter could duplicate, though many had tried. The formula for its making was known to Humilità alone, a secret she had guarded for more than twenty years.

Normally Giulia could lose herself in watching her teacher work, imagining herself into Humilità's hand and Humilità's eyes until it almost seemed it was she who held the brush. But today she was distracted by the malicious wind, the penetrating cold, the restlessness that prickled through her body and made it impossible to stand still. And the bells. She could still hear them, an insistent, chilly chiming that made her feel even colder, for it reminded her of ice, of sunlight shimmering on snow. She'd never heard such a sound at Santa Marta. Where could it be coming from?

At last Humilità set aside her brush and carried her painting indoors, leaving Giulia to clear the worktable. Humilità had taken the pot of Passion blue as well, to lock up in her study; but a residue of the shimmering paint remained on the palette, seeming to draw to itself all the light of the cloudy day. Beneath the hissing of the wind the bells chimed on—fainter now, Giulia thought, as if whoever was ringing them had moved farther away.

In the warmth of the workshop, she returned the paint pots to their places. Still the bells teased at her ears, sounding exactly as they had in the courtyard, and it struck her suddenly that this should not be. Inside, surely, they should be fainter, or clearer—but not the same.

The chiming followed her as she set Humilità's used brushes in a jar of turpentine to soak, then carried the palette over to a table to clean it. Pausing, she closed her eyes, concentrating on the slippery fall of notes. She hadn't realized quite how lovely they were—and, somehow, less like bells than she'd first thought, almost unearthly in their silvery cadences. *They sound like . . .* She groped for comparisons. *A cascade of stars. A rain of crystal.*

She opened her eyes. On the palette, the smear of Passion blue gleamed, as if the candles burning on the table favored it above the other colors. It drew Giulia's gaze like a tether. She let her vision blur, let her eyes fill up with blue, with swirling azure currents and glinting sapphire radiance. The bell-music deepened, reaching into her, resonating inside her head.

It's the paint that's singing. The thought rolled up from indigo depths. *It's the voice of Passion blue.*

Something flashed through Giulia's body, a bolt of cobalt light. The palette snapped back into focus. The blue was just a smear of paint again. But she could still hear the bells, chiming, chiming; and her heart, suddenly, was pounding with dread—at the absurd, no, the *mad* thought that had felt utterly true in the instant it came to her. *True* in a way impossible things should never be.

She snatched up a scraper and dragged it hard across the palette's wooden surface. The soft oil paints came up easily, the colors smearing into mud. Even the jewel essence of Passion blue could not survive such mingling. Again and again she scraped, until the palette was clean.

The bells were silent now. She could hear only the ordinary noise of the artists at their labor. But around her, the familiar landscape of the workshop had grown strange, as if she were looking through someone else's eyes. She was cold, as cold as she'd been in the wind-chilled courtyard.

Am I going mad? She put her hand to her throat, thinking of the talisman she'd worn all summer and then destroyed, of the celestial spirit that had been imprisoned inside it. *Am I being punished for the sin of putting my trust in magic?*

No. They were just bells. Real bells, rung by real hands. I'll never hear them again.

But within herself, she knew differently. And the next morning, when Humilità uncorked the pot of Passion blue and the crystal chiming rose, Giulia understood that something inside her had irrevocably changed. She would never be the same.

Part II

The Bequest

CHAPTER 2

✤ A Secret Revealed ✤

Convent of Santa Marta, Padua, Italy
September, Anno Domini 1488
Ten months later

Giulia paused before Humilità's door, preparing herself. Each time she visited, she found it harder to bear the changes in her teacher, harder to pretend she was not desperately afraid.

She knocked and stepped inside, breathing the chamber's familiar odor—medicine and sickness—imperfectly masked by the herbal infusion simmering on a brazier, a scent she had learned to loathe. As usual, the windows were shuttered and the room was drowned in shadow. The only illumination came from a pair of candles burning on a table by the bed.

Humilità lay propped on pillows, her wasted body hidden under heavy quilts.

"How are you, Maestra?" Giulia knelt by the bed and took the hand Humilità held out to her. The workshop mistress's fingers, once so strong and capable, felt like a collection of twigs.

"Less than I was yesterday." Humilità smiled with a ghost of her old sardonic edge. "More than I will be tomorrow."

She had admitted to her illness in the spring, when she could no longer hide the wasting that was stealing her strength and melting her flesh away like candle wax. There was nothing the infirmarians could do. Through the summer she'd kept working, but toward the end of August she had taken to her bed. She had not left it since.

"Please don't speak like that, Maestra."

"Ah, Giulia. Should I lie to you when you ask me such a question?"

Giulia looked away from the knowledge in her teacher's face. "I've brought my Annunciation to show you."

"In a moment. I have something for you. There's a paper under my pillow. Reach it out for me."

Giulia laid her painting on the floor and obeyed. The workshop mistress unfolded the paper and smoothed it flat. She gazed at it a moment, then offered it back to Giulia.

"This is yours now."

Giulia held the paper near the flickering candles so she could see. It was a paint recipe, written out in Humilità's familiar script. A recipe Giulia had never seen before.

Or . . . wait . . .

She gasped. "Maestra—this is— Is this . . . ?"

"Yes. It is Passion blue."

Giulia felt something terrifying expand inside her chest. "No." She tried to thrust the paper back into Humilità's hands. "I don't want it."

"It's time, Giulia."

"Not yet! It's not time yet!"

"Don't be foolish." Humilità's tone was sharp. "You are stronger than this."

Giulia had never felt less strong. She dropped the paper on the bed and hid her face in her hands, knowing as she did how selfish it was to trouble her teacher with her grief. But the paper and the recipe it held—a secret Humilità had never shared with anyone else, ever—were too much of a shock. Normally she could hold her thoughts away from the inevitability of Humilità's death; but now, all at once, it was a black pit right at her feet.

After a moment she felt Humilità's hand on her head. "Hush," the workshop mistress said. "Calm yourself. I have more to say."

With enormous effort Giulia raised her head, using her sleeves to dry her cheeks.

"This was not an easy decision, Giulia. For more than twenty years I have kept the secret of Passion blue. It has brought me fame, but it has also brought me grief."

Giulia nodded. She knew the grief Humilità meant: her betrayal by her father, Matteo Moretti, also a painter of fame, who had schemed to steal Passion blue for himself.

"I thought perhaps I would let the formula perish with me. But it is beautiful, this thing I created, and beauty should not be allowed to die. So I've chosen to let it live on, with you— with you and you only, Giulia, for you are the most gifted pupil I have ever had, and I know that you will use it well. I cannot make you Maestra after me, as I'd hoped. I cannot give you the workshop. But I can give you Passion blue."

"You honor me, Maestra."

"Be truthful. Don't tell me you did not hope for this."

"Someday," Giulia admitted. "When I became a master painter. Not now. Not like this."

"Now or later, it is God's will."

God's will is cruel. Giulia looked down at the recipe where it lay on the shadowed covers of Humilità's bed—written not in cipher, as she had often seen it in Humilità's leather-bound book of paint formulas, but in words she could read. There was not a painter in Padua who did not covet this formula, even those who would never admit that a woman was capable of painting as magnificently as a man. *How many would give gold to see what I am seeing now?*

"Does Domenica know?" she asked.

"Of course."

"She's not . . . angry?"

"It is not her place to be angry. It is my recipe, and my decision, and she well knows it. But she has accepted with good grace."

I'm not so sure of that. Inwardly, Giulia sighed.

"There is something else, Giulia. I must ask something of you."

"Anything, Maestra."

"It has been more than a year since I've communicated with my father, but I doubt his greed has lessened. He will certainly suspect that I have given you Passion blue, and he may come to you to find out. If he does"—Humilità shifted, turning so she could look into Giulia's eyes—"you must not give it to him."

A chill rolled up Giulia's back. "I never would, Maestra."

"Swear to me." In the past weeks Humilità's gaze had become distant, as if part of her were already gone. But now she was fully present, her dark eyes blazing with all their former force. "Swear on your mother's soul that you will never give him Passion blue."

"I swear it. On my mother's soul, I swear. Maestra . . . do you really think he'll come?"

"He is not one to forget, or to relent." Humilità settled back against her pillows. "Remember, Giulia, he is only a man. He cannot touch you inside these walls. Santa Marta will keep you safe."

Memories unfurled inside Giulia's mind: a dark night, a locked attic, Matteo Moretti's face looming over her like a thundercloud. She bent her head and took up the paper, folding it again into quarters and stowing it in her sleeve.

"Do you ever think of that boy?" Humilità's eyes were closed. "The thief, the one my father hired to steal Passion blue. Ormanno Trovatelli."

For a moment Giulia was too surprised to answer. This was their secret, known only to the two of them, and they never spoke of it. Ormanno's face appeared inside her mind, handsome and sly—a memory that carried a scalding rush of shame, though it had been more than a year since he had beguiled her by pretending that he loved her, then tricked her into telling him the workshop's secrets.

"I try not to, Maestra," she said. "I was such a fool, not to see that all he wanted was to get his hands on Passion blue."

"Don't put him out of your mind completely. Our mistakes shape us. We forget them at our peril." Humilità opened her eyes again. "Show me your Annunciation now."

Giulia bent to undo the canvas that wrapped her painting. Some of the paints were still sticky; faintly, she could hear them singing, dwindling toward silence as they dried. *My own secret,* she thought, wishing with sudden intensity that she could share it with Humilità, as Humilità had just shared Passion blue with her. But who would believe that the paints she made and used sang to her, each with its own voice? Humilità might think her mad, or cursed. She'd never been quite brave enough to speak.

She placed the painting in Humilità's hands and pushed one of the candles closer so Humilità could see. The painting was small, an ashwood panel only two hand spans wide, but even so, Giulia could tell that it was hard for her teacher to hold it.

"I know it needs improvement," she said when Humilità did not speak at once.

"Not so very much," Humilità said. "The folds of the angel's garments hang a little stiffly, do you see? And you've not got the light on the Madonna's face quite right—if your sunlight comes through the window at this angle, your shadows should slant more to the left." She skimmed her finger above the painting's surface, illustrating what she meant. "But overall it is a fine effort. Very fine indeed."

"I'll work on correcting it, Maestra."

"Ah, Giulia." Humilità let the painting fall and reached out both her hands. "How I wish God had allowed me to live long enough to see what you'll become."

Her eyes glittered in the candlelight, and Giulia realized with a shock that they were filled with tears. She had never seen her teacher weep, just as she had never heard her complain about or question or grieve her fate. She took Humilità's hands in her own, resting her forehead on their joined fingers. Her entire body ached with the effort not to cry.

After a moment Humilità pulled gently away.

"I'll rest now. Perhaps you could stop at the infirmary and ask Sapientia to bring me another dose of poppy."

Giulia nodded, for she did not trust herself to speak. She wrapped her painting again, then rose and stood looking down at her teacher. Humilità's hands were folded on her breast, and her eyes were closed. In the shifting candlelight, her face looked like a skull.

A year and a half. Only a year and a half since I came to Santa Marta and she took me as her apprentice. Yet I feel as if I've loved her always.

What will I do when she's gone?

The candle flames fluttered, their light too weak to reach the edges of the room. Giulia felt the loss that crouched in the shadows, an emptiness waiting to devour her.

—

Giulia stopped at the infirmary to relay Humilità's request for poppy. Then, instead of returning to the workshop as she was supposed to, she headed for the little nun's cell where she lived alone, hurrying along as if she were on an important errand and hoping none of the sisters she passed would challenge her. She closed her door and sat on her bed, and carefully pulled the recipe out of her sleeve.

Passion blue. The color that had made Humilità famous, named for the painting of Christ's Passion in which she had first used it. How many times had Giulia seen this formula in Humilità's book of paint recipes—her book of secrets—written out in the incomprehensible cipher Humilità used for the most precious of her colors? How many times had she tried to imagine what special ingredient, what exotic technique, made Passion blue so luminous and alive? And here was the answer.

A list of materials—some expected, some surprising—and a detailed, exacting preparation procedure.

Giulia had not understood, when Humilità had first taken her into the workshop, why a paint recipe should be so valuable. Paint was paint, was it not? Surely it was only a matter of mixing and combining, like making bread or simmering soup. But as Humilità initiated her into the secrets of paint making, Giulia began to realize how difficult it was to create colors that kept their brilliance as they dried, that did not alter or darken under layers of lacquer, that resisted the ravages of cold and heat and damp and time. A single ingredient, a fraction of a measure, was all the difference between a pure color and a corrupted one, a color that endured and one that faded. Color was the painter's language, and Passion blue was a new word in that language, a word of matchless beauty that had not existed before Humilità invented it. A word only Humilità had been able to speak—until now.

It was almost disappointing to see it written out this way, its mysterious essence reduced to black marks on a white page. Yet thrilling too: Humilità's crowning achievement, coveted by so many, and now Giulia's, Giulia's alone. Giulia felt her fingers burning as they did when some face, some scene, some trick of light demanded that she draw or paint it. She imagined following the instructions on this paper, step by careful step. She imagined the paintings on which she'd lavish Passion blue, glowing like stained glass—dozens of paintings. Scores of them. As many as she could make in the lifetime that lay ahead of her.

And I'll hear it singing. I will hear its voice, the first color song I ever heard and the most beautiful, sounding just for me.

For an instant a new world seemed to open at her feet, dazzling. But then she thought of Humilità, skull-like against her pillows, and felt a rush of guilt. How could she take pleasure in the secret when it was hers only because Humilità lay dying? She had the burden of keeping and defending it now too, which Humilità had also passed to her. She thought of Matteo Moretti and shuddered. *Perhaps he's forgotten me. Perhaps she's wrong, and he will not come.*

Oh, how I wish everything could be as it was!

Her throat was full of tears again. She dropped the paper and bowed her face into her hands. At her side, barely audible, the drying paints of her Annunciation sang whisper-harmonies.

At last she straightened. She retrieved the paper and tore away its margins to make it as small as possible, then folded it into a tiny square and stowed it inside the waxed canvas pouch she wore at her neck, concealed beneath her shapeless novice gown. The pouch also held a fragment of her natal horoscope, which she'd carried with her since she was seven years old.

Two secrets, safe against her skin.

She left her cell. In the main hallway she paused, overwhelmed by the desire to return to Humilità, to sit by her in the dimness and hold her hand. Perhaps she'd be sleeping now, with her poppy dose. But perhaps she'd be awake, and Giulia could whisper in her teacher's ear, at last, her own secret of the color song.

Only knowing that Domenica might punish her by forbidding her to visit Humilità at all made it possible to resist. Reluctantly Giulia turned toward the workshop, and the many tasks that waited for her there.

—

Humilità never woke from the poppy she took that afternoon. She lingered for another day and part of another night. Sometime in the dark hours, in the depths of the Great Silence, she died.

And all at once the world was empty, and Giulia was empty too. *I should have gone back,* she thought, curled up on her bed with the covers drawn over her head. *I should have gone back.* In the rawness of her grief, it seemed the worst mistake she had ever made.

CHAPTER 3

❖ The Sin of Pride ❖

Giulia had never wanted to be a nun.

That decision had been made for her when she was seventeen, after her father had died and she became an orphan. Desperate to escape her unchosen fate, she'd paid an astrologer-sorcerer to seal a celestial spirit inside a talisman, bound to her heart's desire: true love, as she believed then, a man to save her from the convent. The spirit's name was Anasurymboriel, and though the sorcerer swore he'd summoned it from the realms of angels, Giulia knew such magic was a sin. Faced with a barren lifetime as a nun, she hadn't cared.

But magic did not announce itself, or come neatly labeled. She'd mistaken fair-haired, charming Ormanno Trovatelli for Anasurymboriel's gift. By the time she realized her mistake, he had gotten what he really wanted: Humilità's book of secrets, and with it, the formula for Passion blue.

Giulia had taken back the book. She'd returned it to Humilità and confessed everything. She was punished for her transgressions: burdened with penances, condemned to live apart from the other novices so she would not infect them with her dishonesty. But for the sake of her talent, she was allowed to remain in the workshop—and by then she had wanted to stay. For she understood at last that painting was her true heart's desire. She'd chosen to embrace it, even though it meant she must become a nun.

She had destroyed the talisman, releasing Anasurymboriel back to the heavens from which the little spirit had briefly been drawn down. She'd been glad to see it go. *No more magic,* she promised herself. She was finished with such remedies, with their tricks and their traps and their risk to her immortal soul.

But magic was not finished with her. When Anasurymboriel departed, it left her changed. At least she thought it must have—for how else could she explain why she'd suddenly become able to hear the colors singing?

—

The workshop reopened the day after Humilità's funeral.

Arriving, Giulia paused before the open doors. The whole world had changed—how could it be that the great chamber looked the same as always, with its vaulted ceiling and red-tiled floor and orderly work areas, and smelled the same as always too, of oil and charcoal smoke and chalk dust and exotic materials? For the first time since she had become Humilità's apprentice, Giulia wanted to turn away, to flee from this place that would never again be filled with Humilità's voice and her genius and the force of her brilliant, restless personality. It took all the will she had to cross the threshold.

Domenica had come in first, as always. She had already tied back the curtains that were drawn at night across the workshop's open north side and brought her easel over to the light. Now she was laying out her palette and brushes with her usual tight efficiency.

"Good morning, Maestra," Giulia said.

Domenica raised her head and fixed Giulia with a raking stare, then returned to her work without replying.

Sighing, Giulia went to tie on her apron. Unlike the other painters, Domenica had never forgiven her for her part in the theft of Passion blue. Domenica had kept her animosity more or less in check while Humilità was well, but once Humilità had left the workshop and Domenica became Maestra in all but name, she'd ceased troubling to hide it. Giulia had never told Humilità about the sharp criticism, the undeserved reprimands, the efforts to deny her any personal drawing or painting time. She wished now that she had not been so reticent.

This is how it's going to be from now on. A grinding depression filled her. *Or perhaps it will get worse.*

She fetched charcoal and lit the braziers as the other painters arrived: kind Perpetua, whom Humilità had promoted from journeyman to master just before she became ill; pretty Angela, formerly an apprentice and now a journeyman, who'd become Giulia's fast friend; lovely, flighty Lucida, one of the wealthiest nuns at Santa Marta and a talented miniaturist. Elderly Benedicta, the workshop's third master painter, was absent. She'd become frail over the past months and often was unable to work.

When they were all gathered, Domenica gave a speech, acknowledging her now-permanent position as the workshop's leader and praising Humilità. She stood stiffly at the center of the room, her hands hidden in her sleeves, her face showing no expression. She might have been speaking about a stranger.

It was a long, grim day. Humilità's absence haunted the workshop like an echo. The painters worked in silence—Perpetua at the drafting table; Angela at her easel; even Lucida, who normally delighted in defying Domenica's prohibition of unnecessary conversation—one of the many new rules Domenica had imposed since she took over the running of the workshop. Giulia prepared paints, welcoming their familiar songs, which distracted her at least a little from her sadness.

She'd learned a great deal since that blustery November morning when Passion blue first sang to her. Raw materials had no voice; it was only in the final stages of the preparation process—after she'd soaked or boiled or crushed them, after she'd strained them and dried them and ground them to fine powder on a marble slab—that their songs began to swell, rising as she added water and oil and other substances to bind them into paint.

There was not a color now that she could not hear. Black, compounded from charred animal bones, thrummed like a drum. Vermilion, derived from the mineral cinnabar, sizzled. Crimson lake, extracted from red-dyed silk, warbled like a flute. The various ochres rasped and hummed, as arid as the earth they were dug from. She could judge the quality of the paints she made by ear now, even better than she could by eye. She'd begun to experiment with pigment combinations and paint layering in her practice paintings, creating harmonies and counterpoints, achieving color effects that impressed even Benedicta, the workshop's acknowledged master of color lore.

The songs' peak was brief. Almost as soon as the paints were mixed, their voices began to dwindle, sinking toward silence as they dried. Giulia knew of only one color that retained a ghost of its former music: Passion blue, whose icy chime breathed almost imperceptibly from paintings years or decades old, as faint as a forgotten dream.

It was a long time since she had feared the voices of the colors. A long time since she had prayed each night to God to take the songs away. For they were beautiful, and their beauty called irresistibly to her artist's soul. Even when she'd been most afraid, she had felt that seductive pull.

There were days when she wondered whether she was sinning by surrendering to the songs, by embracing them in her art—whether the singing of the paints was the stain that magic had imprinted on her soul, ground into her substance like the charcoal dust that blackened her fingers. But there were other days when the songs pierced her to the heart, and her whole being soared with the wonder of perceiving this hidden truth about the world. On those days, the color song felt like a gift. On those days she could not believe that something so beautiful could come from any hand but that of God.

What had changed her so? Anasurymboriel. She could think of no other explanation. The spirit must have left something inside her when she set it free, altered her in some inexplicable way. Or perhaps it had taken something with it, removed some barrier or inhibition to expose what had been there all along.

She could not guess whether the change was permanent, or whether it would someday vanish as suddenly as it had arrived. But the color songs were part of her now, wound as deep into the substance of her being as the roots of the cypresses in the soil of Santa Marta's gardens. Sin or not, she knew that if they left her, she would bitterly mourn their passing.

—

Vespers arrived at last, and with it the end of work. The nuns departed, leaving Giulia to clean up.

She was the workshop's only apprentice now. Humilità had promoted Angela from apprentice to journeyman a year ago, but she had not been able to find a replacement to suit her; and to spare Giulia, she had given all the painters a share of apprentice tasks: the preparation of paints and other materials, the constant cleaning. Once Humilità became ill, Domenica gave those responsibilities back to Giulia. Angela still helped where she could, but Giulia often had to labor far into the evening to get everything done, sometimes leaving tasks uncompleted so she could return to her cell before Compline, when Suor Margarita, the novice mistress, came to lock her in.

This night she finished early. She was blowing out the candles when she heard footsteps. She turned, expecting Angela—but it was Domenica.

"I am glad you are still here," Domenica said, in a tone that suggested the opposite. "I wish to speak with you. Come to my office, and bring a candle."

Giulia obeyed. She felt dread, but no surprise. She'd known this confrontation was coming.

Three days ago, Humilità's possessions had crowded the office: books, painting tools, the chunks of quartz and amethyst she'd used as paperweights, sketches nailed to the walls. Now Giulia saw that they had all been removed. The chests that contained the workshop's papers and accounting ledgers had been rearranged. Only the locked cabinet that held Humilità's book of secrets remained in its old place.

Giulia set down the candle on the newly bare surface of Humilità's desk, waiting as Domenica seated herself in Humilità's chair and folded her hands before her. Domenica's face, gaunt with constant fasting, was as pale as paper within the severe frame of her wimple and veil. The air in the little room was perceptibly chillier than in the workshop, for there was no brazier. Domenica, who strove never to take pleasure in the comforts of the body, preferred to endure the cold.

"Before she died," Domenica said, "Humilità informed me that she intended to give you Passion blue."

"Yes, Maestra."

"You have the recipe, then?"

"I do, Maestra."

The corners of Domenica's mouth turned down. "You should know that I consider her actions highly inappropriate. Her mind was unclear, especially at the end. I believe her judgment was impaired."

"I saw her the day before she died." Giulia had to struggle to keep her tone respectful. "She was as much herself as ever."

"Of course you would say so. Especially if it was your idea."

"*My* idea?"

"You may have fooled Humilità and the others, Giulia Borromeo, but you have never fooled me." Domenica fixed Giulia with a flat, unblinking stare. "I know what you are capable of. You showed your true face last year when you whored yourself to that thief, Ormanno Trovatelli, and helped him steal our precious book of formulas. I think you saw your chance to steal from us a second time by whispering lies into the ears of a dying woman."

Giulia was too stunned to speak. She knew very well that Domenica detested her. She'd been certain Domenica must be angry at Humilità's decision to bequeath her Passion blue, no matter what Humilità believed. But she'd never imagined anything like this.

"So," Domenica said. "You don't deny it."

"I do deny it." Giulia's tongue felt stiff. "She gave it to me of her own free will. I didn't ask for it. I didn't even want it."

"Then you should have no trouble surrendering it."

"Surrendering it?"

"To me and to the workshop, where it should have gone to start with. A workshop is not simply a collection of individual painters. It is a body, with all its limbs connected, no part of it divided from or superior to another. Humilità did not understand that. She separated herself from the rest of us. She raised herself above us, not least by keeping secret what should have been shared with us all."

"But she *did* share with us all! Passion blue is part of all our paintings!"

"That was not *sharing*. That was *husbanding*. Only she could read the cipher, only she could mix the paint or use it. She made sure that it was *she* who became famous, *she* who was acclaimed. She forgot that it is not our own names we glorify by the work we do, but *God's* name. Even in her illness she would not renounce her pride—do you know she tore the recipe out of the book and took it with her to her sickbed, so the secret would not pass out of her hands? And then, knowing herself to be dying, did she bequeath this precious thing to the workshop, whose reputation it sustains? No. She bestowed it upon *you*, her protégé, her pet. A mere apprentice. A girl of proven cunning and dishonesty."

There was a moment of echoing silence. Slowly Domenica relaxed her hands, which had tightened into fists.

"It is in you too," she said quietly. "The sin of pride. It is no wonder Humilità took you for her own, for you are like her. But you must humble yourself or there is no place for you here."

The chilly office suddenly seemed to have acquired a deeper cold. "What are you saying?"

"Give the recipe for Passion blue to me. And since I have no doubt you have already memorized it, you are henceforth forbidden from mixing it or using it, except at my express instruction."

"But—the Maestra wanted me to have it! It was her wish!"

"*I* am your maestra now. I have given you a command. If you do not heed it, I shall have no choice but to dismiss you from your apprenticeship."

All the air seemed to have left the room. "But you can't do that," Giulia said faintly.

Rage flared behind Domenica's rigid face. "*What* did you just say to me?"

"Maestra—I'm sorry—but you know—you know what Maestra Humilità wished for me—for my training and my future—"

Domenica brought both her open palms down hard on the surface of the desk. *"Humilità is no longer here!"*

It shocked them both to stillness for a moment. Then, deliberately, Domenica sat back, clasping her hands before her once again.

"I have made myself clear. You take your final vows in a little less than three weeks. You have until then to follow my command. That is all. You may go."

Numb, on legs that did not feel like her own, Giulia turned to obey. Nearly to the door, Domenica's harsh voice reached after her.

"She believed your gift was God-given. But I know that gifts can come from other sources, and that some have no purpose but to corrupt and to deceive. She should never have let you back into the workshop."

Deep emotion heaved beneath the words, like a fire raging under a stone. Giulia did not pause. But even after she was safe inside her cell, she could feel the heat of Domenica's hatred, and hear the poison of her condemnation.

CHAPTER 4

✣ Matteo Moretti ✣

The next morning, Giulia woke dreading the day ahead. As she put on her clothes and tidied her bed, she felt the tiny weight of the little pouch around her neck: the weight of secrets.

She'd sworn never to give Passion blue to Humilità's father. But Humilità had not forbidden her to give it to others. She was not bound to hold the secret for herself alone as Humilità had done—she could share it, if she chose.

But that's the key: choice. The Maestra gave it to me. Not to Domenica, not to Perpetua or Lucida or Angela or Benedicta— to me. If I pass it on, that should be my decision.

It might have been different if Domenica had simply asked. Instead, she had commanded—and not simply that Giulia share the secret of Passion blue, but that she *renounce all use of it.* If she gave the formula to Domenica, she would never see Passion blue take shape beneath her own hands, its voice rising from the grinding stone. She would never learn what it was like to take it on her brush and lay it on a panel. She would never hear it singing—except perhaps at a distance, when Domenica used it.

It was intolerable. What right had Domenica to make such demands? To impose such ultimatums? And the way she'd spoken of Humilità . . . As inflexible as Domenica was, as self-righteous and intolerant, she'd never shown anything but respect for Humilità, or deference to Humilità's orders. Obviously, this had been pretense—and a skillful one, for she'd completely concealed her judgment until Humilità was gone and she needed to conceal it no longer.

If so much guile and bitterness could hide behind Domenica's controlled façade, could greed be hidden there as well? Domenica already had the gift she wanted most: She was Maestra now, which she would never have become had Humilità lived. But perhaps that was not enough for her. She'd claimed she wanted Passion blue for the sake of the workshop—but she would not be the first artist to covet the radiant color for herself. Or to act on that desire.

If that's so, she's no better than a thief. As Ormanno was a thief. As the Maestra's own father is a thief.

Would she really do it? Would she really dismiss me from the workshop?

Even to think it made Giulia feel ill. She could not remember a time when she hadn't drawn. It was not something she'd been shown or taught, simply something she knew how to do, as instinctive as breathing. Yet until she came to Santa Marta, she had never thought of her sketching as anything but a private passion. The world was ruled by men. Women could become wives or nuns or servants or whores—but only a man could become a painter.

Humilità had shown her a different truth. Convent walls were prison walls, but they enclosed a paradoxical freedom, for within them women must necessarily do all the things men did in the world outside. In Humilità's workshop of painter nuns, the only one of its kind in all the world, Giulia had given herself to the fire that burned in her, opened herself to it and let it consume her utterly.

She *was* that fire now. Painting was her heart, her soul. If it were taken away, there would be nothing left but ash.

—

Domenica ignored Giulia for the first part of the morning. But near noon, as Giulia was measuring a batch of yellow ochre into the little clay pots in which paints were stored, she stalked over to the grinding table and stood watching. In her nervousness Giulia lost her grip on one of the pots, which fell to the floor and smashed.

"Clumsy girl," Domenica said in a voice of ice.

"I'm sorry, Maestra." Giulia kept her eyes lowered. "I'll clean it up at once."

"I can see from what's on the slab that you've not ground the mixture nearly fine enough. Discard what you've prepared and begin again."

"Discard it?" To Giulia's spirit-altered senses, the rasping song of the ochre sounded just as it should, with not the slightest off-note of impurity. "*All* of it?"

"I despair of your future, Giulia, if you cannot comprehend simple verbal instructions. Let me know when you are finished."

Domenica turned away. The other painters, who had been watching, quickly went back to work. Giulia began to clean the grinding slab, anger burning dully behind her breastbone. *I'm sorry,* she told the ochre silently as she scraped it out of its pots and dumped it in the discard bucket, where the muddle of paint already there swallowed up its gentle voice. *I'm sorry.*

The new batch of ochre passed muster. But the brushes Giulia cleaned that afternoon did not; and when she snatched a few free moments to take her drawing board into the court-yard, Domenica called her away almost at once, instructing her to dust the containers on the already dust-free supply shelves.

"What did you do to annoy her so?" Angela asked that evening after Vespers, when she returned to help Giulia finish the day's work.

"What do I ever do?" Normally Giulia shared every-thing with Angela, but she had not yet told her friend about Humilità's bequest. "I feel more like a servant than an apprentice."

"Well, it's a bad time." Angela pulled a worn-out bedsheet from the pile that Giulia was tearing up for rags. "None of us is ourself."

"Perhaps she's free to be herself at last," Giulia said bitterly. "Now that the Maestra's not here."

"Think how difficult it must be for her, Giulia. She must prove that the workshop is still worthy of patronage under her leadership, but she'll never be Maestra Humilità's equal, and everyone knows it. It's no coincidence that we haven't had any major commissions in the past few months."

"You always think the best of people, Angela, even when they don't deserve it."

Angela sighed. "Well, in three weeks you'll be a vowed nun. That will make a difference. Oh, Giulia." She clasped her hands, her brown eyes shining. "I can't wait for your ceremony! We'll truly be sisters then."

Giulia tore another strip of linen. She'd thought she had put away her doubts about becoming a nun a year ago, when she brought Humilità's book of secrets back to Santa Marta. But Humilità was well then, and Giulia's path had seemed clear, a smooth transition from apprentice to journeyman to master painter, eventually even to Maestra. Now the path that had seemed so wide and welcoming had darkened and turned in on itself. Giulia could no longer see with any certainty what lay ahead—except her final vows, each day a little closer. Each day a little more inevitable.

"You're nervous," Angela said, perceptive as always. "Don't worry; it's natural. All I ever wanted was to vow my life to God, but on the day of my ceremony I could do nothing but weep. Then I put on my wedding dress and crown, and it was as if the Savior himself reached down from heaven and took my hand. All my doubts fell away. The ceremony, the feast . . . it was the most wonderful day of my life. It'll be the same for you—you'll see."

Giulia nodded, but only because Angela expected it. There would be no wedding dress or feast for her as there were for nuns of noble birth. Her father had been noble, but her mother was a commoner; and in Santa Marta, as in the outside world, her common blood was what defined her. Her vows would be made in Madre Magdalena's office, in the presence of the abbess and a witness. She would put on her nun's habit and veil, and go back to work.

She felt a surge of dread. Even before Humilità's death, the thought of her final vows had started to make her breathless. Now it was like a hand closing around her heart.

"Giulia." Angela put down the knife she was using to nick the sheets to make them easier to tear. "We've been wondering. Well, Lucida and Perpetua and I have been wondering. Did the Maestra say anything to you about Passion blue before she died?"

"No." The lie was out before Giulia knew she meant to tell it.

"It's just that Domenica . . . Maestra Domenica . . . hasn't mentioned it. And you were closest to Maestra Humilità of all of us." Angela's brows drew together in a frown. "Surely she would have wanted to pass it on."

"I think I have enough here." Giulia gathered up the rags she'd made. "I'll just put them away."

She took the rags to the rag basket, then got a broom and began to sweep. It had seemed easier to lie than to explain, but already she regretted it. Too late, though, to take it back.

—

In the middle of the next morning, one of the novices came looking for Giulia.

"You've a visitor waiting for you in the parlor."

Giulia felt all the blood drain from her face. *The Maestra's father. It has to be.*

"It's a mistake," she said through dry lips. "I know no one in Padua. Tell whoever it is to go away."

"Nonsense," Domenica said from across the room. "I will not tolerate discourtesy in my workshop—you will go, Giulia. At once."

I should have seemed eager, Giulia thought miserably, untying her apron. *Then she would have forbidden me to stop working.*

She was dizzy as she left the workshop, her heart racing as if she were running instead of walking as slowly as she could, putting off the moment when she must see him. She knew it had been foolish to hope he had forgotten her; but she'd allowed herself to hope anyway, and now she felt that she might faint with dread.

The visitors' parlor was a huge chamber, with whitewashed walls and a flagstone floor. An iron grille ran down its center, dividing it in half. On the far side, a door stood open to the street, admitting the brightness of the sunny September morning. Here, in one of the few locations where the outside world was allowed to touch the sacred precincts of the convent, nuns and their visitors could exchange news, share food and drink, even clasp hands—though always with the grille between them, so they would never forget that they inhabited separate worlds.

He stood beyond the grille, among the other visitors: Matteo Moretti, famed painter, chief of the Paduan artists' guild, man of wealth and influence. Betrayer and thief: Humilità's father.

Giulia froze. With every part of herself, she wanted to turn and flee. But Matteo's eyes had already found her. She knew that if she ran away, he would only come again.

She forced herself to approach, halting a safe distance from the grille. It was impossible to breach those iron bars. Even so, she did not want to be within his reach.

"So." He looked her up and down, with his dark eyes that were so much like Humilità's. She remembered him as a huge man, but he seemed even bigger now, as tall and broad as a bear in his velvet mantle and tunic of rich brocade. A cap trimmed with feathers rested on his mane of gray curls. "Here you are, the girl who stole my daughter from me."

"*I?*"

"Except for you, she would never have known the truth. But you told her everything, did you not?"

"Yes, I told her." Anger at his hypocrisy overcame Giulia's fear. "I told her how you paid Ormanno Trovatelli to beguile me and steal her book of secrets. I told her how he abducted me when I discovered his intent and brought me with him when he went to you to collect his pay. I told her how you imprisoned me in your attic when you saw the formula for Passion blue was ciphered, even though I swore I didn't know the key."

"And how you managed to escape? And stole the book from under my very hand as I lay sleeping?"

"*Rescued* it," Giulia said. "She would have guessed. Whether I told her or not, she would have guessed it all."

"Say you so?" The words were icy cold. "Well, it hardly matters now, for she is dead. Do you know how many letters I've sent over the past year? How many times I tried to see her, only to be turned away? Even on her deathbed, *even then*, she would not relent. My only sight of her the whole of this long year past was in her coffin."

Giulia was silent.

"Tell me, since I have no choice but to ask what a father should know of his own experience. Did she have a gentle death?"

"No," Giulia said, wanting to be cruel. "She suffered."

His jaw clenched. He turned away, fixing his eyes on the family group nearby, laughing and chatting through the grille with the elderly nun they had come to visit. Giulia remembered, suddenly, glimpsing him at Humilità's funeral, surrounded by his sons and their wives and children. She'd thought she had seen tears on his cheeks.

"Perhaps you think I did not love my daughter." His voice was quiet. "In fact, I loved her dearly, more dearly than I love my sons—yes, I will admit it, for of all my children, she was most like me. Another man might have let her talent go to waste. But I trained her like a boy, like one of my own apprentices. And then, so she might follow her gift, I arranged for her to be taken into Santa Marta, where she could give her life to painting as no worldly woman ever could."

He turned toward Giulia again, a sudden motion that startled her, and took hold of the grille. She could see the paint under his nails, the charcoal stains on his fingers.

"I gave her everything. *Everything.* All she was and all she became, she owed to me. Yet when I asked for Passion blue, she denied me. Again and again I asked, but always she refused. Was that the duty a daughter owes her father? To refuse the one thing I asked of her after all I'd done, a thing that would not even exist had I not opened the way for her to discover it? She left me no choice but to take matters into my own hands. Yet through it all I loved her, as any parent loves his disobedient child. Had she lived, we would have reconciled. Now . . . now we will never forgive each other, she and I."

His hands tightened on the bars, the knuckles whitening, as if he wanted to wrench the grille apart. In that gesture, even more than in his words, Giulia saw to the heart of the conflict between father and daughter: not just his greed for the fabulous color Humilità had invented, not just Humilità's stubborn determination to keep her creation for herself, but his desire to rule her, her proud refusal to be ruled, Passion blue both the object and the symbol of their battle.

"But I did not come to speak of this." Matteo released the grille and stepped back, rubbing his palms together. "I have another matter in mind. I think you know what that is."

Giulia's heart had begun to race. "No," she said.

"Come now. Let's not pretend we do not understand each other. Did my daughter pass Passion blue to you before she died?"

"No." Giulia could not hold his gaze. She could feel the secret inside herself, and was terrified he would somehow perceive it. "She didn't."

"Ah, but you see, I find that difficult to believe. You were her protégée. The one she hoped would succeed her. To whom else would she have given it?"

"Perhaps she gave it to no one."

"My daughter was endowed with a full measure of womanly caprice, yet not so much, I think, that she would have taken Passion blue with her into death. No." He shook his head. "She would have wanted it to live after her—for the sake of her pride, if nothing else. She passed it on, and you are the one she gave it to. Deny it as you wish; I know I am correct by the way you cannot look at me."

Giulia forced herself to raise her face to his. It was like walking against the wind. His eyes, unblinking beneath heavy brows, seemed to scour the inside of her skull. Was this what Humilità had confronted each time he demanded the secret? But Humilità had been like him. She would have found it easier to resist.

"Truly, you are mistaken." Giulia cursed herself for the quaver in her voice; but she was afraid of him, and she could not hide so many things at once. "She never gave me the secret. She never even spoke of it."

"That is your answer?"

"I can give you no other."

He knew she was lying. She could see it in his face. She felt a terrible despair. He'd come here suspecting she had Passion blue, but he hadn't known for sure. Now he did know. She'd kept the secret, but even so, she had failed Humilità's trust.

"Very well," he said. "But we are not finished, you and I. Think on the answer you have given me today." He aimed a paint-marked finger at her throat. "I will come and ask again."

"I won't see you. I'll talk to the novice mistress. I'll remind her that you are no kin of mine, and it isn't proper for you to visit me."

She sounded weak and foolish, like a child. He regarded her a moment, almost with amusement. Then, without haste, he turned and strolled toward the door, darkening it briefly as he passed into the white light of the sun.

CHAPTER 5

❖ Letters From Venice ❖

He cannot touch you inside these walls. Santa Marta will keep you safe.

Giulia clung to Humilità's words for the rest of the day. But sleep swept all assurances away, and she dreamed of the attic where Matteo had imprisoned her, pitch-dark and alive with menace. She woke with her blanket tangled around her legs and her pillow across her face, suffocating with dread.

The next evening when Suor Margarita came to lock Giulia in her cell, she brought with her a cloth-wrapped package. "For you," she said brusquely, thrusting it into Giulia's hands. "A bequest from Maestra Humilità."

Another bequest? Unwrapping the cloth, Giulia found Humilità's manuscript copy of Leon Battista Alberti's *Delle Pittura*, a text on painting that Humilità had especially treasured, and a bundle of brushes with rosewood handles: Humilità's own. She held them a moment, stroking the silky wood, then set them aside and picked up the last item, a fat packet of letters tied with cord. Accompanying these was a note in Humilità's sickness-weakened hand:

> *Giulia:*
>
> *I leave you my letters from my dear friend Gianfranco Ferraldi of Venice, which extend over most of the years I have been at Santa Marta. He is a painter of intelligence and worth, and it is my wish that you should write to him in your turn, not only to continue the friendship that he and I have maintained for so long, but to keep cognizant of the world that exists beyond our walls. A mind grows narrow if it cannot reach beyond itself, and art grows stale if it is not refreshed by new ideas. He may be a mentor to you, my dear Giulia, even if only from afar.*
>
> *Your devoted teacher,*
> *Humilità*

Giulia's eyes filled with tears. When had Humilità written this? Perhaps she had guessed, at least a little, about Domenica.

Giulia pulled her candle closer and began to read. She knew about Humilità's friendship with Ferraldi, for he had sometimes sent prepared pigments from Venice, where the finest painting materials in the world were sold. He'd been an apprentice in Matteo Moretti's workshop while Humilità was training there but had left soon after Humilità entered Santa Marta.

Now she learned of his dissatisfaction with Matteo's autocratic leadership, of his decision to seek his fortune in Venice, of his struggle to establish his own workshop and his eventual success. The letters were full of technical details—discussions of his work, responses to Humilità's descriptions of her own—but there were also many lively accounts of people and happenings, with deft, quick sketches to illustrate the stories.

Ferraldi's affection and respect for Humilità shone clearly through this one-sided conversation. Giulia could find no trace of condescension in his writing; he addressed Humilità not as a nun and a woman but as a fellow painter, as an equal. And possibly, Giulia thought, as something more.

In the final letters Giulia found her own name. It gave her a little shock to see it, in a letter received soon after Humilità took her into the workshop: just a brief reference, Ferraldi congratulating Humilità on finding a talented apprentice. She read the subsequent letters with apprehension—would there be mention of the theft of Passion blue and her part in it? But though Ferraldi responded several times to Humilità's reports on Giulia's progress as a pupil, there was nothing at all about Matteo Moretti's plot. It seemed Humilità had kept that secret even from her oldest friend.

The last letter was dated two months before Humilità's death.

As for your extraordinary apprentice, Giulia, I am glad to learn that she continues to blossom. I cannot tell you how it delights me to know that you have found a pupil whose ability is worthy of your own—no easy feat within the walls of a convent, where you do not have the luxury of choice, as we artists do in the world outside. It is my earnest wish that she will fulfill all your ambitions for her. I hope to see her work when I visit Padua next spring. By then, God willing, you will be in good health once more.

It seemed Humilità had not told him the truth about her illness either.

Giulia let the letter fall into her lap. She felt closer to Humilità than she had since her teacher's death, as if Humilità herself had spoken through the words of this man Giulia had never met. The evidence of her teacher's faith in her was both joy and pain. For in the new world of Domenica's workshop, she was no longer certain she could fulfill it.

At last she wiped her eyes and placed the final letter with the others, and tied the bundle up again in its cord. She'd write soon to let Ferraldi know of Humilità's death. It would be a sad introduction, but perhaps they could indeed become friends, as Humilità had wanted. It would be a small spark of hope to light the days ahead.

—

Giulia was not surprised when, a week after Humilità's funeral, Domenica confronted her again.

"Have you considered our discussion?" As before, Domenica had waited until after Vespers, when Giulia was alone. She stood in the workshop's doorway, her white habit and black veil falling in perfect, sculpted folds. "Are you ready yet to do your duty?"

Giulia clutched the broom she was holding. "You said I had until my final vows."

"So I did." Domenica turned to go. "You would be well-advised not to delay so long."

Giulia began sweeping again, scraping the broom across the tiles, her anger burning hotter and hotter as she thought of Domenica's ultimatum and the petty persecutions of the past days. Yet what choice did she have? If she didn't obey, Domenica would take everything away.

What if I give her Passion blue and she dismisses me anyway? It struck her like a blow. She stood frozen, broom in hand. *No. She wouldn't be so faithless.*

But then she thought of how skillfully Domenica had concealed her resentment of Humilità. Of how she'd pretended to bow to Humilità's wishes, including the bequest of Passion blue. Of the hard, flat stare she'd turned on Giulia that night in Humilità's office, and the hatred in her final words: *She should never have let you back into the workshop . . .*

Nausea surged into Giulia's throat. She dropped the broom and fled the workshop, ignoring the nuns' disapproving stares as she ran through the hallways. Reaching her cell, she fell onto her bed, curling up on her side, taking deep breaths to calm her thudding heart and roiling stomach.

After a little while she felt better. She sat up, realizing that she was still wearing her apron, which in her haste she'd forgotten to remove. She took it off, then carried her stool over to the cell's high window and climbed up onto it. Resting her elbows on the sill, she gazed at the sky, seeking reassurance, as she'd done most of her life, in the ancient, unchanging beauty of the stars. Orion was rising, the three stars of his belt rolling up above the roofs of the convent. Taurus hung just above him.

She'd learned the constellations from Maestro Carlo Bruni, her father's astrologer, with whom she'd forged a secret friendship after her mother died—he a lonely man held in small regard by his employer, she a bereft child suspended between worlds: neither commoner nor noble but something awkward in between. Maestro Bruni had taught her how to read and write. He'd given her used paper to scrape clean for drawing.

He'd told her the names of stars; and though he'd never shared his own art of astrology, she had absorbed some of his knowledge from the copying she'd done for him.

On impulse she pulled the little pouch at her neck from beneath her gown and teased it open. Reaching past the recipe for Passion blue, she drew out the other paper inside and unrolled it on the windowsill, using the very tips of her fingers, for it was as old as she was and brittle with the years. She hadn't looked at it in a long time—not since just after she'd brought Humilità's book of secrets back to Santa Marta. The starlight was too dim to make out the writing on it, but that did not matter, for she knew it by heart:

> . . . *major affliction by Saturn, and the Moon and Sun in barren signs, there is thus no testimony of marriage, or of children. She shall not take a husband's name, nor shall she bear her own at the end of life, but shall . . .*

The words were part of her natal horoscope, commissioned for her by her mother just after she was born: a prediction of the entire course of her life, written in the stars by the hand of God at the moment of her birth. It was one of the few gifts her mother had ever been able to give her, intended to protect her against misfortune by warning her of what was to come. But her bullying foster brother, Piero, had destroyed it soon after her mother died. This fragment was all Giulia had managed to save.

She hadn't learned to read until long after the horoscope was gone. She'd never known the horoscope's full prediction— just this small part of it. The lonely life the broken sentences seemed to promise terrified her. Never to have the love of a man . . . never to bear children . . . to lose even her name. What could it mean but that she would live and die alone, like a beggar in the street?

Yet from Maestro Bruni, who had taught her so much, she had learned that the stars could be defied, through God's own gift of free will. With determination, she might be able to change her fate, find a way to seize for herself the love and comfort her stars wanted to deny her.

For most of her life she had been fighting to do just that. When her father died and she was sent to Santa Marta, she was certain the stars had won, for to become a nun was surely the most perfect possible fulfillment of the fragment's desolate promise. Purchasing the talisman, with the little spirit Anasurymboriel sealed inside it, had been a final, desperate effort to escape. But then Humilità had taken her into the workshop. And in that extraordinary place she had seen the possibility of a future that turned the horoscope's prediction on its head: a life without the love of a man, yet not without passion. A life without children, yet not without creation. A life without her true name—yet the religious name she would receive when she took her final vows would live on through her art.

If Domenica banished her from the workshop, the prediction would turn again. She'd be face-to-face once more with the destiny she feared. Her final vows would seal her to it forever: to the loveless, barren, nameless life of an ordinary nun, who would never hold a brush again.

Oh, Maestra. How could you not know that this would happen? Anger turned in Giulia, bitter and unreasonable. *Why did you never see Domenica for what she is?*

"I wish . . ." she whispered, then stopped. *I wish you'd never given me Passion blue.* But in spite of everything, that was not true.

She thought of Gianfranco Ferraldi and his workshop in Venice. How easy it would be if she were a boy. She could pack up her brushes and her sketches, make her way to Venice, and apprentice herself to Ferraldi—and if he wouldn't have her, she could search out another artist, and another, until she found someone who would agree to take her on.

Of course, if I were a boy, I wouldn't be in this situation. I'd have apprenticed myself to a master long ago. I might even be a journeyman by now.

A journeyman.

A boy.

A mad idea unfolded in Giulia's mind, a flash of inspiration like a star exploding in the night. For an instant she stood dazzled. For an instant it made perfect sense.

Then she remembered who and where she was.

"Don't be ridiculous," she whispered to herself.

She shivered. The September nights were growing chilly. She rerolled the delicate horoscope fragment and concealed it in the pouch again. Then she lit her candle and knelt before the crucifix on the wall.

"Almighty God," she whispered, "I'm a sinner, I know. Almost all my life I've fought the destiny You wrote for me in the stars on the night of my birth. When I broke the talisman last year, when I committed myself to the workshop and to painting, I swore I would stop fighting and accept my fate as it came to me. I want to keep my promise. But please don't let painting be taken away from me. You gave me my talent. You gave me this fire inside me. Please let me use it."

She felt the hollowness of the words even as they left her lips. For it wasn't in her simply to accept. She had to fight. She would always have to fight.

CHAPTER 6

❖ Words Set Free ❖

At night in her cold cell, Giulia lit her candle and reread Ferraldi's letters. She wanted to know him before she wrote to him, so she could compose a letter intelligent enough to make him want to write her back.

She pored over his discussions of technique. She memorized the layout of his workshop, of which he'd provided many sketches. She tried to build an image of the great city of Venice from his drawings and descriptions: an impossibly exotic place where the streets were made of water, where magnificent palazzi and richly furnished churches spoke of centuries of wealth and power, where the Piazza San Marco, home to the vast golden-domed Basilica, was as big as an entire village and one might, walking across it, hear a dozen different languages spoken at once. Where sometimes the *acqua alta,* the high tide, swamped the streets and the squares and the ground floors of the palazzi so that the city seemed to rest not on hundreds of wooden pilings driven deep into the mud of the lagoon, but on the surface of the ocean, raised not by man but by magic.

Now and then as she read, her mad idea would stir, nudging like an insistent finger. It was just a fantasy, and fantasies were useless. But it was a relief sometimes to escape into dreams of what could never be.

At the end of another seven days, Domenica cornered her again, reminding her that only a week remained until her final vows. *I can surrender*, Giulia thought, staring at the floor so she would not have to meet Domenica's angry glare. *Right now, I can give her what she wants.* But her mouth refused to open.

That evening she returned to her cell to find it had been searched. The bed had been dragged out from the wall, the mattress and pillow slit and their stuffing pulled out onto the floor. For a long moment she stood in the doorway, too shocked to move. Then she remembered the bundle with Humilità's bequests, which she'd kept under the bed, and forced herself to go in. She found the bundle beneath a tangle of bedclothes. It had been opened. The Alberti manuscript was still inside, and Humilità's rosewood brushes. But Ferraldi's letters were gone.

Giulia didn't know how long she knelt there. Her knees were numb by the time she got up and began to set things to rights. She was still shoving straw back into her mattress when Suor Margarita came to lock her in.

The next day was Sunday. Giulia passed it in a daze of misery and uncertainty, imprisoned in her cell as she always was when the workshop did not open. On Monday morning she arrived at the workshop to find a servant nun waiting for her, with a summons from the abbess, Madre Magdalena. Light-headed with dread, she made her way to the abbess's office.

"It was I who ordered the search of your cell yesterday." Madre Magdalena paced back and forth before her desk. She was a small, gaunt woman with pinched features and a dislike of being still. She'd been elected just two months earlier, after the sudden death of the previous abbess, Madre Damiana. "I think you know why."

Giulia swallowed against the dryness of her mouth. How could she have been so foolish as to think the struggle would remain between herself and Domenica? That Domenica, her patience at an end, would not look beyond the workshop for help?

"A bundle of letters was found, left to you by Maestra Humilità. I've only glanced at them, but I believe I am correct in guessing that they do not contain what we seek."

"No, Madre Magdalena," Giulia whispered.

"Tell me now, and do not think to lie. Where is the recipe for Passion blue? Where have you hidden it?"

Giulia felt the tiny weight of the pouch at her neck. "It's somewhere safe, Madre Magdalena."

"Somewhere safe? *Somewhere safe?* Do you dare answer me so slyly, girl?"

Giulia stared down at the red tiles of the floor, biting her lips against the tears that wanted to fall. Even if she'd wished to surrender the recipe, she could not reveal the existence of the pouch, for then she would lose her horoscope fragment too.

"I order you to produce it without further delay," Madre Magdalena said. "I am giving you this one last chance to do your duty willingly; but willing or not, we will have that recipe. Do I make myself clear?"

"Yes, Madre Magdalena," Giulia said, because there was nothing else to say.

"I have no wish to dishonor Maestra Humilità's memory, but her actions in this matter defy comprehension. The workshop is the glory of Santa Marta, not only for the beautiful paintings it gives the world, but for the income it contributes to our community. And the reputation of the workshop is built largely upon Passion blue. To give so valuable a thing to a mere apprentice, a girl of questionable character, is scarcely less disgraceful than your defiance."

"I'm sorry, Madre Magdalena," Giulia whispered.

"God knows what is truly in your heart. I do not. Whatever discipline Maestra Domenica decides for you, you should know that I myself will be evaluating whether it will be possible for you to continue in your current situation once you take your final vows."

Giulia's head snapped up. The abbess had paused in her restless motion. Her lips were pinched together, her gaze deeply cold.

"You understand me. Good." Madre Magdalena began to pace again. "Now, there is something else I wish to discuss with you. I have had a letter from Signor Matteo Moretti."

Giulia gasped.

"He wishes to share with you reminiscences of his daughter, whom he loved so dearly, as a comfort for his grief. He has asked that you be allowed to visit him occasionally in his house, as his daughter used to."

"*Visit him?*"

"As you may imagine, I am not inclined to grant you any privileges. But Signor Moretti is a generous donor to this convent, and he has just suffered a grievous loss. I do not feel I can refuse his request. Accordingly, I have arranged for you to go to him on Friday."

"*This* Friday? But—Madre Magdalena—please, I can't!"

Madre Magdalena wheeled around, fixing Giulia with a flinty glare. "*Can't?*"

"He's not . . . Signor Moretti is not my family." Giulia trembled with desperation. Madre Magdalena, like the rest of the convent, knew of Ormanno's theft of Passion blue and Giulia's part in it; but the truth about Matteo, and what had happened to Giulia in his house, had been Giulia's and Humilità's secret. "It isn't proper for me to be . . . to be alone with him."

"Don't be foolish. I shall make sure you have a chaperone."

"It won't be enough! Please, Madre Magdalena, he's not the man you think he is. He's lying about why he wants to see me—he only wants to force me to give him Passion blue—"

"Wicked girl! Matteo Moretti is a leading citizen of Padua, a man of reputation and piety, a famous painter in his own right. How dare you slander him so?"

"It is the truth, if you'd only let me tell you what he did last year when the Maestra's book of secrets was stolen—"

"Be silent!" Madre Magdalena stepped forward and slapped Giulia hard across the face. "You will be fetched at noon on Friday. If I learn that you have shown Signor Moretti anything but the greatest humility and gratitude, you will have cause to regret it. Now get out. I shall expect soon to hear from Maestra Domenica that you have done your duty."

Clutching her throbbing cheek, Giulia fled.

—

Giulia returned to the workshop. She tried her best to hide her distress. But when Domenica decided that the quills she'd just sharpened were not satisfactory and ordered her to recut them all, she startled herself and everyone else by bursting into tears.

"Go into the courtyard and compose yourself," Domenica snapped. "And don't come in until I summon you."

Domenica did not call Giulia back, and she sat on the edge of the fountain for the rest of the afternoon. She was aware of the sympathetic glances of the other painters, but no one was brave enough to intercede.

At last the bell rang for Vespers, and the workshop emptied. Giulia hurried inside and stood over one of the braziers, trying to get warm. Her teeth were still chattering as she began the nightly ritual of putting away the artists' materials. Everything she touched seemed to be made of lead. The very air weighed on her. She wanted to fall to the floor and howl with desperation and despair.

The bell was tolling Angelus when Angela appeared, her pretty face determined.

"Sit down this instant," she commanded, "and tell me what's wrong."

"Oh, Angela, it's just . . . Domenica, you know. I'm tired today, and those quills . . . it was too much."

"No." Angela shook her head. "There is something you're not telling me. I can see it, Giulia. Don't pretend, not with me."

Giulia hesitated, but only for a moment. She let it all pour out: Humilità, Passion blue, Domenica's ultimatum, Madre Magdalena's order. After so many days of keeping the truth to herself, it was an incredible relief to share it.

Angela listened without interrupting.

"So," she said at last. They were sitting side by side at the drafting table. The curtains were still open, and candle flames dipped and swayed in the drafts from the courtyard. "You lied to me about Passion blue."

"I'm sorry. I should have told you. I wanted to, but then Domenica threatened me. I didn't know what to do."

"Domenica's behavior is disgraceful. Still . . . Giulia, I can understand why she's angry. She must feel terribly slighted."

"That is not my fault." Someone had left a pot of pigment open—azurite, Giulia could tell from its song, like a silver hammer tapping against a cymbal. She reached for it and corked it, silencing it.

"I know. But Giulia, there is something to what she says. Maestra Humilità created Passion blue. She had the right to keep it for herself. But she's gone now, and we must carry on her legacy, all of us together. I don't want to say she was wrong in giving it to you, but I think it was . . . unfair. Passion blue should belong to the workshop, not to one person."

"But that's not why Domenica wants it." The blood was hot in Giulia's cheeks. She had expected Angela to understand. "I think she wants it for herself. And I'm afraid . . . I'm afraid that if I give it to her, she'll dismiss me anyway."

"No, Giulia. I know there is no love between the two of you, but you can't think she would be so base."

"Angela, Domenica *despises* me. She called me a whore. She accused me of lying to the Maestra on her deathbed in order to get my hands on Passion blue. She said the Maestra should never have let me back into the workshop."

Angela stared at her. "She said that?"

"That and more." Giulia realized she was still clutching the pigment pot. She loosened her fingers and put it down. "Even if she allows me to stay, Madre Magdalena may not—she said as much today. And oh, Angela, that's not all. The Maestra's father has asked that I be allowed to visit him—to share memories of the Maestra, he says, but that's a lie, and Madre Magdalena has said I must go, and I can't be in his house again, I can't—"

"Wait, wait! What do you mean, a lie?"

"There's something else you don't know, Angela. Last year when Ormanno Trovatelli kidnapped me, I told everyone I never found out who hired him to steal the Maestra's book of secrets. But I did find out. It was the Maestra's father."

"Signor *Moretti*? Giulia, are you sure?"

"Ormanno brought me with him when he went to collect his pay."

"But why?" Angela's eyes were huge. "Why would Signor Moretti do such a thing?"

"Because of his greed for Passion blue. You know how he pressed the Maestra to share the recipe. He could no longer bear that she refused him, so he took matters into his own hands. Of course, once he got her book of secrets he couldn't read the cipher, and when I swore I couldn't read it either, he did not believe me. He locked me in his attic—to question me, he said."

"Oh, Giulia!"

"I'd never been so terrified. I'd learned too much, and if he could betray his own daughter so, what would he not dare do to me? But Ormanno came in the night and set me free. I stole into Signor Moretti's bedchamber and took back the book."

"And the Maestra knew this? You told her?"

"Yes. She was ashamed. She didn't want it known that her father had betrayed her and so I promised to keep it secret. But now she's gone, and I'm the only one who knows what he did. What he's capable of. And he wants Passion blue as much as ever. Do you remember last week, when I had a visitor?"

Angela nodded.

"It was him. The Maestra made me swear an oath never to give him the recipe—I tried to lie, but he didn't believe me. And now I must go to him. I must be in his house again . . . What if he gets me away on some pretext and locks me up again? Oh, Angela, I'm so frightened. I'm afraid . . . I'm afraid I won't be strong enough to stop myself from giving him the secret, no matter how I try."

"Giulia." Angela reached to take Giulia's hands. Her face was grave, her brown gaze steady. "You must talk to Madre Magdalena. You must tell her everything."

"I tried, this afternoon. She wouldn't hear me."

"Then we'll go to her together. I'll vouch for you."

"But all you can say is what you heard from me, and she thinks I'm a liar." Giulia felt the burn of tears behind her eyes. Something terrible was expanding inside her chest, a choking storm of dread and desperation. "Oh, Angela, I never wanted to be a nun. I never wanted to renounce the world and live behind walls and never know what it was to . . . to love a man. But I was willing to take vows if it meant I could paint, if it meant I could be the Maestra's pupil. But the Maestra is gone, and if I can't . . . if I can't paint . . ."

"No, Giulia. I can't believe Domenica would dismiss you. Not if you give her Passion blue."

"You're wrong. Maybe if I'd given it to her at the start . . . but I've left it too long." Giulia recognized the truth of it even as she said it, a stony certainty beyond any possibility of denial. "She'll never forgive me now."

She pulled her hands from Angela's. There were words in her mouth—words she had never imagined saying, words she'd never even allowed herself to think before. Yet now, this moment, she understood they had been inside her for weeks, waiting to be uttered.

She drew a breath and set them free.

"Angela. I don't know if I can take my final vows."

The shadows, the candle flames, the draft-stirred curtains—all for an instant seemed to go completely still.

"What do you mean?" Angela's voice was hushed.

"If I take vows . . . and I lose the workshop . . . I'll be trapped. Trapped at Santa Marta for the rest of my life. I'll be a servant, a *conversa,* despised even by other *conversae* for what they all think they know about me: the girl who ran away with a thief and came back without her virtue. I'll never paint, I'll never even draw unless it's with a charred stick on a whitewashed wall. I'll never—" *Hear the colors singing.* "I couldn't bear it."

"No." Angela was shaking her head, her black veil moving on her shoulders. "No, Giulia, I know you have doubts—"

"More than doubts." It was terrifying, and yet strangely exhilarating, to admit it. "Angela, I have no vocation. Not for religious life. My vocation is for painting. Only for painting."

"But how will you paint if you leave Santa Marta? The world does not allow such things to women. Where would you go? You have no family, no friends outside these walls. How would you survive?"

The fantasy woken by Gianfranco Ferraldi's letters whispered an answer. *I'd disguise myself as a boy. I'd go to Venice and find Ferraldi. I'd talk him into taking me as an apprentice. I'd have a real teacher then, not an angry enemy who hates the sight of me. And Matteo Moretti . . . Matteo Moretti couldn't touch me, because he wouldn't know where I'd gone.*

"You see?" Angela was angry now. "You have no idea. What do you know of the world, the wicked world that has so many dangers in it? Santa Marta is your *home.* We are your *sisters,* we painters. You're my best friend, Giulia! You can't throw away all the Maestra's hopes for you just because you are frightened of something that may never happen. And if

Domenica does do what you fear—and I don't think she will, I don't, but if she does—I will help you! I'll bring you paper and charcoal and brushes and paint. I'll teach you myself! And Lucida will too, and Perpetua, because they love you, Giulia, just as I do."

She was so passionate, so certain. Giulia looked down at the scarred surface of the worktable, at the litter of materials she still had to clear away.

"Here's what we'll do. Tomorrow morning I'll go to Madre Magdalena and tell her everything you've told me. I'll beg her to rescind permission for the visit to Signor Moretti. And you'll give Domenica Passion blue—and, Giulia, you will give it to her as if she had never threatened you. You will beg her to forgive your defiance. You will promise to renounce your pride. You'll convince her she has won—and you will go on convincing her for as long as she is Maestra." Angela's eyes were filled with tears. "You must save yourself, Giulia. Domenica won't be Maestra forever. Your day will come. I promise it will."

Giulia leaned forward and put her arms around her friend, feeling Angela embrace her tightly in return. She was suddenly conscious of how tired she was, weary to the bone.

"It's late." Angela pulled away, raising her hands to wipe her eyes. "You go. I'll finish here."

Grateful, Giulia slid off her stool.

"Don't worry." Angela took up one of the candles, holding it so that her face seemed to be lit from within. She looked like a resolute angel in one of Humilità's paintings. "We'll make things right."

CHAPTER 7

❖ The Orchard Wall ❖

Despite her exhaustion, Giulia lay open-eyed after Suor Margarita locked her in her cell. She could feel the fearful thing she had admitted to Angela spreading through her like ink on wool, transforming everything.

I have no vocation.

It was to Humilità she'd been willing to swear herself. Humilità and the workshop and all she could become there. Not Santa Marta. Not religious life. Deep inside herself, she'd known it all along. She'd just never allowed herself to admit it. There had been no reason to do so until now.

She thought of Ferraldi's letters, which she hadn't had the courage to ask Madre Magdalena to give back. She'd dismissed the idea they'd woken in her as fantasy. But was it really so impossible?

She could escape through the orchard, the same way Ormanno had crept in a year ago. She'd need a boy's disguise, but surely she could manage that—steal washing from a line, perhaps. She knew Venice lay east of Padua and that the two cities were not terribly distant from each other; maybe the journey would not take so very long. Once in Venice, she'd convince Ferraldi to apprentice her. And if he refused—well, Venice was a city of painters, or so Ferraldi had said. Surely there was an artist who would take her.

Of course, she had no experience of travel. She hadn't grown up cosseted and sheltered, not as a noblewoman did, or a girl like Angela, who had been born into a wealthy merchant family—she'd always had to fend for herself. But she'd never been entirely alone before, had never been without a home to return to. She had no money, not so much as a single soldo. And though a boy on his own was safer than a girl on her own, even a boy was vulnerable to thieves, and sickness, and starvation, and a hundred other possibilities that threatened life and limb.

But you've done impossible things before, her rebellious imagination whispered. Had she not found her way to the house of an astrologer-sorcerer and paid him to make her a spirit-haunted talisman? Hadn't she escaped from Matteo Moretti's attic and crept into his rooms by moonlight, and taken the secret he had stolen from under his very hand?

Wasn't Santa Marta dangerous for her also, as long as Matteo knew she was inside it?

You've made mistakes before too. Ormanno's smiling face appeared in her mind. And all at once her thoughts turned, and she saw her plan through Angela's eyes—as the madness it really was, the daydream of a desperate girl. At Santa Marta there were some certainties—if nothing else, of shelter and of

Angela's support. Outside it there were no certainties at all, not even that she would reach Venice safely.

She heard Angela's words again: *You can't throw away all the Maestra's hopes for you just because you are frightened of something that may never happen.*

"What should I do, Maestra?" she whispered. "What would you want me to do?"

Of course there was no answer—only her own thoughts, turning and turning in the dark.

—

Hollow-eyed and exhausted, Giulia made her way to the workshop on Tuesday morning. Angela arrived late; as she'd promised, she had gone to Madre Magdalena to speak on Giulia's behalf.

"You were right," she told Giulia in a quiet moment that afternoon. "She said I was not a witness to the events you described. And with no corroboration, she could give no credence to such an accusation, or insult Signor Moretti by denying his request."

"I told you." Foolishly, Giulia had allowed herself a sliver of hope that Angela might succeed.

"Wait, I'm not finished. You must still go to him this coming Friday, but Madre Magdalena will give you two chaperones, not just one, and she will instruct them never to leave your side. So she did heed me, at least a little." Angela was smiling, pleased with her accomplishment. "Do you feel better now, Giulia? There's surely nothing that can happen with two chaperones watching over you."

Giulia did not have the heart to tell her friend that all the chaperones in the world would not make her feel safe.

"She said I was to remind you of her command." Angela was serious now. "Have you talked to Domenica yet?"

Giulia shook her head.

"Oh, Giulia! You must! You must do it at once!"

But by the close of the workday Giulia still had not spoken. She hurried through her tasks, managing to get back to her cell before Vespers ended and either Angela or Domenica could return. For a long time she stood at her unshuttered window, gazing at the sky. She'd prayed for guidance and had received none; the stars could not help her either. She was so confused and weary she hardly knew what she was thinking any longer.

She did not expect to sleep. But almost as soon as she closed her eyes, exhaustion claimed her. She was back in Milan, where she had grown up, in Maestro Bruni's study in her father's palace. Maestro sat behind his untidy desk, dressed in his shabby velvet robe and felt cap, his quill scratching across a sheet of paper. He rose when he saw her, smiling his sad smile. "You have a question for me, child?" Giulia realized that she did have a question, and she spoke it, though as the words left her mouth they lost their meaning and she had no idea what she had said. Maestro shook his head, looking grave. "There are no stars. I cannot take a sighting for your horoscope." He gestured to the windows of his study, through which the sun streamed gold. Giulia was puzzled, for he could have taken a sighting on the sun. But then his face brightened and he reached toward her, plunging his hand into her chest. There was no pain, only a coolness like the kiss of water on a hot summer's day. He pulled back, smiling. In the cup of his palm were stars—not diamond white, but lapis blue, pulsing with indigo brilliance, shedding sapphire sparks. "I can take a sighting after all," he said, and tossed the stars up in the air so that they came down again in a rain of cobalt, singing as they fell, the icy, unearthly song of Passion blue.

And then Giulia was awake, her eyes wide open in the darkness of her cell. Blue shadows swam at the edges of her vision. She could still feel a little of the coolness of Maestro Bruni's dream-touch.

She thought of the question she had asked in her dream, the question she hadn't understood as she was speaking it. And all at once it was as if a wind blew through her, sweeping away the clutter of question and doubt, leaving only the hard, flat clarity of truth behind.

Angela was right. If she surrendered Passion blue, Domenica might not banish her. Yet what she'd said to Angela was also true. Too much had passed between them ever to be healed. In Domenica's workshop, she would labor each day under a woman who despised her. Who looked at her gift, the fire at the core of her being, and saw only something ugly and unnatural. Who would never teach her how to become the painter God had created her to be.

That was not what Humilità had wanted for her. It was not what she wanted for herself.

What, then, will I win by staying at Santa Marta? Only the safety of my body. While outside in the world, the wicked world with all its dangers, I may lose that and more . . . but possibly, just possibly, I may have everything to gain.

The bed seemed to tilt, as if the Earth had shifted underneath it. Terror swept her. For the rest of the night she lay open-eyed, her heart beating and beating, the dark around her like the impossible distance between stars.

—

When Giulia rose on Wednesday morning, she was still terrified. But something inside her had changed. She could feel it. It was as if she'd crossed the border into another country.

She was not supposed to go to Matteo until Friday. And Domenica's ultimatum ran until Sunday, when she would take her final vows. But she knew she would be foolish to test Madre Magdalena's patience.

I can't wait. If I am leaving, I have to leave tonight.

In the afternoon, when Domenica vanished into her study, Giulia went to the shelf where she kept her own drawings. She could not say good-bye to the other artists, but she couldn't bear to leave without acknowledging their trust, their friendship, their forgiveness. She wanted to do something that, looking back, they would realize had been farewell.

She'd drawn them all many times. She sorted quickly through the sheaf of sketches, picking out the best: Lucida in charcoal with white chalk highlights, her face alight with laughter. Perpetua in black chalk on gray paper, concentration smoothing away her homeliness. Old Benedicta dozing in the sun, contented as a cat. Angela in profile—a simple sketch, just quill and ink, yet none of the more finished drawings Giulia had done captured her friend so well.

She went first to Angela's easel. "For you," she said, laying the portrait on the little table where Angela kept her pigment pots and other materials.

"What is it?" Angela set down her brush. She was highlighting an angel's wing feathers with vermilion; Giulia heard the color's voice, a musical sizzle like oil in a hot pan. "Oh, Giulia, what a lovely drawing! But you've made me look so . . . so . . ."

"Beautiful? You are, you know."

"Oh, well." Angela made a dismissing gesture. "Thank you. What made you think of it?"

"I thought you might like it. Angela . . ."

"Yes?"

I never imagined I'd have a friend like you. Someone who cared about me, who stood up for me. I'm going to miss you so much.

"Nothing. I love you, Angela."

"I love you too." Angela frowned. "Giulia—"

But Giulia, already hurrying away, pretended she had not heard.

Lucida was delighted with her portrait and kissed Giulia on both cheeks for thanks. Perpetua was embarrassed, blushing as she looked down at herself. Benedicta had stayed in her cell that day; Giulia placed her portrait by her easel, where she would find it the next time she came in.

For the rest of the afternoon, Giulia went about her duties with a calm efficiency that amazed her, while fear vibrated in her like a swarm of bees and her pulse beat high and fast against her throat. She felt outside herself, unable to believe what she was about to do.

The Vespers bell rang at last. She stood by the grinding table after the artists departed, counting to a thousand to make sure they were truly gone. Then, half-certain she was dreaming, she crossed to the supply shelves, where she spread a square of linen on the floor and stacked it with her Annunciation painting, the best of her drawings, a supply of unused paper, a pouch of charcoal sticks, and a knife for sharpening them, which she could also use to cut her hair. She added Humilità's bequests: the Alberti manuscript and the rosewood brushes. She'd left the workshop earlier to retrieve them, smuggling them back in under the bodice of her gown.

Last, she fetched a small silver plate from one of the chests that held the costumes and other items the workshop used for the models who posed for drawings. She hated stealing. But she had to have something to sell or barter for the clothing and food she'd need on her journey.

I'll pay it back, she promised silently. *I swear I will.*

She folded the linen around the items and tied the bundle with cord. She loosened her belt and pushed the bundle up under the front of her gown. It was bulky; but if she clasped her arms around her midsection and hunched forward as though her stomach pained her, it was more or less hidden.

She was ready.

She stood a moment, looking around. The candle flames shook in the draft from the courtyard, sweeping light and shadow across the big room so that everything in it seemed to shift a little, to breathe a little, as if the workshop were a living thing. At the grinding table, the marble slab was still smeared with bone black, the last paint she'd mixed: She could hear its thrumming, drumlike voice, rising and falling in steady rhythm. *How long will it be before I hear the color songs again?*

For an instant she was sure she sensed Humilità's presence, as if her teacher were standing just behind her. Approving? Accusing? She could not tell.

This is the only way I can think of to become what you wanted me to be, Maestra. I wish I could see another. But I can't. I can't.

She blew out the candles and left the workshop. The torch-lit corridors were deserted; the noble nuns were all in church, singing Vespers, and the servant nuns were at their duties. She was aware of the bundle, uncomfortable beneath her clothes—and of the other treasures she was carrying out of Santa Marta: the secret of Passion blue, the bright flame of her own gift.

She reached the last of the convent's garden courtyards and hurried along its paths, gravel crunching under her feet. Then she was in the orchard, the branches a dark tracery against the starry sky, the smell of windfall apples all around. She was trembling now, shaking with the chill of the night and with fear, her teeth chattering so hard they hurt.

The breach in the wall, where Ormanno had climbed in a year ago, had been repaired. But the repair was rough, and the sloppily mortared bricks offered hand- and footholds. Giulia pulled the bundle from under her gown and slung it by its cord over her elbow, then tucked her skirts into her belt and began to climb.

The top of the wall was wide, embedded with tile shards all down its center to deter intruders. The drop on the other side seemed huge, and the ledge at the bottom was narrower than she remembered. The canal lapped below it, a heaving black surface stinking of sewage.

Carefully she crawled over the tile shards and twisted around, thinking to lower herself by her hands to make the distance to the ground a little less daunting. But as she tried to walk her feet down the wall, her sandals slipped and the whole weight of her body dropped. Her grip broke and she fell, landing on the ledge with a jolt that snapped her teeth together. Bolts of pain shot through her ankles. She staggered, tipping sickeningly backward toward the filthy water of the canal, but at the very last second managed to grab hold of a sapling that had sprouted from a crack in the ledge and haul herself to safety.

She rested against the wall, gasping, as her pounding heartbeat slowed. Her knees burned where she'd scraped them, and there was pain in her left hand. When she turned her palm to the sky, she saw darkness there: blood. She'd cut herself when she lost her grip.

She wrapped the wound with a strip torn from her chemise. Then she pulled her skirts out of her belt and, still shaky, set off along the ledge, keeping her shoulder to the wall. The wall gave way to the backs of houses; she began to worry that the ledge would end before she found a way up into the city. But soon she reached a stone dock, jutting out into the canal. A set of stairs connected it to the street.

At the top she paused. The cobbles of the street glinted faintly in the starlight. Arcaded housefronts rose on either side, twin walls of shadow, candlelight glimmering between drawn shutters.

Padua lay before her. Then Venice. Then the world.

With no warning, panic roared out of the night, a black terror that felt as if it would rip her apart. What was she doing? Had she lost her mind? What madness possessed her, to imagine she could succeed?

It's not too late. Compline hasn't rung. If I hurry, I can get over the wall and back to my cell before Suor Margarita comes. No one will know I've been outside . . .

She wheeled around. She stumbled down the stairs. But by the time her feet touched the dock, she felt sense returning; and as she stepped onto the ledge, she remembered her decision and why she had made it.

She stopped then, closing her eyes, letting the turmoil in her settle until she could feel again the familiar fire at her core—the passion that had driven her from Santa Marta, and must drive her farther still.

She returned to the stairs. As she reached the end of the street, she heard the Compline bell begin to ring.

Too late now.

She put her head down and walked on.

Part III

The Daughter
of the Sea

❖❖❖❖❖❖

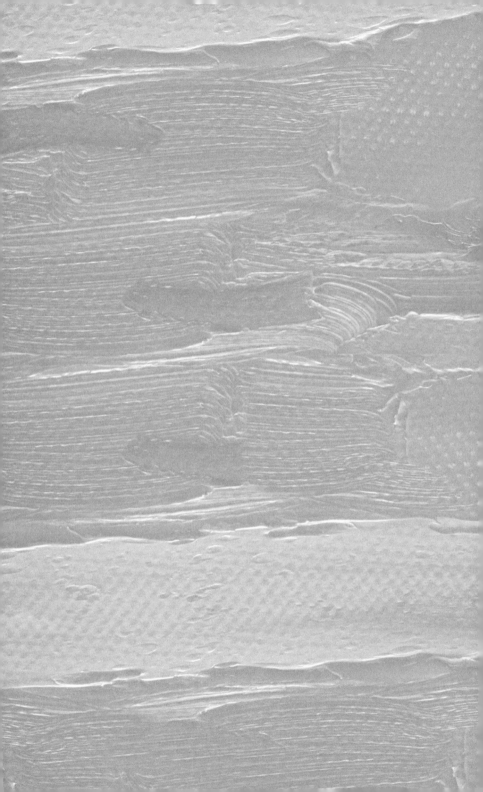

CHAPTER 8

❖ Girolamo Landriani ❖

Padua, Italy
October, Anno Domini 1488

Giulia passed the night crouched in the doorway of a church. Shortly after leaving the dock, she'd realized that trying to find her way to the market in the dark, in a city she did not know, was foolish. The church steps seemed as safe a place as any to wait for morning.

The air was autumn-chill and the steps were cold. Even so, she managed to doze, jolting awake from time to time, her heart pounding as she remembered all over again what she'd done and why.

As dawn began to gray the sky, she climbed to her feet, her body aching. The bandage on her injured hand was stiff with dried blood; she peeled it away, making the cut bleed again. The torn flesh gaped. With nothing to clean it, the best she could do was to tear another strip from her chemise and wrap it up again.

She untied her belt from around her waist and knotted it below her breasts so her novice gown would look a little more like an ordinary woman's dress. She unwound the kerchief that hid her hair, pulling it over her shoulders like a shawl and letting her long braid fall free. From the bundle she took the silver plate, which she slipped into her bodice. Then, hooking the bundle's cord over her arm again, she set off into the city.

Her fear was still with her. But it was far too late for second thoughts. If she returned to Santa Marta now, there was not a chance in the world she'd ever be allowed to set foot in the workshop again. She could only go forward. Knowing this was oddly liberating. As she moved toward the next hurdle of her journey she felt, if not brave, at least determined.

The city was waking: housewives throwing back shutters, laborers hurrying to work, tradesmen bringing their wares to market. Giulia followed the flow of traffic, and in less time than she expected found herself at the edge of Padua's great market piazza, with rows of stalls being set up for the day and the long bulk of the Palazzo della Ragione rising above them, the lead plates of its vast domed roof gleaming in the first light of the sun.

She began to wander among the stalls, already thronged with early shoppers. The clamor of commerce beat against her ears, and with every breath she drew in the market's odors: produce fresh and spoiled, wood smoke, animal dung, crowded humanity. At last, among the stalls crammed into the palazzo's ground-floor portico, she found a seller of metal and leather goods. She paused a moment, gathering her resolve, then approached the stallholder.

"Do you buy?" she asked, trying to sound confident.

"I might." The stallholder, a skinny man with a mouthful of bad teeth, eyed her skeptically. "Depending on what's being offered."

She pulled the plate from her bodice. He took it, turning it in callused fingers, biting it and examining the mark.

"Silver," he said. "Not the best quality. Still, it's a decent piece. I'll give you twelve soldi."

Giulia knew nothing of the value of silver; but she knew good quality from bad, and she could see that the stallholder was more eager than he wanted to appear. "Twenty soldi," she said boldly. "It's very good quality, I know it for a fact."

"Thirteen soldi, six piccoli. That's a better offer than I'd make to most."

"Give it here, then. I'll sell it somewhere else."

"Fifteen. You're robbing me, my girl."

"Eighteen."

"Sixteen and six, and not a piccoli more."

Giulia hesitated. "Done."

The stallholder counted out the coins, fingering each one as if reluctant to let it go.

"You're not as innocent as you look," he said as he put them in her hand. "If I was the kind of man who stuck his nose into other people's business, I might wonder where you got that plate."

Giulia felt the blood rising to her cheeks. She turned away, holding tight to the money.

There were several stalls selling rags and old clothes. At the biggest, she sorted through piles of garments laid out on a trestle, selecting a mantle, a cap, a shirt, a pair of woolen hose, a doublet, and a peasant's thick woolen tunic. The clothes were patched and darned, but otherwise whole and reasonably clean, and not infested with fleas as far as she could tell.

"How much?" she asked the stallholder's wife.

The wife, a plump, pretty woman with red hair escaping from beneath a kerchief, turned Giulia's choices over with one hand, balancing her little daughter on her hip with the other. "Two soldi for the lot," she said.

"Would you barter?"

"Barter what?" asked the wife, suspicious.

"I'm a painter. I can make your portraits—you and your husband and your daughter. All of you together or each separately."

"You? A painter?" The woman laughed. "What would the likes of us want with portraits anyway? We're working folk, not nobility."

"Wouldn't you like to remember your little girl as she is today?" Giulia nodded toward the child, as plump as her mother, with the same red hair. "Or your husband? I can draw them to the life. Look here." She knelt and unknotted the cord of her bundle, awkward with her one good hand, and shuffled through her drawings, pulling out a sketch of Lucida that she'd done several months ago without her nun's wimple and veil. "I drew this of a friend of mine."

"Oh!" The wife gazed at the drawing. "You made that?"

"I did. I'd charge more than two soldi for it if I was in my . . . my workshop, but since I'm not I'll give you all three drawings—you and your husband and your daughter—for just these clothes here." The words tumbled forth, fast and breathless; Giulia was astonished at what was coming out of her mouth. "They're for . . . they're for my brother, he has had some hard luck lately, there are many things he needs, but clothes are what he lacks most."

She stopped herself, afraid the lies were becoming too obvious. But the wife's attention was still focused on the sketch.

"Jacopo," she called. "Come see."

The husband finished with a customer and came to peer skeptically at the drawing. The wife pulled him aside, speaking in a voice too low for Giulia to hear. The husband listened, his arms folded, frowning. Giulia held her breath. She'd never in her life done anything like this and had no idea what would happen.

The husband shook his head. He reached out and set his hand on his wife's shoulder, then turned away, glancing at Giulia as he did, a quick flash of hard brown eyes that told her she was about to be sent packing. But the wife was smiling as she came forward.

"My husband says yes. These clothes for a portrait of me and my little Carmela."

"Truly?" Giulia could hardly believe it. "I mean, good. That's good."

She took one of the smaller sheets of blank paper and a stick of charcoal from the bundle, and also the Alberti manuscript, which had a leather cover that would do for a drawing board. She was grateful it was her left hand she'd cut rather than her right.

The wife cleaned her daughter's face with a corner of her apron and smoothed the little girl's curling hair. "What should I do?" she asked.

"Just stand and hold her. Turn your head a little, to look at her. There, that is exactly right."

Giulia examined them, assessing the light and the angles. Then she set charcoal to paper. Drawing was the one thing in her life she was always certain of; but what she was doing now was new and strange, and her hand was shaking. She pressed too hard on the first stroke, snapping the point of the charcoal stick.

"Sorry," she muttered, fumbling out her knife to sharpen it. Her cheeks were burning. Any moment now the wife would see through her pretense, would realize she was not a painter but only a runaway novice with no idea of what she was doing. But when she looked up, the wife was still waiting, her head turned as Giulia had instructed, as serene as a saint. The little girl, Carmela, had laid her head on her mother's shoulder and closed her eyes.

This time Giulia's hand did not falter. She roughed in the outlines of the two figures, a linked geometry of shapes and angles, then began to add detail, crosshatching the shadows and smudging them with her fingers to blend the strokes. She finished quickly. In the workshop, she would have spent much more time on such a drawing, accenting the highlights with white chalk, adding dimension to the shadings with ink wash. But for what it was, it was a good effort, an excellent likeness that captured something deeper: the little girl's utter trust as she dozed against her mother's shoulder, the mother's radiant love for her child.

She held the drawing toward the stallholder's wife. The wife caught her breath.

"Is that—is that really me?"

"To the life," Giulia said.

"And Carmela—oh, it is exactly like her! What a wonder, to see her there on the paper!" The wife reached out, took the drawing from Giulia's hand. "I had a little boy," she said. "Jacopetto, we called him, after my husband. He died of the fever this winter past, and it's growing hard to remember his face. But now I'll have Carmela with me always." She raised her eyes to Giulia's. They were shimmering with tears. "What is your name?"

"Giulia," Giulia said, knowing she should use a false name but unwilling to lie in the face of the wife's sadness. "Giulia Borromeo."

"You have magic in your hands, Giulia Borromeo. Wait there a moment."

The wife went to lay Carmela, still dozing, on a heap of blankets in a corner of the stall, placing the drawing carefully beside the little girl. She piled the things Giulia had chosen on the mantle she'd selected, then reached under the trestle. When she straightened, she was holding a pair of boots.

"For your brother," she said. "My husband won't mind, once he sees Carmela on that paper."

She placed the boots on top of the clothes and tied everything up in the mantle.

"May God bless you," she said, pushing the bundle toward Giulia. "And your brother too."

"Thank you for your kindness."

Giulia had taken no more than a few steps when she felt a hand on her arm. She jumped, startled.

"I saw what you did for that rag seller there." It was a woman in a sober gown of good cloth, her neatly dressed hair covered by a veil. "Could you do the same for me?"

"You wish me . . . to draw you?"

"My sons." She gestured to the two boys who stood behind her. "They're to travel with my husband on business, and I would like to have a likeness to look at while they are gone. I'll give you a soldo to show them both on one paper."

"I—well—that is, yes. Yes, I'd be glad to."

Near the boundary of the piazza, where there were not so many people, Giulia seated herself on the edge of a fountain, balancing the Alberti manuscript on her knee and the drawing paper on the manuscript, her charcoal scratching as she sketched the two boys, trying to capture the edge of mischief in the face of the younger, the older's watchful seriousness.

A little crowd gathered as she worked. As the woman, delighted, pressed a silver soldo into her hand, a young man came forward with his sister, and then a father with his son. Giulia heard her own voice, as self-assured as if she'd been selling sketches on the street for years; she watched her own hands flying over the paper. Inside herself, she was amazed.

I can sell portraits all the way to Venice. I can support myself while I look for Ferraldi. I won't have to sleep in the gutter, and I won't starve.

Could it really be that easy?

She might have had customers all morning. But she knew her absence would have been discovered soon after sunrise; by now Madre Magdalena might have searchers out combing the streets. Already, she had stayed too long. She accepted the father's soldo, then packed up her things and hurried away from the market, back into the winding avenues.

At the end of a dark and malodorous alley overlooked by blind walls, she dragged off her dress and chemise and, standing naked and shivering, bound her kerchief tightly around her breasts to flatten them, glad for once that she wasn't better endowed.

She put on the garments she had bartered—first the shirt, then the doublet, then the hose, tying the points, the laces at their top, through the holes at the doublet's waist to hold them up. A good thing she had been trained as a seamstress before she came to Santa Marta: She knew how men's clothing went together, as a more privileged girl might not.

The boots the stallholder's wife had given her were too big, but better than the sandals she had been wearing. She pulled the tunic over everything, belting it with her own belt, and wrapped the mantle over that. She'd already stowed the money she had made that morning in the pouch sewn into the inside of the doublet, counting it first: twenty soldi, six piccoli—four soldi earned by her own labor. A good sum with which to start a journey.

There was just one thing left to do.

She took the knife she'd brought from Santa Marta and leaned forward so that her braid fell over her shoulder. Not giving herself time to think, she set the knife to her hair, sawing at the thick rope of it.

The knife was sharp. The braid came off quickly. What remained of her hair swung free, just touching her shoulders. It had hung below her waist, thick and waving and glossy black, the one thing about herself that she considered beautiful. She felt its loss like a wound.

Stop it, she told herself. *It's only hair. One day you can let it grow again.*

She sheathed the knife and stowed it in her boot. Using a stick, she poked her severed braid and her novice clothing under the piles of rubbish that heaped the alley's corners. She settled the cap on her head and slipped her bundle over her arm.

At the alley's mouth she paused, bracing herself. Then she stepped into the street, into the light of the sun—no longer Giulia Borromeo, fugitive novice, but Girolamo Landriani, apprentice painter. Landriani for her mother, whose family name it was, Girolamo because it was close to her own real name.

Girolamo Landriani. A boy.

—

Taking those first steps was one of the most difficult things Giulia had ever done. The tunic covered her to midthigh, but still her legs felt as exposed as if she were naked. The binding around her breasts was uncomfortably constricting, and her shorn head felt strangely light. She'd been reasonably confident that her height, her strong features and level brows would pass for a boy's—but now she felt utterly ridiculous, an obvious imposter. Surely anyone looking at her would immediately see through her absurd attempt at disguise.

But no one looked at her. She realized this once she found the courage to raise her eyes, which at first she'd fixed on the cobbles of the street. The tradesmen, the beggars, the young men lounging under the arcades—all were busy with their own affairs. Most didn't spare her a glance, or if they did, their eyes slid across her and then moved on. She had actually attracted more attention earlier, when she'd still been dressed as a girl.

She felt a burst of confidence. This morning she'd had nothing, nothing but her plan. Now she had the disguise she needed, money that would see her on her journey, and the means to earn more.

I can do this.

Her stomach reminded her that she hadn't eaten since yesterday noon. She bought roast mutton from a man selling skewers from a brazier, and devoured the greasy meat. Then, boldly, she stopped a passerby and asked how she might travel to Venice, trying to deepen her voice so it would seem more masculine.

"Best way to go's by river." The man's eyes lingered on her face, but there was no suspicion in his gaze, only ordinary curiosity. "If you've got the price of passage."

Giulia shook her head. She wanted to save her money if she could. "I don't."

"Well, then, go out of the city by the Porta Molino, cross the Molino bridge, and head east."

He gave her directions to the Porta Molino. Giulia moved on, reminding herself not to walk as a girl did—with small steps, hands clasped at her waist, eyes downcast—but like a boy: in long strides, her shoulders thrown back, her unencumbered arm swinging freely. The too-large boots flapped annoyingly at her toes—she'd have to find something with which to stuff them—and she was realizing that she needed to tie up her hose more loosely, to allow more slack in the fabric when she bent her knees. But she could attend to those things later.

It was midafternoon by the time she reached the Porta Molino. Beyond it, the Bacchiglione River embraced Padua's northern walls, its banks lined with flour mills. On the river's far side a tumble of houses made a brief continuation of the city. In the distance, Giulia glimpsed planted fields.

She crossed the bridge, joining the stream of travelers heading out of the city. Her cut palm had begun to throb, and the ill-fitting boots were raising blisters on her heels. She could feel the exhaustion of her sleepless night settling over her.

A cart trundled past, raising a cloud of dust. She hailed it, but the driver ignored her. The next driver ignored her also, and the one after that cursed and flicked his whip, forcing her to dodge aside.

Her feet were agony. She needed to do something about them or she wouldn't be able to continue. She was starting to limp to the roadside when another cart overtook her—and this time the driver heeded her wave and reined to a halt. She hurried to catch up.

"Are you—" She cleared her throat, lowered her voice. "Are you traveling east? Toward Venice?"

"Could be." The driver, a burly young man with a rough stubble of beard, looked Giulia over, his eyes lingering on the bundle at her elbow. Beside him sat a younger companion—his brother, by the resemblance.

"Can you give me a ride? I can barter. I'm a painter. I'll draw you two portraits on fine paper if you'll take me as far as you're going."

"Portraits?" The driver turned his head and spat. "What would we want with portraits?"

"For your parents, or your sweethearts. For remembrance."

"My sweetheart sees me every day. You got anything else to offer?"

Giulia sighed. She hadn't wanted to pay for passage, but even if she wrapped her feet, she knew she couldn't walk much farther.

"A soldo," she said. "I'll give you a silver soldo if you'll take me as far east as you're going."

"That's more like it. Show us your money."

Turning her back, Giulia extracted a soldo from the pouch sewn into her doublet. She turned back to the cart, holding it up. The driver reached for it. She snatched her hand away.

"You'll get it when I get off."

"What d'you say, Santello?" The driver addressed his brother. "Will we carry this painter boy here for just one silver soldo?"

Their eyes held, some wordless communication passing between them. The brother shrugged. The driver jerked his thumb at the back of the cart.

"Jump in, then."

Giulia hesitated, suddenly unsure. The brothers' unkemptness, the neglected appearance of their horse, the look they'd exchanged . . . But then it occurred to her that she was thinking like a girl. A girl was vulnerable to men like these. But she was a boy now. She was Girolamo Landriani. She would have to keep her wits about her—but she did not have to fear these two as a girl would.

"What're you waiting for?" the driver demanded. "Get in or get gone."

Giulia's burning feet made the decision for her. She hoisted herself into the cart, making a clumsy job of it with her injured hand and her too-tight hose. The brothers had been at market—she shared space with a trestle and its supports, a folded canvas awning, and a heap of rotten onions.

I've done it, she thought as the cart bumped back into motion. She felt Padua falling behind her, sloughing away like a heavy garment, leaving her cold and unprotected but much, much lighter. *I'm on my way.*

The sun was sinking, probing the fields with fingers of shadow. The urge to sleep was overwhelming, but Giulia knew she had to stay awake. She flexed her wounded hand, concentrating on the pain, and slipped her other hand under her mantle, closing it tightly around her purse.

It was the last thing she remembered doing.

CHAPTER 9

✤ A Portrait In Darkness ✤

Asleep in the cart, Giulia dreamed. Santa Marta had found her. Domenica's face loomed over her, distorted with rage; she felt Domenica's hands, tearing at her clothing. She tried to resist, for she knew Domenica meant to claw through not just her garments, but her skin and bone, to plunge her fingers into Giulia's heart and rip free the secret of Passion blue—

And then Giulia was awake, and for an instant dream and reality blurred, for there really *were* hands on her and faces above her, and she was utterly bewildered; but then she remembered where she was, and she saw that the faces were the brothers' faces, the men who had let her ride in their cart, and the whites of their eyes were glinting in the moonlight, for it was full night now, and one of them was holding her down while the other was pawing at her doublet—

She began to struggle. But the younger brother had her hands over her head, gripped fast by the wrists, and as she tried to whip her body to the side, the driver, the one who had offered her the ride, planted a knee across her thighs, immobilizing her.

"Help!" she shouted. "Help!"

The driver laughed. "Shout away, boy, there's no one to hear."

He'd slit her tunic so he could get at her doublet. His fingers closed on the knot of the purse sewn into the inside. He yanked at the doublet's laces, wrenching them loose. She heard a ripping sound, felt the purse tear free.

"There." He held it up, shaking it so it clinked. "I knew there was more where that silver came from."

He tossed the purse aside, then leaned over her, his weight crushing her thighs, his breath foul.

"Got any more on you?" She turned her face away; he seized her chin, jerked it back. "We'll strip you to find out, so if you don't want to be walking to Venice naked, you'd better tell us."

"No," she gasped. Her arms were stretched so high over her head she could barely breathe. "I don't have any more."

"Strip it is then." His hands went to her hose, fumbling at the ties that attached them to her doublet. Panic burst inside her; she screamed, unable to help herself. The driver laughed again.

"Screams like a girl, don't he?" Then suddenly he paused. "Wait a moment. Wait . . . just . . . one . . . moment."

His hand moved down her belly. She writhed, trying pointlessly to pull away. His fingers slid between her legs, closed hard on the tender flesh there. She gasped, every part of her desperate to escape the violation of it. He began to laugh, really laugh this time, great chortling peals of mirth.

"Oh, so that's the story, is it? We've caught ourselves a different fish than we thought, Santello. Not some soft, stupid painter boy at all but a girl. A real girl." His free hand went to Giulia's chest, probing. "Yes indeed, there's tits under there, they're bound up tight but I can feel 'em. We're going to have us a good time tonight, and no mistake!" His fingers dug brutally between her legs. She cried out. "See, Santello? She likes it!"

He bent forward, taking his weight off her thighs. He was grinning, the moonlight glinting off his teeth. Santello, the silent brother, was breathing hard through his mouth. Giulia could see his face upside down: his wet lips, his avid eyes. She felt his grip on her wrists slacken as the driver thrust his hand down the neck of her shirt and took hold of the binding around her breasts.

In a moment of complete clarity, she saw that she had one chance. There would not be another.

She whipped her legs up, twisting her body as violently as she could. Her arms came free. She bolted upright, lunging at the driver with clawed hands. Her nails raked his cheeks; he bellowed in surprise and pain, rearing back as she scrambled toward the end of the cart. One of them grabbed her foot. She kicked out and the too-large boot slid off. Then she was falling, tumbling off the cart, landing on the ground with a thump that knocked the breath out of her. Gasping, she scrambled to her feet and ran.

"She's blinded me!" Behind her, she heard the driver shouting. "The bitch blinded me! Go after her, Santello, you idiot, go after her and get her back!"

Then all she could hear was her own panting, her own uneven footsteps pounding against the earth. She ran and ran, falling now and then, clambering to her feet and running on. At last she fell and could not rise. Her last thought before consciousness slipped away was to hope that the brothers, when they found her, would leave her alive.

—

She woke to cold. Opening her eyes, she saw an infinity of gray. Her first thought was that she'd lost her sight, but then she realized she was lying on her back, looking up at an overcast sky.

For a moment she could not recall where she was or why. Then memory returned in a terrible rush. She gasped, sitting up, her hands flying to her hose. They were ripped at the knees but otherwise whole, still tied firmly to her doublet.

They didn't catch me. I got away.

She felt a huge relief, but only for a moment.

Where am I? How far did I run?

She'd come to rest in a meadow. There was tall grass all around, brown and dry. Some distance away, blurred by mist, she could see a fence, and beyond it a dark mass of trees.

She climbed carefully to her feet. She could feel the aches and bruises of her flight. The cut she'd gotten on the wall of Santa Marta, still wrapped in its dirty bandage, was hot and throbbing. She'd lost her cap, her tunic was slit all the way down the front, and she had only one boot. Her money was gone. And her bundle, the precious bundle with her artwork and the Alberti manuscript and Humilità's rosewood brushes—that was gone too, left behind in the brothers' cart.

I've lost everything. She felt a dreamlike disbelief. *I've got nothing but the clothes on my back.*

How had things gone so wrong? She remembered her rash confidence of yesterday. What a fool she'd been. Angela had predicted this—predicted it so exactly that now that it had come to pass, it did not seem real.

She was shivering, her teeth chattering, as cold as death. She couldn't stay in this meadow. She had to move on—find a road, find a farm or a village, discover where she was. Beg for something to eat—for she was hungry, terribly hungry, the hollow pain of it drilling through her. And then what? Turn her face to Venice again. Pick up the pieces of her plan and resume her journey.

But I've no work to show Ferraldi now. I've no way to earn money, for I have no charcoal or paper or coins to buy them. And my clothes are in shreds, and my hand is getting worse . . . and I don't even have a knife to defend myself, because it was in the boot I lost . . .

Hopelessness overwhelmed her, buckling her knees and dragging her down again onto the damp ground.

She had no idea how long she sat, her hands loose, her head hanging. Her mind was clouded, as if the drifting mist had seeped inside her. But at last she became aware that she was thinking about turning back—back to Padua, back to Santa Marta, where the high brick walls would imprison her forever, but also promised warmth and shelter and no rough men to abuse her. Where the outside world was held away—the huge and terrifying world in which she was a speck, a mote, unknown and unregarded by anyone but herself.

It was like a blow to the face, shocking her back to clarity. Of course she could not go back. She knew what waited for her at Santa Marta. She'd made her choice; for good or ill, it had brought her here. She could sit in this meadow and wait to die, or she could get up and continue. But she could not go back.

One thing at a time. I'll do one thing at a time, and see where it takes me.

She dragged off her remaining boot, hissing as her hose ripped away from her heel, where burst blisters had pasted the fabric to her skin. Miraculously, the cloth on her bootless foot was whole. With her teeth she tore the hem of her mantle, ripping two long strips from the bottom to wrap around her feet and a narrower strip to use as a belt to hold her tunic together. She removed her doublet and shirt to rewrap the band around her breasts, then tied up her hose more loosely than before, letting them sag at the knees. The shortened mantle she draped over her shoulders.

That's one thing done. What next?

The fence and the trees seemed as good a direction to choose as any. She began to walk, the dry grass rustling with her passage. The bindings on her feet felt lumpy and uneven, but cushioned her steps well enough, and the motion warmed her.

The fence was made of woven willow boughs, higher than her head. She followed it till she found a stile that let her cross to the other side. In the wood beyond, the trees were going gold with autumn, the ground beneath them knotted with roots. The mist was thicker here, enclosing her in a damp, white world through which the trunks loomed like phantoms.

The sound of water led her to a stream frothing over mossy rocks. She crouched down to drink and to bathe her hand. The cut was inflamed, the flesh swollen and hot to the touch. Since she could do nothing else, she wrapped it up again and moved on.

The day was darkening toward dusk by the time she came out of the trees. Before her lay another meadow, the grass scythed to stubble and dotted with hay ricks. Nearby was a farmhouse; she could smell the smoke rising from its chimney. Mist lay across the scene, lending everything a misleading semblance of softness.

She could hardly think of anything now but her hunger. She plunged into the meadow, the stubble sharp under her sore feet. A track began at the meadow's edge, straggling toward the house. Its shutters were all drawn, but she could see the glint of candlelight through the cracks.

She knocked. After a moment she heard someone approaching.

"Who's there?"

"I'm a traveler," Giulia called. "I've been robbed by bandits. I need help."

"And if I open the door, you'll help yourself." The man's voice was hoarse. He spoke Veneto, as everyone in this part of the world did, but with an accent different from that of Padua. "We know that trick round these parts."

"It's no trick. Please, I just want something to eat. A crust, anything you can spare."

"There's nothing for you here. Get you gone."

"Can you at least tell me where I am?"

The only answer was his footsteps, heading away. Giulia hit the door with her good hand. Silence.

Beyond the muddy pigsty at the side of the house she found a well, and near it several ancient apple trees. All the apples had been harvested; but, scrabbling on the ground in the deepening dusk, she scavenged a few windfalls, mushy and spoiled smelling but edible. She slaked her thirst at the well, then returned to the meadow, devouring the apples as she went. The black sky showed through rents in the mist, shimmering with stars.

She made a nest for herself in the side of one of the hay ricks and curled up in its springy, sweet-smelling softness, warm for the first time since she'd left Santa Marta. She thought perhaps she should pray as she was accustomed to doing before sleep, but no words would come. At last she simply crossed herself.

God preserve me.

Sleep sucked her down like quicksand.

—

She woke at first light. She lay a moment, feeling the ache of her abused body and the pain of her hunger, her wounded hand pulsing with heat. Yet, strangely, she felt better. She had faced her fear and forced herself to move on. If she could do it once, she could do it again—and again, and again, as many times as necessary until she reached Venice.

She climbed from the warmth of the hay. The farmhouse was still closed up tight; she could see no sign of life except for the pigs rooting in their sty and a few chickens scratching in the dirt. She drank again from the well, then, her teeth chattering from the coldness of the water and the chill of early morning, turned toward the sun, just tipping up over the horizon. *East,* she thought. *To Venice.*

The air warmed a little as the sun rose. The landscape was as flat as a tabletop, a patchwork of fields and vineyards and orchards, broken by occasional stands of uncultivated trees. Giulia followed meandering tracks where she could and tramped across the fields where she could not, her feet catching on stubble or sinking into raw earth, pushing through hedgerows and jumping drainage ditches.

Flocks of blackbirds, gleaning the leavings of the harvest, rose like ebony curtains at her approach; and now and then she spotted cows, grazing in autumn-hued meadows. Otherwise, she saw no living soul. Except when she'd traveled to Santa Marta a year and a half ago, she'd never been outside city walls. She had never imagined the world could be so wide or so empty of people, or that the sky could be so huge, a vast blue helmet clapped down upon the Earth.

Sometime after noon she came upon a family tending a field of cabbages. She called to them, begging for something to eat. They were suspicious, like the farmer, but more charitable. The wife came forward to offer the heel of a loaf. Giulia crouched where she was to gulp it down, aware that she was tearing at the bread like an animal but too ravenous to care. The wife watched.

"You're a foreigner," she said when Giulia had finished. Her accent was similar to that of the farmer, her face so weathered Giulia could not guess her age.

"I'm from Padua. I was set upon by bandits. I escaped, but now I don't know where I am."

"Near the town of Mestrino."

Giulia shook her head; the name meant nothing to her. "Is there a road anywhere near?"

"North." The woman pointed. "The Vicenza road."

"Vicenza?" Giulia said, dismayed. Vicenza lay north of Padua, but also west. How had she gotten so far off course? Had the brothers lied about traveling east?

The woman nodded. "It isn't far."

Giulia thanked her and moved on, charting her course as best she could by the path of the sun. She was aware that her pace was slowing—she'd never walked so much in her life, and pain flared in her clumsily bound feet at every step. At another farmhouse she asked directions again; the farmwife pointed her on and gave her a handful of small green pears to take with her.

The sun had set and the stars were beginning to show by the time she came upon the road. She paused among the trees that bordered it, steadying herself against a trunk. Her exhaustion was like a weight of stone. A little distance away she could see a camp, five or six carts with several tents pitched alongside and mules and horses staked out to graze. Men moved about the space. There was a fire; she smelled roasting meat.

Hunger stabbed her. She pushed away from the tree and limped toward the camp. One of the men, tending to a horse, spotted her and raised his lantern.

"Who's there?"

"A traveler," Giulia said, or tried to say. Her throat was as dry as dust, and the words came out as a croak. "Please, could you let me have something to eat?"

"We've nothing to spare for beggars," the man said, not unkindly. He was young, with dark hair to his shoulders. "There's a farmstead not too far back. They may help you there."

"I'm not a beggar." Giulia's head seemed to be floating somewhere above her body. "I'm a painter. I met with—with bandits, they stole everything I had. Please, signor—I'm so hungry."

"What's the matter here, Bernardo?"

A woman had emerged from the nearest tent. She was clad in a flowing garment of some kind, her hair loose over her shoulders.

"Another vagrant," said the young man. "Begging for a meal. You needn't trouble yourself."

"But he's only a boy. Can we not spare a crust of bread? And did I hear him say he is a painter?"

"He might as well have said he is a duke," Bernardo replied. "There'd be as much chance it was true."

The woman came forward. In the light of Bernardo's lantern, Giulia could see that she was beautiful and that her hair was coppery gold. The wrapper she wore, almost the same color, showed the unmistakable luster of silk.

"Is it so, boy? Are you a painter?"

"Yes, madonna," Giulia said faintly. "There's an apprenticeship waiting for me in Venice. If I had paper and charcoal, I could show you."

"I have paper and pen. Will that serve?"

"God's bones!" Bernardo exclaimed. "What's the point of this?"

"Hush, Bernardo. It's a dull journey. Don't begrudge me a little diversion."

He shook his head, irritation clear on his face, but did not interfere as the woman rustled back to her tent. Giulia, not sure what would happen next, found that her legs no longer wanted to support her. She sank to her knees.

The woman emerged after a few moments, carrying a portable writing desk. She set it down before Giulia. A sheet of paper lay ready on its wooden surface.

"Give me the lantern, Bernardo."

He sighed and did so. The woman placed the lantern beside the desk. "Draw," she said, holding out a quill.

Numbly, Giulia took it. "What should I draw?"

The woman tilted her head and smiled, keeping her lips closed. The skin around her eyes crinkled, and Giulia realized that she was quite a bit older than she had first appeared.

"Whatever you like."

Giulia dipped the quill into the inkwell set into the top of the desk, holding the paper still with her bandaged hand. The incident had taken on the feeling of a dream—surely she could not really be kneeling on the cold ground, preparing to make a drawing for the entertainment of a woman she'd encountered in a camp by the roadside. She was shivering, and her hand was shaky, and she did not try for fine detail as an impression of the woman's face emerged upon the paper—hatched with shadows, mysteriously smiling, with those telltale creases at the outer corners of her eyes.

"It's finished."

The woman took the drawing, holding it to the lantern. For a moment she was silent.

"I have been told," she said at last, "that in candlelight I appear no more than twenty-five. I am well aware that this is flattery. There are few who are willing to give an aging woman the truth—except of course for Bernardo, who never flatters anyone." Her eyes flicked up. "You are not a flatterer either, young man."

Giulia knew then that she was about to be sent back into the night. "I'm sorry. I draw . . . what I see."

The woman rose to her feet. "If you are to make a career as a painter, you must learn to draw what others *wish* you to see." She regarded Giulia. "I am Sofia Gentileschi. This frowning beast is my son, Bernardo. What is your name?"

Her *son*? Giulia had guessed the woman was not as young as she looked, but she hardly seemed old enough to have a grown son.

"Your name," the woman—Sofia—repeated.

"Giu—" Giulia caught herself. "Girolamo. Girolamo Landriani."

"And you say there is an apprenticeship waiting for you in Venice, Girolamo Landriani?"

"Yes."

"I am Venetian, born and bred. What is your master's name? I may have heard of him."

Giulia drew a breath. "Gianfranco Ferraldi."

Sofia regarded her, a clear, assessing look that seemed to reach beneath the skin. Giulia was certain her deception must be written on her face, but she was too exhausted to care.

"Come," Sofia said. "I will give you something to eat, and a new dressing for your hand."

"Mother." Bernardo caught his mother's arm. "This is folly. Give him some bread if you must, but then send him on his way."

"Where is your charity, Bernardo? He is alone and injured. It would be cruel to banish him into the dark."

"You know nothing about this boy. You cannot assume he is what he claims."

"Then you will have to keep watch, will you not, my beast?" Sofia smiled into his frowning face, then turned and beckoned to Giulia as she might have to a child or a pet. "Come, Girolamo."

Giulia climbed to her feet. The image of the brothers flitted through her mind, and she wondered if she were walking into some new danger. But she was at the end of her strength. She had nothing for anyone to take anyway—she truly was a vagrant. A beggar, as Bernardo had named her.

"Come," Sofia repeated. She was holding aside the flap of her tent. The interior glowed gold, a promise of warmth Giulia could almost feel. "Don't be frightened."

On wobbly legs, Giulia moved toward the light, leaving the night behind.

CHAPTER 10

❖ Sofia Gentileschi ❖

The opulence of Sofia's tent made Giulia wonder if she were dreaming. Straw mats hid the ground. A patterned rug lay atop them. A cot heaped with crimson covers stood against one wall, a pair of painted chests along the other. Candles glimmered inside glass globes strung from the roof frame, filling the space with trembling light.

"Maria," Sofia said to the woman who sat sewing on one of the chests, close by a glowing brazier. "Fetch a bowl of water."

The woman rose. Her skin was the color of burnt sienna, her hair a night-black cloud. Giulia could not help staring. From Maestro Bruni she'd learned about the dark-skinned inhabitants of Africa, but Maria was the first she had ever seen.

Sofia pushed Giulia down on the chest and began unwinding the bandage. When Maria returned with the water, Sofia plunged Giulia's hand into the bowl and started to clean the wound, a process that made Giulia go cold and faint.

"Put your head between your knees," Sofia ordered.

By the time Giulia felt strong enough to raise her head, Sofia had finished with the water and was applying some kind of stinging unguent. "It only burns for a moment," she said, tearing a strip of linen for a clean bandage. And it was true. The stinging faded, leaving Giulia's palm feeling cool and soothed.

"There." Sofia knotted the ends of the bandage. "Better?"

Giulia nodded.

Sofia replaced the pot of ointment in a wooden case that held other medical supplies and shook back her coppery hair. Even in the candlelight, with the lines around her eyes and the slight looseness beneath her chin clearly visible, she was one of the most beautiful women Giulia had ever seen, with smooth milky skin, a bow-curved mouth, and eyes the shape and tawny color of roasted almonds. The silk of her wrapper glistened, shadow pooling in its folds. Despite her exhaustion Giulia could not help imagining how she might paint it . . . She could almost hear the rich, slow voice of the raw umber she'd apply first, the sour, metallic resonance of the orange realgar she'd layer on top.

"How old are you, Girolamo?"

"Fifteen." Giulia had decided on this lie before setting out, to explain her high voice and lack of beard.

"I have heard of your master, you know."

"You have?"

"Yes." Sofia's lips lifted in the enigmatic, closed-lipped smile Giulia had drawn outside in the dark. "It is one of the reasons I do not share Bernardo's suspicions of you. A mere thief might have the skill to draw a portrait, but how would he know the name of a true Venetian painter? Where is your home, Girolamo?"

"I was born in Milan, *clarissima.*" This, Giulia knew from Maestro Bruni, was how the nobility of Venice preferred to be addressed—and this beautiful woman, with her silk garments and rich furnishings, was surely noble, or at least very wealthy.

"I would not have guessed it. You speak Veneto like a Paduan."

"I learned from my tutor." That much was true. "He studied at the university in Padua."

"Your family has means, then."

"Yes," Giulia said, thinking of her childhood, divided between the servants' quarters in the basement, where her noble blood had made her an outcast, and Maestro Bruni's study on the *piano nobile* above, where her common blood had barred her from nearly all the benefits of her father's wealth.

"How did you meet with bandits?"

"I was foolish, clarissima. I accepted a ride on a cart. I fell asleep, and when I woke they were robbing me. I had my artwork and some money—they took everything, even my boots."

"You were traveling alone, then? A dangerous thing for a boy like you."

"There was no one to accompany me, clarissima."

"What of your family?"

"My parents are dead. I have no brothers or sisters."

"Or cousins? Or guardians? Or friends?"

Giulia shook her head, uneasy under Sofia's cool, assessing gaze.

"It seems a long way to travel for an apprenticeship. Could you find no painting master in Milan to teach you?"

"I had a master. But . . . he . . . died." Giulia was horrified to feel her eyes filling with tears. She ducked her head, letting her tangled hair fall forward to hide her face.

"Poor boy," Sofia said gently. "You are weary, and I am pressing you with questions. I'll have Maria fetch you some food and find something for your feet." She gestured to the maidservant, who got up again. "She'll mend your hose as well, if you'll leave them with her tonight."

"No!" Instinctively Giulia drew up her legs. "That is, thank you, but if I can borrow a needle I can mend them myself."

Sofia raised perfectly plucked brows. "I've not met many males in my life willing to do their own sewing when there's a woman to do it for them. But very well."

Giulia hung her head again, cursing herself. Of course a boy wouldn't darn the knees of his own hose.

"You've had a hard time of it, haven't you. And not just at the hands of bandits, I think. I believe . . . yes. I believe I will bring you with me."

"With you, clarissima?"

"To Venice. Bernardo will not approve. But he knows me well, so he also will not be surprised."

Giulia was scarcely able to believe it. "I don't want to cause trouble, clarissima."

"I do not wish that either." Sofia's expression had sharpened. She seemed older suddenly, closer to what Giulia knew must be her true age. "Let me be plain, Girolamo. For pity, and also for the skill you showed tonight, it pleases me to help you. But you must not mistake my kindness for weakness. I know more of the world than you might think, and I am not a fool. Do you understand?"

"Yes, clarissima," Giulia said. "Thank you. I'm more grateful than I can say."

Maria returned with a bowl of stew and part of a loaf. Giulia ate, trying not to gulp the food as her hunger urged her to do. When she was finished, Sofia gave her one of the mats from the floor and a blanket from her own bed, and Maria led her outside and pointed her to a spot beside the tent, close to the fire.

The ground was hard under Giulia's weary body. But the mat blocked its chill, and the blanket was thick and warm. It smelled of cedar. The scent, spicy and exotic, followed her into sleep.

—

Giulia opened her eyes on the great arch of the sky, where the gray of dawn was just overtaking the pinpoint brilliance of the stars. She smelled wood smoke and animal dung, heard the whickering of horses and the voices of men.

I didn't dream it, she thought, marveling.

She pushed back the blanket and rose, shivering in the early morning chill. She could see men gathering by the camp's main cook fire, their forms shadowy in the rising light of dawn. There was a rustling nearby: Maria, ducking out of Sofia's tent, carrying her mistress's chamber pot covered with a cloth. She cast Giulia an inscrutable look and moved on.

A pair of wooden peasant clogs had been placed nearby. Giulia unwound the clumsy bindings around her feet and slipped them on, then left the camp, heading for a nearby copse of saplings. Of all the difficulties of managing her disguise, she could already tell that finding privacy to relieve herself was going to be the most troublesome. Finding time too—for the hose, with a codpiece at the front, were designed for male convenience. She, on the other hand, had to untie all the points attaching hose to doublet so she could take them down, and then knot everything up again. At least her fingers were less stiff than they'd been yesterday. Her hand was still painful, but she could tell that the swelling had gone down.

By the time she returned, the sun was rising and the camp was readying for departure. She passed Bernardo, hitching the horse he'd been tending last night to Sofia's cart.

"Good morning," she said.

He glanced up. In daylight, she saw how young he really was—not much older, perhaps, than her own true age. He dipped his head, a single curt nod, and went back to what he was doing.

Someone—Maria—had left a hunk of bread on Giulia's blanket. As she swallowed the last of it, she looked up to see Bernardo approaching. She felt a surge of apprehension. She hadn't forgotten his objections last night.

"My mother says you are to travel with us." His voice held the cool hauteur of someone accustomed to command. "There's room at the back of the cart with the baggage, or you can walk. We halt once a day for a meal, and as necessary to water the horses. It's up to you to keep pace. If you fall behind or wander off, we won't wait for you. Is that clear?"

Giulia looked up at him, acutely conscious of her tangled hair, her torn and dirty clothing. "Yes."

"Do not mistake your situation. My mother enjoys collecting stray creatures, but her tolerance extends only as far as this journey. Once we reach Venice, you'll be on your own."

"I understand. I'm very grateful to clarissima Sofia and . . . and to you."

In his hard mouth and unblinking eyes she read his opinion of her gratitude. "Just see that you keep up."

Stung by his condescension, but relieved he hadn't banished her, Giulia knelt to roll up her bedding. She'd just gotten to her feet again when Sofia emerged from the tent, dressed in a dark mantle and a gown of red wool, both garments plainly cut but obviously of the finest quality.

"Good morning, Girolamo," she said, smiling her secretive smile.

"Good morning, clarissima."

Bernardo handed his mother into the cart, settling her beneath the awning that spanned the front. She touched his cheek in thanks; he smiled at her, a brief softening of his stern face. Returning to the tent, he began to break it down, collapsing the poles and dragging the canvas flat so he could fold it.

"Can I help?" Giulia asked, reasoning that this was something a boy would do, wounded hand or no.

"No need." He did not bother to look up.

Maria had already joined her mistress under the awning. Giulia tossed her bedroll up behind it, then climbed in herself, pushing at the bundles and boxes to make a place where she could sit. Bernardo heaved the folded canvas into the rear of the cart and stowed the tent poles in brackets along the side, then vaulted into the driver's seat.

With much shouting and creaking, the caravan got under way. It was a merchant train, Sofia had told Giulia last night, returning to Venice from trading in Milan. Sofia and her companions were not part of it but were following it for safety on their way home from Vicenza, where Sofia had been attending the birth of a friend's second child. Venice was not far: forty miles, maybe a little more. But according to Sofia the roads were bad, and it would be more than a week before the party reached the Venetian lagoon. The contents of the carts would then be loaded onto boats, the mules and horses and the carts themselves left behind—for as Giulia had learned from Ferraldi's letters, nothing came to Venice except by water.

It was a long, dull, bone-rattling day. By the time the caravan halted to make camp, Giulia was grateful to escape the cart. Maria assisted Bernardo with the baggage and the tent; again Giulia offered to help, and again Bernardo turned her curtly away. At Sofia's insistence she shared the evening meal, perched awkwardly on one of the painted chests while Sofia and Bernardo discussed their stay in Vicenza and Maria knelt by the brazier, her dark face as still as a painting.

Later, wrapped in her blanket, Giulia lay awake, staring at the red eye of Maria's cook fire. She was still mistrustful of this sudden turn of luck. But she was warm. Her belly was full. And she was one day closer to Venice.

—

By the third morning the cut on Giulia's hand had scabbed over, and she'd begun to believe, cautiously, that her luck might hold after all.

That afternoon Bernardo gave Maria the reins and jumped down into the road to stretch his legs. He kept pace with the horse for a time, then jogged back and hoisted himself into the rear of the cart, settling down on the other side of the pile of baggage. His eyes passed over Giulia as if she were just another bundle. He took a book from his belt pouch and began to read, shading his eyes against the sun.

Giulia craned her neck, trying to see the print. Growing up, she'd had access to books, for Maestro Bruni had allowed her to borrow as she pleased from his small library of printed and hand-copied volumes. She'd read Ovid in the original Latin, and Plato in translation. She'd read Dante in Italian, and

suffered nightmares of his vision of Hell. At Santa Marta, however, there had been no opportunity to read, other than the
formulas in Humilità's book of secrets. She missed it.

She craned too far. Bernardo raised his head and fixed her
with a flat stare. "Do you want something?"

"No," Giulia said, remembering to lower her voice.

"Keep your eyes to yourself, then."

He returned his attention to the book. Giulia felt a rush of
anger. As herself, as a girl, she might have swallowed it, but she
was a boy now. She did not have to be so deferential.

"I was only wondering what you were reading."

He looked up again. "Why? It would mean nothing to
you."

"I can read. I have book learning."

She saw the skepticism in his face. Like his mother, he was
extraordinarily good-looking; but where Sofia was gold, he
was iron, his eyes too dark to see the pupils, his glossy hair as
black as the charred animal bones Giulia had so often ground
up for paint. It was cut in the Venetian fashion, with short
bangs across the front, angling down to fall below his shoulders at the back. His clothes were conservative, made of plain
dark materials, though the fine cloth and meticulous cut, as
well as the silver at his belt and at the pommel of his dagger,
spoke of wealth, as surely as did the luxurious furnishings of
Sofia's tent.

"Read this, then." He held the volume toward her in the
manner of someone calling a bluff.

Giulia could not resist the lure of the book. It was small,
beautifully bound in leather, with a silver clasp that caught the
sunlight. The text was Latin, printed on creamy paper: poetry,
though she did not recognize the poet's name.

She leafed through it, turning the pages with care—a book like this, she knew, might cost as much as a week's wages for a notary or a clerk. Picking a poem at random, she began to read—haltingly at first, for it had been nearly two years since she'd held such a volume in her hands, but then more fluently, taking pleasure in the words. It was a love poem, the lament of a lover pining for his absent beloved. She read to the end, then closed the book and offered it back to Bernardo. He took it. She could see that he was trying to hide his surprise.

"Where did you learn Latin?"

"I had a tutor, growing up."

"Yes, my mother said you told her that." *And I assumed you were lying.* He didn't need to say it. "Is he the one who taught you to draw?"

"No. I've always known how to draw, ever since I can remember."

"Tell me the truth." That flat stare again. "Are you really apprenticed to Gianfranco Ferraldi?"

"Yes."

"But that's not the whole story, is it?"

The cart passed over a deep rut, jolting them both. Giulia shoved away a bundle that had shifted. "What do you mean?"

"There's something else. Something you haven't told my mother. Did you run away? Did you steal something?"

His regard was almost as penetrating as Sofia's. Giulia forced herself to meet his eyes. "I stole nothing. Everything I've said is true."

She braced herself for another harsh question. But all he said was "Lucky for you my mother has so soft a heart."

"She's very kind."

"You needn't call her 'clarissima,' you know. She'll let you do it because it flatters her, but in truth she has no claim to any title of respect."

"Oh. I assumed . . ."

"Because she is wealthy? She built her wealth herself. And kept it too." Giulia heard the pride in his voice. "Few in her profession can say the same."

"Her profession?"

"Did she not tell you?"

"Tell me what?"

"My mother is a courtesan. Retired now, but for a few of her oldest clients. In her prime, though, she was famous."

Giulia's mouth had fallen open.

"Be careful," he said, deadpan. "You'll catch a fly."

"I'm sorry." Giulia found her voice. "I meant no offense."

"Offense?" Contempt twisted his lips. "In her youth she was called La Fiamma, for the beauty that burned men's hearts to ash. She was a confidante to members of the Council of Ten, even to one who became doge. Giovanni Bellini himself begged to paint her portrait. How could the ignorance of a boy like you give offense?"

Giulia's face was on fire. Angry retorts filled her mouth. Instead of speaking them she turned away, reminding herself that she was dependent on this haughty young man's tolerance, just as she was on his mother's.

I should have held my tongue when he first spoke to me. She stared at the sunlit countryside rolling past the cart, hearing the rustle of pages as Bernardo opened his book again. *I won't make that mistake a second time.*

—

That night in Sofia's tent, as the three of them shared a meal, Giulia looked at Sofia with new eyes. It had been obvious that Sofia was rich—though whether by birth or marriage, Giulia had not been able to guess—and, for a woman, unusually highly educated, for she carried with her several printed books and wrote daily in a journal. Giulia had gathered, from Sofia's and Bernardo's conversations in the evenings, that Sofia was a widow—or at least that she had no living husband—and that she owned a house in Venice along with a number of properties rented out to tenants, which Bernardo managed for her.

Now these things took on new significance. Giulia was not unfamiliar with Sofia's profession—in her father's household, it had been common knowledge that in addition to the mistresses he kept under his roof, he visited a courtesan called Emilia alla Tresca. Emilia was no common whore: She was beautiful, accomplished, equal in intellect to any man—or so said the gossips in the sewing room where Giulia worked. They also said that Emilia's career had made her wealthy—that she wore silks and velvets, that her throat was wound with gold, that she received her admirers in chambers as magnificent as any noblewoman's.

Giulia had listened to these stories as she might have to tales of angels or two-headed calves—things so improbable that there was no likelihood of ever actually encountering them. Yet here was Sofia, so close Giulia could have touched her, talking with Bernardo about repairs that needed to be made to the roof of one of their properties. Giulia thought of the seamstresses at Palazzo Borromeo, some of whom had spat at the mention of Emilia alla Tresca. She thought of the priest at Santa Marta, who would certainly denounce Sofia as a harlot. She thought of Suor Margarita, who would say that the proper response to such a corrupted soul was revulsion, and of Angela, who would counsel compassion. And then she thought of Bernardo—of the pride in his voice as he spoke of the rewards Sofia's profession had won her, as if they were accomplishments to be envied rather than the fruits of sin.

He must be illegitimate. Like me.

Or maybe not like me. For my mother had only one lover, while Sofia . . . Does he even know who his father is?

Later, Bernardo left the tent to bed down in the cart, and Sofia allowed Giulia to sketch her. As a form of payment for the journey, Giulia had offered to make Sofia a portrait—a real portrait, not a simple sketch like the one she'd done the first night. Sofia had given her six precious sheets of paper from the store in her writing desk, and Giulia had made charcoal sticks by burying willow twigs, cut with a knife borrowed from Maria, in the embers of the cook fire overnight. In the morning before starting out, in the pauses during the day, by the ruddy light of the dying campfire at night, she worked not just on the promised portrait, but on images of her own: a tumbled wall, a ruined cottage, a line of cypresses. It was an entirely unexpected blessing to be able to draw again; she'd resigned herself to days or even weeks without charcoal and paper. To conserve space, she made the drawings tiny, filling up both sides of the sheets.

Sofia's loosened hair, which Maria braided each day into elaborate arrangements, rippled past her waist. The candles in their swaying globes gilded her milky skin. Her ability to hold a pose with perfect immobility was amazing; she knew, also, how to flatter herself by the positions she chose, her head angled so that the skin of her throat and the flesh beneath her chin seemed taut and smooth. Giulia had thought her merely vain, but now she saw even this with different eyes. Sofia's livelihood depended on her beauty. She had no choice but to be vain.

At last Sofia yawned. Over the past days, Giulia had discovered why she kept her lips closed when she smiled: Her teeth were discolored at the front and gapped at one side, the only part of her that was not beautiful.

"Is it enough, Girolamo? I am tired."

"Yes, *cla* . . . " Giulia caught herself, but then thought, *Why not?* "Yes, clarissima. Thank you."

"Good." Sofia extended her arms above her head, stretching like a cat. "Sleep well, Girolamo."

No, Giulia thought as she passed from the tent's warm illumination into the chill blackness of the night. It wasn't horror or disgust or pity that she felt now that she knew what Sofia was. It was only what she'd felt before: curiosity. And respect.

CHAPTER II

❖ La Serenissima ❖

The distant mountains rose higher as the caravan approached
the coast, their peaks now crowned with snow. Fog gathered
during the night, muffling the campsite at dawn, burning off
later in the day. Giulia's blanket was always damp when she
climbed out of it in the morning.

She was growing used to her disguise. Her exposed legs no
longer felt so naked, and she was beginning to enjoy the freedom of not being encumbered with long skirts. She was even
starting to appreciate the convenience of shorter hair, which
she could simply untangle with her fingers and tuck behind
her ears, rather than spend the time to comb and braid and
bind it up.

But there was so much to remember. Lowering her voice.
Walking with her shoulders back and her eyes focused boldly

straight ahead. Sitting with her knees apart. The binding around her breasts was a constant irritation—too tight and it was hard to breathe, too loose and she worried it would slip. She was becoming anxious about her monthly courses, though they were not due for another couple of weeks. She borrowed Maria's knife again and cut another strip from the bottom of her mantle, wrapping it around her waist under her doublet to have it ready.

And then there were her several-times-daily excursions away from camp. She tried to leave only when others were not watching, but that was not always possible. Sofia had noticed— Giulia was aware of her gaze sometimes as she returned, the cool regard that seemed to perceive so much yet revealed so little. The merchant's teenage apprentice and son had noticed also. They'd begun to tease her, whistling and making rude comments.

On a gray afternoon, with only two or three days remaining in the journey, the caravan halted to water the animals, and Giulia made use of a handy hedgerow. When she came back, the two boys were waiting for her, a little distance beyond the gathering of carts. The minute she saw them, she knew she was in trouble.

"If it isn't the whore's charity case," the merchant's son drawled. "Have a nice walk?"

Giulia ducked her head and kept going. If she ignored them, perhaps they would let her pass. Instead, they moved to block her.

"Think you're too good to talk to us?" the apprentice demanded.

"Too good to piss alongside us, that's for sure," the merchant's son sneered.

"I don't want any trouble." Giulia's heart had begun to pound.

"Maybe he's not pissing," said the apprentice, making a lewd gesture at his groin. "Maybe he's doing something else."

"Four times a day? He doesn't look the type."

"Let me by," Giulia said.

"Let me by," mimicked the merchant's son. "I know what it is. He's ashamed. He's got a tiny little prick, and he doesn't want anyone to see."

"Maybe he's one of those whatdoyoucallits, the ones that get cut," said the apprentice. "Maybe he's got no prick at all. Maybe he has to piss like a girl."

"Come on then." The merchant's son stepped toward Giulia. "Let's have a look."

"Leave me alone." To Giulia's horror, her voice cracked. The apprentice grinned like a wolf.

"Grab him!"

They rushed at her. Giulia sank to her knees, folding in on herself, protecting the parts of her body that could betray her. But when rough hands seized her arms, searing memories came over her—of the brothers and their cart, of all the times in her childhood when she'd been bullied for her bastardy. She wrenched free, scrabbling along the ground, staggering to her feet. Wildly she struck out, the side of her fist connecting solidly with the apprentice's face. He howled and leaped away. The merchant's son darted in and punched her in the ribs. All the air went out of her. For a moment the world went dark.

"What's this?"

Giulia discovered that she was on the ground again. She heard someone gasping: herself, she realized, clawing for breath. Bernardo stood nearby, holding the merchant's son by the back of his doublet. The apprentice was crouched on his haunches, moaning, his hands covering his nose. Blood seeped from between his fingers.

"Two against one, is that it?" Bernardo shook the merchant's son like a puppy.

"Just having a bit of fun. What's it to you?" The merchant's son tried to twist away. "Let me *go!*"

"Go on then." Bernardo pushed the boy so hard that he stumbled to one knee. "You too." Bernardo aimed a kick at the apprentice, who scuttled out of reach. "Get back to the carts."

"I'll tell my father you laid hands on me," the merchant's son said, climbing to his feet.

"And I'll tell him you enjoy beating younger boys."

"Whore's son!" the merchant's son yelled, backing away. "Bet you don't even know your father's name!"

He turned and ran. The apprentice stumbled after him, still clutching his face.

"Blood will out," Bernardo said quietly, though the merchant's son was by now too far away to hear. "Whether or not it has a name."

He smoothed his clothes and shook back his hair, then turned and held a hand down to Giulia. "Come. Get up."

She tried to push herself up on her own, but pain burst like fire along her ribs, and she subsided to the ground again, gasping. Before she realized what he meant to do, Bernardo stooped and gripped her under the arms, heaving her easily to her feet. She cried out, with shock this time as well as pain, pulling free and staggering back, hunching over as she did, for the sudden motion had caused the binding around her breasts to slip.

Bernardo stared at her, his hands still outstretched. *Please God*, she thought, *don't let him notice anything.*

"You're hurt," he said.

"It's nothing." Giulia forced herself to straighten. She pulled her mantle close, hiding in its folds. "Just bruises."

"You should let my mother have a look. She's sure to have something in her box of remedies that would help."

"No! Truly, it's not necessary."

"Well." He shrugged. "If you're certain."

"I am. Thank you for helping me."

"I despise bullies." His face went cold as he said it, and Giulia wondered what experience lay behind the words. "Fortunate for you I spotted what was going on."

"I would have managed."

"I doubt it. Though you gave a decent account of yourself, considering. That boy will be swallowing blood for some time." He eyed her. "I wouldn't have thought you had it in you."

"I'm not a weakling," she said, stung by his tone.

"I didn't mean—" He stopped, frowning. There was a beat of silence. "Well. The caravan will be moving on. We'd best get back."

Giulia found her clogs, which had come off when she fell. The bottoms of her hose were soaked. The fabric bunched uncomfortably under her feet as she began to walk.

"What was it about anyway?" To her surprise, Bernardo fell in beside her. "The fight."

"Nothing." It had begun to drizzle, a fine, cold spray that chilled Giulia's hot cheeks. She drew up the hood of her mantle.

"I've noticed they've been teasing you."

"It's nothing," she said again, wishing he would stop watching her, that he'd let her go on alone.

"You are asking for it, you know," he said. "Always going off alone to do your business. Boys like that are like dogs. They can't bear anyone who breaks from the pack."

"I just like to be private."

"You'd be better off—"

"I'm grateful for your help." She rounded on him, the sudden motion making pain flare along her side. "But it's none of your business. In fact, you've probably made things worse. They'd have beaten me, and that would have been the end of it. Now they'll want revenge."

His obsidian eyes narrowed. She turned away, more carefully this time, and trudged on. Surely now he would leave her alone. But he walked beside her in silence all the way back to Sofia's cart.

—

Giulia feared she would have to argue with Sofia about inspecting her injury and was surprised when Sofia did not even suggest it. Instead, she prepared a draft of some sort of medicine, which made Giulia dizzy but helped her sleep. The draft had worn off by morning; she had to grit her teeth against the pain as she climbed to her feet. Later, in the seclusion of some bushes, she found that a lurid purple bruise had bloomed all down her side.

She caught sight of the apprentice when the caravan paused at midday. His nose was twice its normal size, his eyes ringed with black. It gave her a surprising amount of satisfaction to see the damage she'd done. She was wary as she left the camp, but he did not follow her, nor did the merchant's son. She wondered if Bernardo had talked to them, then dismissed the thought. Why would he bother?

"We'll reach the lagoon the day after tomorrow," Sofia said that night. "Can you smell it, Girolamo? The ocean?"

"Is that what it is?" Giulia had begun to be aware of it that day: a briny, slightly sulfurous odor that she noticed when she drew a deep breath.

"Yes." Sofia smiled, the rare full smile that showed her bad teeth. "How I've missed it. Have you ever seen the ocean?"

"No, clarissima. Though my tutor told me of it."

"All the words in the world cannot compare to the reality." Then, seeing Giulia shifting about, trying vainly to find a comfortable position: "I'll make you another draft. Be sure you drink it all."

The sun shone the next day. Giulia was still sore, but the stiffness had lessened, and she could move more easily.

During the noontime halt, she brought out Sofia's portraits and laid them in front of her, side by side. She'd made two, in a combination of homemade charcoal and borrowed ink, with a gray wash she had created by diluting the ink with water.

In the first Sofia was turned slightly away from the viewer, her eyes cast down as if she were reading, her expression inward and serene. In the second she was looking back over her shoulder as though someone had called her name, smiling her closed-lipped smile, her eyes alight with laughter. In both she wore her rich silk wrapper, her hair flowing loose across her shoulders; in both, she looked exactly what she was: a beautiful woman just beginning to lose the battle against age. Giulia had hesitated over this, remembering what Sofia had said, the first night, about flattery. In the end she'd drawn the truth, as much of it as she was capable of perceiving.

The portraits were as good as anything she'd ever done. She knew that without vanity, in spite of the difficult conditions and improvised materials. But she also knew that they were flawed—criticisms that came to her in Humilità's voice,

as if she were in the workshop again and Humilità was standing at her shoulder: the stiffness of Sofia's bent neck in the first
portrait, her not-quite-in-proportion left arm in the second.
This sense of Humilità's presence had visited Giulia often over
the past days. She knew it was really only her own voice she
heard, speaking her teacher's wisdom back to her. But at Santa
Marta she'd felt only the black void of Humilità's absence. It
comforted her now to feel something else—to imagine that
she carried a little of her teacher with her as she ventured out
into the world.

Her hand went to her neck, where the canvas pouch hid
beneath her clothes. *Are you angry with me, Maestra, wherever
you are, for running away? For abandoning the workshop you
gave your life to? But it wasn't your workshop any longer. And if
I'd stayed, I wouldn't have been able to save Passion blue.*

With an effort, Giulia pulled her mind away from the past.

Flawed or not, the portraits were finished; she'd only harm
them if she tinkered with them further. Now she needed to
sign them—but how? Not as Girolamo; that felt too much like
attributing her work to someone else. Yet her artist's pride
demanded that she mark them as her own. In the end she simply inscribed them with the letter *G*, the initial of both her true
name and her false one.

That night at supper, Giulia sat as usual on one of Sofia's
clothing chests. Sofia was gracefully arrayed nearby on a folding chair, while Bernardo lounged on the cot, his long legs in
their fine boots carelessly extended. The smell of the wood
burning in the brazier masked the scent of the sea, which was
stronger than it had been yesterday.

Sofia drew in her breath when Giulia put the portrait into
her hands—the first one, without the smile. "This is beautiful,"
she said. "Truly, Girolamo, it is exquisite."

"And you thought him not a flatterer," Bernardo said dryly.

"No, Bernardo, you cynical beast." Sofia was usually tolerant of his occasional needling, but now she sounded almost angry. "That is not what I mean. Look."

She thrust the drawing toward him. For a moment Giulia thought he would refuse to take it. But then he leaned forward and twitched it from his mother's fingers.

"I knew you had ability." Sofia turned to Giulia again. "But this is beyond anything I imagined."

"It's a small enough repayment for your kindness, clarissima." Giulia was pleased, and also relieved. She'd learned that people did not always enjoy seeing themselves through an artist's eye.

"One day, I wager, it will be you who'll be paid, and far more than the price of a journey. Have you always had it? This sorcery in your hands?"

"Not the skill, clarissima. That has come with time and teaching. But I've always been able to draw. One of the first things I remember is scribbling on a flagstone with a bit of chalk. I was punished for it after my mother died—the woman who fostered me thought it a waste of time. But I never stopped. I couldn't stop, any more than I could stop breathing."

"I think perhaps I understand you better now." Sofia tilted her head, embracing Giulia in her cool, amber gaze. "Why you would leave your home and travel so very far alone to a city where you are a stranger in order to apprentice yourself to a master you do not know. It is your gift that demands this of you, is it not? Your gift demands *everything* of you."

Giulia felt a prickling down her spine at how exactly Sofia had touched upon the truth. She was suddenly acutely aware of her disguise—her exposed legs, the binding at her chest, the loose hair around her face.

"You have looked enough, my beast." Sofia reached toward Bernardo, who all this time had been staring at the portrait. "Give it back to me."

His eyes came up, as if she'd startled him. For an instant he didn't move. But then he placed the drawing in his mother's hand and sat back, turning his head to look at Giulia, not haughtily or dismissively, but in a way she couldn't read.

"I see you've signed it," Sofia said. "But only with an initial?"

"It's the way I've always done it, clarissima."

"*G*," Sofia said in a musing tone. "Well. I shall treasure it." Reaching for her writing desk, she slipped the portrait carefully inside. "Do you need another sleeping draft? I've nearly used up my stock of herbs, but there should be enough for one more night."

"No," Giulia said, even though she knew it meant she wouldn't sleep. "But thank you."

She rose carefully, and escaped into the dark.

—

They reached the coastal town of Mestre the next morning. There, Giulia knew, Sofia and her party would separate from the merchant train, leaving behind the cart, the horses, the tent poles and canvas, all of which had been rented for the journey. Bernardo, who'd seen to the unloading of the baggage, went off to hire boats, while Giulia and Sofia and Maria waited on the dock.

It was another damp, overcast day. The tide was out, exposing mudflats and salt marshes, which gave off a sulfurous stench of brine and rot that stung the inside of Giulia's nose. A mist lay across the ocean and the town—not thick enough to obscure objects close by, but completely obliterating the horizon. Huddled in her mantle against the chill, Giulia felt a keen disappointment. Sofia had told her how, on a clear day, it was possible to see Venice from the shore, rising like a mirage from the green waters of the lagoon. Now, Giulia thought, she might merely have been standing by a large lake, or on the banks of a tidal river.

Bernardo returned. He'd found two boats, but they would have to wait for the tide. He'd purchased food and drink, and they made a meal of roast fowl and thin wine in the open air.

They embarked at last, Sofia and Maria in the first boat, Bernardo and Giulia in the second, the baggage divided between them. Giulia had traveled in a boat before, on the night Ormanno had kidnapped her—but that had been a brief ride on the calm waters of a canal. This was the sea, its choppy swells much bigger than they appeared from land, tossing the boat sickeningly up and down. She clung to the side, her knuckles white, rigid with fear as Mestre vanished behind a wall of fog and the clean saltiness of the ocean replaced the stench of the marshes. She could see Sofia's boat a little way ahead, but apart from that there was only the mist and the heaving water—not rich blue green as Sofia had described, but as dull and gray as lead.

Without landmarks she had no way to judge their progress. How could the boatman tell where he was going? But at last she glimpsed something within the obscurity ahead: light, at first just a single point, but quickly joined by others. In the space of a sigh Venice appeared, melting through the mist, a line of close-packed buildings that seemed to rise directly from the waves, as if they had grown like trees from the bottom of the ocean.

Giulia felt wonder thrill through her. It was as if the city had not existed before that moment, as if a spell or a wish had conjured it into being.

"*La Serenissima*," Bernardo said, startling her; he hadn't spoken a word since they'd cast off. "The daughter of the sea. What do you know of her?"

"Only a little," Giulia said.

"She is not simply a city, but the heart of a great republic." Pride filled his voice. "She has never been conquered, not once in all her history—how many places can say the same? Her trade extends across the sea, her dominion across the land. There is no city in Europe to match her for wealth and beauty. You'll see as we travel down the Grand Canal."

The boatman pulled steadily at his oars. They were so close now that Giulia could count the windows of the houses.

"Look." Bernardo pointed. "There is where we enter."

Ahead, Giulia saw a forest of poles rising from the ocean. *Channel markers*, she thought, remembering Ferraldi's sketches. Sofia's boat was already passing between them, into the canal beyond.

The swells diminished, the boat slipping along more smoothly. Long brick buildings—warehouses?—rose on either side, their contours softened by the mist, interspersed with smaller structures crowded as close as teeth. There was water traffic here: barges, other rowboats, and slim, curve-prowed craft guided with a single rear-mounted oar by a boatman standing on a platform at the back. These too Giulia recognized from Ferraldi's letters: gondolas.

Ahead, where a great church towered above the buildings alongside it, she saw another waterway.

"The Grand Canal," Bernardo said. "It runs through the city from north to south, all the way to the Molo and the

Doge's Palace. It used to be a river—that's why it bends so, in the shape of an *S*. But long ago our engineers dammed the source and turned it into a canal."

Giulia braced herself against the tipping of the boat as the boatman steered left. The Grand Canal was much wider than the canal they'd come from, and the traffic was heavier; the air was filled with curses and shouts of warning as craft drew too near one another.

Ferraldi had written of the splendid palazzi that adorned the entire length of the Grand Canal, and sketched them, too, in all their astonishing variety. Now Giulia saw the reality, more amazing than words or drawings could convey: palazzo after palazzo, two and three and even four stories tall, their façades of patterned brick and colored marble embellished with columns and balconies, their immense windows framed in elaborate stonework, and their red-tile roofs crowned by a forest of trumpet-shaped chimney pots. Torches and lanterns burned in water-level entryways, gilding the mist. Many of the entryways had steps or landings extending out into the water, but others opened onto internal docks, so that the canal seemed part of the palazzo itself.

Giulia had grown up in a great palace. But never in her life had she seen so many magnificent buildings together in one place, or imagined such a display of opulence and grandeur. She forgot she was cold, forgot she was queasy from the motion of the water. Bernardo, grown suddenly talkative, named the palazzi as they passed: Barbarigo, Foscari, Morosini, Gritti— the names, he said, of Venice's great families; but she barely heard him. She had become a pair of eyes: painter's eyes, entranced by mist and shadow, by form and color. Her hands burned with the desire to put brush to panel. In her mind, she could hear the singing of the paints she would use.

Just past the Ca' d'Oro—so startlingly ornate, with its blue- and gold-painted stonework and its rooftop crenellations clad in gilding, that Giulia had to blink to be sure she wasn't imagining it—Bernardo leaned forward with an instruction for the boatman. They steered left, into a narrow canal—a *rio*, Giulia corrected herself, seeing the word in her mind in Ferraldi's handwriting: the Venetian term for smaller waterways. Houses closed in like cliffs, not palaces now, but modest dwellings with fronts of unadorned brick or stucco—yet in their way no less extraordinary, with their feet in the water and their doors opening directly off the rio. The air smelled of brine and sewage, an odor that intensified as they glided beneath a bridge. She coughed. Bernardo chuckled.

"If you think that's bad, wait until the summer. It's so strong sometimes it will scorch your throat."

The boatman steered around a turn into a rio so constricted that when a gondola glided by, both boats scraped against the walls. Giulia trailed her fingers along the brick, damp and a little slimy. She'd begun to feel as if she'd passed into a dream.

They turned again, entering a wider canal lined with more substantial houses, with a broad, paved walkway running along one side.

"There."

Bernardo pointed to a house just ahead, its yellow-stuccoed front pierced by graceful pointed windows. The boatman steered toward the landing and tied the boat to one of the painted mooring posts that jutted from the water.

Sofia's boat had already docked. She stood at the door, Maria beside her. As Giulia left the boat—stepping carefully, for the landing was slippery with waterweed—the door opened and a gray-haired man in a belted tunic bowed low. He gave Sofia the lantern he carried, then came forward to assist Bernardo, who was starting to unload the baggage.

"May I help?" Giulia asked her customary question, to which Bernardo gave his customary response.

"No need. Go with my mother."

Sofia and Maria had disappeared inside. Giulia hurried after them, down a dark passageway that ended on a paved courtyard with a wellhead at its center. A flight of steps rose to the second floor, the *piano nobile*; Giulia followed Sofia and Maria up into a wide hallway that appeared to run the length of the house from front to back. The pointed windows she'd seen from outside opened at one end, admitting the light of the fading day.

A middle-aged woman was waiting, holding a candle. She curtsied when she saw Sofia.

"I've ordered a room prepared for you, Girolamo." Sofia turned to Giulia. "Chiara will show you where it is and bring you something to eat. She'll clean your clothes as well—just leave them outside the door. Sleep well. I will see you in the morning."

With Maria, she moved down the hall. Chiara led Giulia in the other direction, showing her into a small chamber that contained only a copper bathtub and a pair of chests pushed against one wall. But if it was poor in furnishings, it was rich in other ways, with a floor of patterned marble and walls covered in embossed leather. Windows were set on either side of the fireplace, glazed with glass disks set into a lattice of lead.

Giulia crouched in front of the fire, holding her hands to the warmth. After a little while Chiara returned, first with a tray of food and then with water for the tub: two buckets of hot, two of cold. Giulia turned the key in the door lock, then pulled off her boy's clothes and sank into the tub, feeling the warmth soaking all the way down to her bones. Never before in her life had she experienced the luxury of a heated bath. She wondered if she shouldn't find it strange, to be lying in hot water in this little room . . . actually to be in Venice, the city she had run away to find. But the sense of dream was stronger than ever. Or perhaps she'd simply exhausted her capacity for amazement.

She leaned her head against the tub's high back and closed her eyes. Images of mist-wreathed palazzi filled her mind. Faintly, she could still feel the heaving of the boat.

She woke abruptly. The water had gone cold. Outside, gray day had yielded to black night. The only light came from the fire and the candles flickering on ledges by the door.

Giulia climbed out of the bath and dried herself on the towels Chiara had left, then pulled her ragged mantle around herself and dropped her clothing in the hall outside, as Sofia had instructed. She ate the cheese and sausage Chiara had brought. At last, utterly weary, she blew out the candles and climbed into bed—not the kind of bed she was used to, free-standing on the floor, but a cabinet built into the wall, with a mattress on a platform and a curtain to pull across. The mattress was stuffed with feathers, the coverlet and pillow filled with down. It was like being wrapped in clouds, and she sank quickly into sleep.

CHAPTER 12

❖ Revelations ❖

Giulia woke to a rattling at the latch. For a moment she could not remember where she was.

"Who's there?" she called, forgetting to lower her voice.

"Your breakfast" came the answer, muffled through the door.

Leaving the cloud-like comfort of the bed, Giulia wrapped herself in her mantle again and turned the lock. It was Chiara, carrying a steaming bowl in one hand and the clothes Giulia had left in the hall last night in the other.

"The mistress will receive you in the *sala* when you've finished," Chiara said.

The bowl held grain porridge, sweetened with honey and dried fruit. The shirt was beautifully clean, and the other garments had been brushed and sponged. Giulia redressed, then got into bed again to eat, for the fire had burned out and the room was cold.

I'm in Venice, she thought, astonished. *I am really here.*

But it was too soon to feel triumphant. The most crucial part of her plan still lay ahead. She felt a thrill of apprehension and wondered if she could delay—surely Sofia would let her stay a day or two, at least until her ribs were fully healed. But then she thought of Bernardo and his warning at the journey's start. Two days of rest, in any case—or three, or four—would not make facing Ferraldi any easier.

She had everything she needed: Ferraldi's address, memorized from his letters. Five sheets of work to show—the tiny sketches she had done on the journey, her studies of Sofia, and a finished portrait: the second one, with the smile. The story she planned to tell, conceived at Santa Marta and rehearsed along the journey.

No. There's no good reason to delay.

For the second time she threw back the covers. She finger-combed her hair, thrust her feet into her heavy wooden clogs, and slipped out into the hall.

The clouds had pulled away overnight. Sun flooded through the windows facing the canal, printing their latticed images on the shining marble floor. In the light, Giulia could better appreciate the opulence of the furnishings: the tapestries with their floral motifs, the carved and gilded chairs along the walls, the great glass chandelier bristling with candles.

She headed toward the front of the house, the direction in which Sofia had gone last night. All the doors she passed were closed except the last. It opened onto a comfortable sitting room, where Sofia sat in a cushioned chair in the sun, her head thrown back to reveal the long arch of her throat. A yellow cat dozed in her lap; two others sprawled by her feet. A crackling fire warmed the air.

Sofia looked around, smiling, as Giulia entered.

"Girolamo. Welcome." She leaned back her head again and closed her eyes. "It's wonderful to be home. I pine for Venice when I'm away from it, like a plant uprooted from its native soil."

On the wall opposite the door, a portrait hung—Sofia herself, in a high-waisted dress of brilliant red-gold brocade, her tawny hair wound with pearls, a white Easter lily in one hand. In the exquisite detail, the glowing colors, Giulia recognized the work of a master. It drew her like a flame. Before she knew it she was across the room, bending close to see if she could identify the paints the artist had used. *Orange realgar, for certain, mixed with . . . what?* If the portrait had been wet, she might have been able to guess. But it was long dry. The colors no longer sang.

"You like my Bellini, I see."

Giulia turned. "I didn't mean to presume, clarissima. It's just that it's so beautiful."

"The lily and the pearls were his idea. He enjoyed the irony—symbols of purity, on a courtesan." Sofia smiled, caressing the cat's ears. "Did you sleep well?"

"I did." Giulia came forward, halting in a patch of sun. "Clarissima, I thank you for your hospitality, and for everything you've done for me these past days. I'm more grateful than I can say. But I need to be on my way."

"You're welcome to remain, Girolamo, for as long as you wish."

"My master is expecting me. I shouldn't delay."

"Very well." Sofia lifted the cat off her lap and got to her feet. "I have something to give you before you go."

"You've already been too generous, clarissima."

"Nonsense. Come with me."

She led the way through an adjoining door. The chamber beyond had a coffered ceiling and walls painted to imitate fabric hangings. A great bed occupied the center of the room, with a scarlet canopy and heaps of snowy linens, its gold-embroidered coverlet tossed casually aside. Giulia's cheeks grew warm at the thought of what happened there, in that bed.

"These were Bernardo's." Sofia bent to pick up a pile of clothing that sat atop the long chest at the bed's foot. "Two shirts, a cap, and a good wool cloak to replace that torn rag of yours. They'll be large on you, but they are all nearly as good as new. My beast is particular about his clothing." She gave Giulia the garments, then knelt to open the chest. "And I believe you will need these soon, if you do not already."

She rose. In her hands she held several folded cloths of thick, absorbent wool. Giulia stared at them, an icy flood of understanding spreading through her. Her eyes rose to Sofia's—those amber eyes that saw so much, including, apparently, what Giulia had most wanted to keep hidden.

"Do not fear," Sofia said gently. "I've told no one. Nor will I, you have my word."

"When did you . . . how did you guess?"

"A day or two after you found us. It's nothing you did or said, only a sense I had, which grew surer as time went on. The night you gave me the portrait was when I became certain. I saw the nature of your gift, and understood why you would be driven to conceal yourself in order to follow it."

"But if *you* could see it—"

"No, no." Sofia shook her head. "You make a convincing boy. People see what they expect to see, in any case, and most will not think to question the story told by your clothes and hair. It's simply that I am better versed than most in wearing masks. It's easier for me to recognize them when they are worn by others."

"I've wondered . . ." Giulia hesitated. "Why you've been so kind to me."

"I would have helped you reach Venice regardless of your sex. As Bernardo likes to point out, I have a weakness for abandoned creatures." She gestured to the yellow cat, which had followed them into the room. "Having been one myself, long ago. But if you were what you pretend to be, I would not have invited you into my house. What is your true age?"

"Eighteen."

"And your name?"

Again Giulia hesitated, reluctant to reveal more than Sofia had already guessed.

"No matter. I won't press you." Sofia stepped forward and laid the cloths atop the clothing Giulia held. "Early in my life I learned that though it is God who makes men and women, it is men alone who make the world. I've done the best I can with the gifts God gave me—better, I will say, than most in my profession. I've even won a kind of freedom for myself. Yet it is only as much freedom as a woman may possess, to live in comfort without complete dependence on the whims of men. And the price was very great. You too will pay a price. But if you succeed, the freedom you gain will be a man's. I admire you, *Girolamo*"—lightly, she stressed the false name—"for what you are attempting."

Giulia, overwhelmed, could not reply.

"I have this for you too." Sofia held out a leather purse, heavy with coins.

"Clarissima—that is too generous—"

"I have it to spare, as you can see. Take it. I will not permit you to refuse."

Softly Giulia closed her fingers around the purse. "I don't know how to thank you."

"Thank me by becoming what you were born to be. And Girolamo—if ever you require help, come to me. Ask for the house of La Fiamma, on Rio dei Miracoli in Cannaregio. Will you promise?"

"I promise, clarissima."

It was a lie. Giulia already knew she would never come back. Her secret was perilous enough when she was the only one who knew it. Safer to let Sofia forget her.

"Good." Sofia took Giulia by the shoulders and kissed her on both cheeks. "I'll send for Bernardo now, to escort you."

Giulia felt a pulse of alarm. "I don't want to put him to the trouble."

Sofia laughed. "Venice is a labyrinth, capable of defeating even those born and bred to it. If you go out on your own, God alone knows where you'll find yourself. I have already told him he must accompany you. You may wait for him in the courtyard. Good-bye, Girolamo. I will keep you in my prayers."

—

Calle del Fruttariol, off Salizzada San Lio, in the parish of San Lio in the *sestiere* of Castello. That was Ferraldi's address. Giulia spoke it to Bernardo, who gave it to Sofia's steward, who was waiting on the landing by the gondola.

The steward steered the gondola back toward the Grand Canal. Bernardo sat in the shade of a *felze,* the canopy that arched over the craft's midsection, while Giulia sat facing him in the bow, wrapped in her mantle against the cold rising off the water—her old mantle, for she had no desire to wear Bernardo's castoffs in front of him. In her arms she clutched the bundle she'd made of the things Sofia had given her, except for Sofia's purse, which she'd stowed inside her doublet with her drawings.

At the Grand Canal, where the sun dazzled the water and the palazzi mirrored themselves in ever-fragmenting reflections, the steward turned the gondola toward the Rialto, Venice's great commercial district—a noisy, teeming region of warehouses and markets and quays where masted ships lay at anchor. The water traffic here was the heaviest Giulia had seen; the steward navigated deftly around gondolas ferrying passengers, barges crammed with bales and barrels, boats piled with fresh-caught fish wafting the odor of the sea.

Bernardo, who had been so talkative yesterday, sat silent. When Giulia made the mistake of glancing at him, she found him watching her, a brooding expression on his face. Hastily she looked away. Sofia had guessed her secret—might he have done so too? He'd never given any sign, but then neither had Sofia. She wished again that Sofia had let her go alone.

The canal curved hard to the right, delivering them into the shadow of the Rialto Bridge. Giulia glimpsed its great wooden pilings as the gondola sped past, and then they were steering toward the canal's left bank, where the mouth of a rio admitted them back into the city. At last, where a bridge carried a street over the rio and a set of steps descended to the water, the steward drew the gondola to a halt.

"Campo San Lio lies just down there." He pointed. "Salizzada San Lio leads off it."

Giulia felt her stomach turn over. A few moments, no more, and she'd be at Gianfranco Ferraldi's door.

Bernardo ducked out from beneath the felze. Giulia realized he meant to leave the boat.

"No!" she exclaimed. He paused, his eyebrows raised. "I mean, you needn't trouble yourself. I can find my way from here."

"My mother asked me to see you all the way."

He stepped onto the slippery landing and began to mount the steps to the street. Since she had no choice, Giulia followed.

Campo San Lio was a sunlit square, with an ancient church on one side and a stone wellhead at its center. Children played on the paving. From a baker's shop came a delicious fragrance of baking bread, seasoned with the ever-present tang of the canals.

"Wait!" Giulia called to Bernardo, who was already halfway across the *campo*. Then when he did not pause: "Bernardo!"

Had she ever spoken his name before? He turned.

"Please," she said, catching up to him. "Tell your mother you brought me all the way. But let me go on alone."

He regarded her a moment, then shrugged. "Very well. If you're certain."

"Thank you for escorting me."

He nodded.

"Good-bye, then," she said.

He made no move to go. Some kind of struggle seemed to be happening behind his face.

"Was it worth it?" he asked abruptly.

She looked at him, unsure. "Was what worth it?"

"Running away. Leaving everything and everyone behind."

She thought of the afternoon in the cart, when she'd read to him from his book and he'd asked questions that came too close to the truth. This time there seemed to be no point in lying.

"I don't know yet," she said. "I hope so."

"I didn't believe you were what you said you were. Oh, I saw that you could draw, but still I thought you only meant to take advantage of my mother's kindness. But you never asked her for anything, did you? Not even to stay with us." His obsidian gaze probed her face. "She would have allowed it, you know. You could have had much more from her if you'd wanted."

Giulia thought of the coins hidden in her doublet. "All I ever wanted was to get to Venice."

"What is it you're running from?"

"A . . . master . . . who would not teach me."

"Why would he not teach you?"

Giulia hesitated. But his voice held neither skepticism nor mockery. He sounded as if he really wanted to know.

"My old master died. The one who inherited the workshop hated me. I was ordered to . . . to do something I thought was wrong, or else be banished. I realized that even if I obeyed . . . even if I was allowed to stay . . ." She took a breath. She'd never thought she would say any of this aloud. "I could never learn from such a master. Not as I want to learn. So I left."

"As easily as that?"

She shook her head. "It wasn't easy at all. But I had no choice."

"I thought of running away." He was not looking at her now, but at his fine leather gloves, which he was drawing through his fingers. "Last year, when I turned nineteen."

She stared at him. It was, perhaps, the last thing she might have expected him to say. "Why?"

"I've been managing my mother's affairs since I was fourteen years old." He spoke quietly; it was hard to hear him over the noise of the campo. "But I want to attend the university at Padua. I've always wanted to be a scholar—to read books, to write them myself. Perhaps to teach. I thought of just . . . leaving. Dropping everything, leaving everything behind. But in the end I couldn't betray my mother so."

"Would she not agree to let you go if you asked?"

"I cannot ask."

"Why not?"

"If she said no, I fear I would hate her for it." He breathed in, deeply, then out again. "She needs me. She has no one else."

She heard the resignation in his voice. This was a Bernardo she had never seen before, had never even suspected existed. She did not know what to do or say.

"Well." He slapped his gloves into his palm and held out his free hand. "Good luck to you, Girolamo."

Without thinking, Giulia took his hand. His fingers were smooth, his grip strong and warm. Their eyes met. And she felt something in her shift, as if the touch and the look and the new, yearning part of himself he'd just shown her had worked some kind of alchemical transformation. For the first time, her body understood what her eyes had been telling her all along: that he was a beautiful, desirable young man.

The blood rushed to her face. Perhaps he noticed. Or perhaps he was simply drawing back into himself, closing a door he regretted cracking open. He pulled away, more sharply than seemed necessary. Without another word he turned and left her, striding back toward the canal.

Giulia watched him go. The sense of his hand lingered in hers, his palm and fingers as soft as only those of a man who'd never done manual labor could be.

I'll never see him again. To her surprise, the thought carried something almost like regret.

CHAPTER 13

✛ Gianfranco Ferraldi ✛

Bernardo was gone. Giulia turned away from the canal, her mind shifting to what lay ahead. Her heart, immediately, began to race.

Ignoring the curious glances of passersby, she crouched on the paving of the campo to undo the bundle of clothing she carried. She freed Bernardo's mantle and pulled it over her shoulders, then rolled everything up again in her own ragged cloak and tucked it under her arm.

Salizzada San Lio opened directly off the campo. Giulia plunged into the crowd of pedestrians jostling in the narrow space between the shop fronts and taverns that lined both sides of the street. The air was alive with the voices of trades-people and housewives, ripe with the odors of food and refuse. Laundry flapped from upper windows, draped on long poles.

She found the Calle del Fruttariol without trouble—barely wide enough for two men to walk abreast, its brick paving slimy with the overflow from blocked gutters. At its end, a rio cut across at a right angle. Ferraldi's house was the last one on the left. Giulia recognized its stucco façade from the sketches he'd done for Humilità: the odd placement of the third-floor windows, the plaque of the winged Lion of San Marco inset above the door.

This is the end of my journey, she thought, looking up at the lion—his paw resting on a book, his jaws open in a roar. *Everything I've come to find lies behind that door.*

For an instant she wanted nothing more than to turn and run.

She drew a deep breath, steadying herself, then raised her hand and knocked. No response. She knocked again, harder than she intended, her nerves seizing hold of her muscles.

"Give it up, would you?" A voice from inside, muffled by the wood. "I'm coming!"

The latch rattled. The door swung a little way open, revealing a skinny boy in a paint-stained smock, his hair sticking out like straw around his face.

"What do you want?"

"I'm here—" Giulia cleared her throat, pitched her voice lower. "I'm here to see Gianfranco Ferraldi."

"What for?" The boy swiped his hand under his nose, which was running.

"My name is Girolamo Landriani. I've come from Padua on the recommendation of an old friend of Maestro Ferraldi's, Maestra Humilità Moretti."

"Saints! You'd better tell him yourself."

The boy pulled the door open all the way. The windowless area beyond was unlit; Giulia had the vague impression of a large space, a jumble of chests and shelves. The air smelled dankly of stone and canal water—but also, clear and distinct, of sawdust and varnish and oil and exotic materials, the mingled odors of a painter's trade. They halted her on the threshold, so deeply familiar that she wanted nothing more than to stand and breathe them in.

"You coming or not?"

Hastily she stepped inside. The boy relatched the door, plunging them into darkness, except for a faint illumination from above, where a set of stairs rose to the second floor. Giulia followed the boy up to a hallway. A window on her right looked down into the street. On her left, a single doorway gave onto a long, high-ceilinged chamber.

The workshop.

Because of Ferraldi's drawings, it was familiar to her piece-meal. Now, seeing it whole, she realized it was bigger than she'd thought, nearly as big as the workshop at Santa Marta. Its wood-plank floor was cluttered with tables, stools, chests, and cabinets. Two artists stood in the light of a long window arcade, their easels turned away from her so she could not see what they were working on. An apprentice polished a gessoed panel set on a pair of sawhorses, while another banged at something with a hammer and a third labored at a grinding stone. Near the far wall, two men bent over a drafting table.

The noise of this activity filtered out into the hallway: thumps and scrapes, voices raised in conversation. Things anyone might hear. But for Giulia there was something more, woven through the ordinary sounds like threads of gold in a tapestry of duller hues: the musical sizzle of cinnabar vermilion. The acid whine of malachite green. Lead white, purring like a great cat; crimson lake, trilling like a silver flute. All these paints and more were in use here, each singing with its own singular tone and tempo: the color song, which Giulia had not heard since the night she'd left Santa Marta, and had feared—though she could not have admitted it to herself, not until this very moment—she might never hear again.

"You coming?"

Once more she had forgotten to move. The boy was looking back at her, a peculiar expression on his face; she had the feeling she might have made some sound or gesture without realizing it.

"Yes," she said.

She followed him into the workshop. The singing of the colors intensified as she passed the artists at their easels and dwindled again as she neared the drafting table.

"Uncle," the boy said. "Someone's here to see you."

"Who?" asked the older of the two artists, his attention still on the drafting table, where a large sheet of paper was spread out, its curling edges held down with stones.

"Um, Girolamo something. From Padua."

"Girolamo *something*?" Annoyance snapped in Ferraldi's voice. "Did you not ask his surname?"

He looked up. Giulia had studied the little self-portraits he'd drawn for Humilità; she'd thought him ugly in those sketches, with his high domed forehead, hooked nose, and thin-lipped mouth. She saw now that he had maligned himself. His features were just as he'd portrayed them; but his living face, framed by silver hair falling to his shoulders, was somehow not ugly at all.

"Who are you, young man?" Ferraldi's eyes were a vivid blue green, another thing his sketches had not conveyed. "What's your business with me?"

Everything Giulia had planned to say flew out of her head. She heard herself blurt out: "I want to be your apprentice."

"Ah." Ferraldi straightened and put down the quill he held. The man beside him—muscled like an athlete, with a hard face and close-cropped hair—folded his arms, watching. "Unfortunately, I've no need of an apprentice at present."

"Please, signor. Maestra Humilità Moretti gave me your name. If you'd take just a moment to look at my work—"

"Humilità?" Ferraldi interrupted, his face lighting up. "You are acquainted with her? How does she fare?"

"I'm sorry, signor. She . . . she died in September."

"Ah," Ferraldi said again—this time an exclamation of pain. He closed his brilliant eyes briefly, then reopened them. "Come with me, young man."

He led the way to the end of the room, glancing back once to make sure Giulia was following. He was slight—not even as tall as she was—and very slender, and moved with a decisive swiftness that reminded her of Humilità, who before she'd fallen ill had possessed a similar air of overflowing energy.

He ushered Giulia into a small chamber that was obviously his study. It was a riot of disorder: chests half open; rags and other objects littering the floor; the desk heaped with sketches, ledgers, quills, and other objects. An easel was turned to the light of a window; the painting on it was hidden by a cloth, but Giulia could hear the cymbal song of azurite, so clear that she knew it had only recently been laid on.

"Sit down." Ferraldi seated himself behind his desk, gesturing that Giulia should take the stool opposite. "Tell me who you are and how you know Humilità Moretti." He corrected himself, the spasm of pain passing across his face again. "*Knew* her."

"My name is Girolamo Landriani." Giulia's heart was pounding again as she spoke the first of the lies she planned to tell. "I'm . . . cousin to one of Maestra Humilità's pupils, Giulia Borromeo."

"Are you indeed?" Ferraldi said with interest. "Humilità wrote to me about your cousin. She believes—believed—she has great promise as a painter. You are from Padua, then?"

"From Milan, signor. I apprenticed with a master there, but he died, and there was no place for me in his workshop after that. My cousin had already been sent to Padua, and I decided to follow, since my parents are dead and I have no other family."

"That is how you met Humilità, then? Through your cousin?"

"Yes, signor. Maestra Humilità was interested to learn I had apprenticed as a painter, and she accompanied my cousin sometimes when I went to the convent to visit. She was kind enough to look at my drawings, and . . . and to praise them. When I could find no master in Padua, she gave me your name."

"I am surprised she did not recommend you to her father."

Giulia felt a cold finger slide up her spine. "I would have been honored to apprentice with him, but he had no room for me."

Ferraldi turned his ugly-pleasing face toward the window. "We trained together, she and I," he said softly; and in what she heard in his voice, Giulia knew she had guessed right: He had loved Humilità and, perhaps, loved her still. "Her father taught her as though she were a boy—and well he should, for her talent was the equal of any man's. The apprentices were jealous—they could not accept that God had given such genius to a woman. Their scorn only made her labor harder. Such strength she had. Such will." He sighed. "But no will is stronger than death. She made light of her illness in her letters, but I suspected it was more serious than she said. Do you know what sort of end she had?"

"It was not without pain. But she was at peace. So my cousin told me."

"May God have mercy on her soul." Ferraldi crossed himself. "What will become of your talented cousin?"

"Signor, my cousin is also dead." Giulia felt the touch of ice again as she spoke the lie, though in a way it was true enough. "Suddenly, of a fever, at the end of September."

"Madonna. What cruel fortune. I am sorry, Girolamo."

Giulia looked down at her hands. "Thank you, signor."

"So you have come to me," Ferraldi said. "Hoping to find a new master. I would help you if I could, for Humilità's sake, but as I said before, I am not looking for an apprentice."

"Signor, I'm a hard worker. I can do any task you need, from grinding pigments to purifying oils to preparing panels. I can draw with charcoal, chalk, pen, or brush. I have some experience with paint, and I can use both tempera and oil." Giulia reached into the neck of her doublet and pulled out the roll of her drawings. "I've brought drawings to show you. Please, signor, look at them—they will prove I have a gift."

"I'm sorry, Girolamo. This is a small workshop, as you can see. I have three apprentices already, and though I would gladly rid myself of one of them, I cannot, for he is my sister's son. I have not the wages for a fourth."

"Signor, you don't have to pay me, not a penny. I'll work for free."

"Why would you do that when you could find another master? I can suggest a few names, if you like."

"Signor, I don't want another master. I will do anything. I'll scrub floors, run errands, polish gesso till my fingers bleed. I'll work day and night. I will work harder than any apprentice you've ever had. Just look at my work." Giulia heard her voice break, as no boy's would, but in that moment she didn't care.

"Please, I beg you, don't send me away without looking at my work. Give me that chance at least before you make up your mind."

He fixed her with his blue-green gaze. She could see no softening in his face; and with utter despair she knew that the worst had happened, and she had failed.

But then he sighed. Shaking his head in the manner of a man acting against his better judgment, he reached for the drawings and unrolled them. Giulia had placed Sofia on top, glancing back over her shoulder, smiling her enigmatic smile. Ferraldi's face changed when he saw her. Giulia saw the shift, the sudden sharpening of attention.

"You drew this," he said.

"Yes, signor. I will prove it if you let me."

He laid the portrait aside. One by one, he examined the other sheets: the portrait studies, the tiny sketches of trees and animals and the men of the merchant caravan. Giulia waited, her heart beating, every muscle tense. From beyond the door, faintly, she could hear the sound of the artists at work.

"How old are you, Girolamo?"

"Fifteen, signor."

"Who was your master in Milan?"

"Marco Signorelli." It was the name of a painter with whom Maestro Bruni had been acquainted.

"I don't know the name. How long did you study with him?"

"A year and a half. But I've been drawing all my life, ever since I can remember."

"Describe how you would go about making gesso."

Giulia did. Other questions followed: purifying oils, preparing tempera, the qualities of various pigments. Giulia answered as fully as she could. A flame of hope had kindled inside her, flaring a little brighter with each query.

At last Ferraldi rose. "Wait here."

He went out into the workshop again, returning after a moment with a sheet of paper and a stick of black chalk. Shoving aside some of the clutter of his desk, he laid them in front of Giulia.

"Draw," he said. "One thing, whatever you choose."

Giulia took up the chalk, her fingers curving around it with the same deep sense of familiarity she'd felt as she crossed the threshold of Ferraldi's house, and began to shape Humilità's face. She drew her teacher as she had been in health: round-cheeked and robust, her deep-set eyes meeting the viewer's in her customary expression of challenge. It was the image Giulia carried in her mind's eye—the image that she hoped, one day, would blot out the memory of the gaunt ghost Humilità had become at the end of her life.

She laid down the chalk and offered the paper to Ferraldi, who'd seated himself across from her again. She could read nothing in his face as he looked at it. This was her last chance, she knew. Whatever he decided now would be final.

He set down the portrait at last and folded his hands on top of it.

"Very well, Girolamo. You may stay."

The rush of relief was so powerful that for a moment Giulia feared she would lose consciousness.

"Understand that I am not agreeing to take you as an apprentice—not yet, at any rate. You are gifted, that is clear, but a gift is only part of what makes a painter. For now, you may work with the other boys, doing as they do and learning as they learn. We shall see how well you get along."

"I understand, signor. Thank you. Thank you!"

"Am I correct in guessing that you do not have a place to stay?"

"I'm sure I can find one, signor."

"Well, you may make a bed for yourself downstairs in the storeroom. I have a blanket I can spare for you, but otherwise you are responsible for your own equipment and expenses, and that includes food. Do you understand?"

"Yes, signor," Giulia said, more glad than ever for Sofia's purse, secure beneath her doublet. "You won't regret it, I swear."

"Only God can make such promises." Ferraldi rose. "Now, let me introduce you to my painters."

—

That night Giulia spread her borrowed blanket on a make-shift platform of scrap lumber, which she'd scavenged from the storeroom and arranged in an empty corner. The store-room occupied the whole of the ground floor, with the weight of the upper floors supported on columns. In addition to the entry from the street, big double doors opened onto a wide paved walkway, known in Venice as a fondamenta, alongside the canal. From the smell, Giulia guessed that the room had flooded more than once in the past. But the floor was dry, and she was alone, without the need to guard her secret from pry-ing eyes.

She'd been introduced to the apprentices: Stefano, a husky young man of eighteen with narrow blue eyes and long blond hair; thirteen-year-old Marin, with the face of an angel in a Nativity painting; and Alvise, Ferraldi's nephew, the scruffy, unfriendly boy who'd let her in. She'd met the painters: Lauro, the workshop's second in command, the hard-faced man to

whom Ferraldi had been talking when she arrived; Zuane and
Antonio, cousins who looked almost alike enough to be twins.

Introductions finished, she'd been handed over to Stefano,
who showed her around the workshop and took her up to the
third floor, where Ferraldi, who was unmarried, had his living quarters and the apprentices slept crammed into a single
room. Though curious about where she was from and how
she'd convinced Ferraldi to accept her, Stefano was more interested in talking about himself, making sure she knew that he
was nearly at the end of his apprenticeship and working on
studies for his master painting—which, to hear him tell it, was
certain to be a masterpiece.

The tour finished, he'd brought her back to the workshop
and put her to sweeping up. Work ended for the day as soon as
the light began to fail; Lauro and the other painters departed,
while Ferraldi and the apprentices retired to the third floor
and Giulia was dismissed downstairs. She'd built her scrap-
lumber platform, then ventured out to find a tavern and used
a little of Sofia's money to buy bread and cheese and sour wine,
which she'd consumed by the light of the candle Ferraldi had
given her.

Now, with everything silent, she longed to creep back up
to the workshop—to wander among the materials and tools, to
hold her candle close to the half-finished paintings, to uncork
the pigment pots. She hadn't realized how deeply she missed
the voices of the paints until she heard them again this afternoon, or how dull and quiet the world was without them. She
wanted nothing more now than to listen to them sing, and if
that was a sin, as she had sometimes feared, she did not care.
Better, though, not to risk it. Tomorrow would be soon enough.

"Do you see me, Maestra?" she whispered to the shadows and the flickering candlelight. "I have a master. I have a

workshop. I will be a painter, not a slave under Domenica's command."

All afternoon and evening she'd been repeating this to herself, trying to believe she had actually, against all the odds, achieved everything she had planned. Well . . . not quite everything, for Ferraldi had not yet made her an apprentice. But that would come. Warm under the blanket and Bernardo's mantle, her stomach full and her head buzzing pleasantly from the wine, she could finally allow herself to admit how much, in her heart of hearts, she had doubted she would get even as far as this.

In the time she'd been traveling, she had only vaguely considered the future. All her planning, all her energy and hope, had been bent on reaching this moment. Now her mind leaped forward: to the days she would spend in the workshop, proving herself to Ferraldi so that the last piece of her plan could slip into place. To everything she would need to do and learn in order to survive in this unfamiliar workshop, this alien city. And to the challenge of guarding her secret, of maintaining her disguise. Of pretending every moment to be someone— something—she was not.

A thread of cold rippled through the drowsy warmth enclosing her. Had she ever thought of her disguise as anything but temporary? But the reason for it was not temporary. If she could not apprentice as herself—as a female—would she ever be able to paint as herself?

Will I have to wear this disguise forever?

Something unfurled inside her chest, the same trapped, breathless feeling that had seized her at Santa Marta when she had considered her final vows. She thought of the words of her horoscope fragment, God's will for her life written in the stars of her birth: never to love or marry, to die without her name. A nun at Santa Marta, Girolamo Landriani in Venice—was it not the same? How many times had she tried to outrun her fate; how many times had the stars brought her back? Would every choice she made always bring her back?

But Girolamo Landriani will paint. That must be God's will as well, for did not God give me my gift? And if I must spend my life alone and unloved, shall I not at least spend it painting?

She thought of what Sofia had said to her on the night she presented the portrait: *Your gift demands* everything *of you.* It was so. She could feel it: her gift, the core of fire that was the heart of her. Burning, always burning, no cold or doubt or cruelty enough to put it out.

Only God knew the future. As in the meadow after the brothers robbed her, she would do one thing at a time, take one step at a time, and see where it led her.

I'm here, with Ferraldi. For now that's enough.

She blew out the candle. The room fell dark. She curled into the shelter of Bernardo's mantle, feeling the presence of the great city around her, and herself within it, a new seed cast on fertile ground, ready to grow.

Part IV

The Music of
the Spheres

✤✤✤✤✤✤✤

CHAPTER 14

❖ King David ❖

Venice, Italy
Early January, Anno Domini 1489

The great voice of the Marangona bell, which pealed each morning from the Campanile in the Piazza San Marco to summon Venetians to work, and again each evening to send them home, rang out as Giulia turned the corner into the narrow street where the color seller had his shop.

The spice vendors and jewelers who did business in this part of the Rialto were only just starting to raise their shutters, but the pavement was already crowded with shoppers and tradespeople. Shouts, voices raised in bargaining, the sound of hammers and other tools echoed from the housefronts; whiffs of cinnamon and clove caught at Giulia's nose, mingled with the smell of charcoal smoke and the metallic odors of the forge. Her breath plumed out in front of her as she walked. She'd never experienced anything quite like the cold of the Venetian winter: damp, raw, incredibly penetrating.

The color seller's shop was near the end of the street. She pushed open the door and stepped into the welcome warmth.

"Master Landriani!" A smile of welcome creased the color seller's plump cheeks. "I have your order ready."

"I also need twenty sticks of black chalk, if you've got them."

"I do indeed. Just give me a moment."

The color seller bustled over to the crowded shelves that held his goods. Giulia warmed her hands over a brazier as he counted out the chalk, then counted it a second time for good measure. She breathed deeply, savoring the shop's distinctive aroma: the dense, mixed scents of the hundreds of items sold here, overlaid by the sharp tang of vinegar boiling in another room, where an apprentice was steaming lead to extract white pigment.

In other cities, pigments were sold by apothecaries. Only in Venice, Giulia had learned, were there shops such as these, for nowhere else was there such a wealth of raw materials, or such an army of artisans to use them: painters, textile dyers, potters, even glassmakers from the vast glassworks on the island of Murano. Precious minerals from Persia, rare woods from Africa, oils and plants and earths and even insects from all over Europe and the Orient: All passed through Venice, the queen of trade, and all could be found on the color sellers' shelves.

"The fresco progresses well?"

The color seller was an avid gossip, with an astonishing store of knowledge about all his clients. He pressed Giulia shamelessly for information every time she visited. But he was honest, and the colors Ferraldi bought from him sang true, without any taint of adulteration. And he often tipped a little extra onto the scale when Giulia purchased supplies for herself.

"Well enough," she said. "Three days should see it finished, assuming the plasterer shows up."

"A drunkard, that one, or so I've heard. But he's your master's cousin, is he not? Family. What can one do?" The color seller shook his head. "I can recommend a man if you need one."

"I don't think that will be necessary. But I'll tell my master."

The color seller tied the chalk up with cord, then brought out a larger bundle, which he opened so Giulia could inspect its contents: an array of raw pigments, ground and dried and compressed into little blocks that only needed to be broken up and mixed with the painting medium of the artist's choice. Accustomed as she was to a workshop where the paints had almost all been prepared by the artists themselves, Giulia had been surprised at first at how many of his pigments Ferraldi bought ready-made. But she knew now that in Venice, this was common practice.

"That'll be two scudi for everything," the color seller said. "Shall I put it on account?"

"Yes. Thank you."

"Don't forget that plasterer." The color seller placed both bundles in Giulia's hands. "Just let me know."

Giulia pulled up the hood of Bernardo's mantle—no matter how she tried, she couldn't stop thinking of it as his—and plunged back into the cold.

—

If, on her first night in Venice, she had been able to look ahead three months and see herself as she was today—easy in her disguise, confidently negotiating the crowded streets and *campi* of the Rialto—she would hardly have recognized herself.

She wore her boy's clothes without a thought—better clothes than when she'd arrived, for Sofia's purse had allowed her to replace her travel-worn garments and buy a proper pair of boots. She no longer needed to remind herself how to walk and speak, no longer forgot to respond when someone called her false name. She'd grown skilled at coping with the inconveniences of her masquerade: the privacy she always needed, the excuses and accommodations she had to make. She could untie her hose in scarcely more time than it took a real boy to unlace his codpiece.

It was true, what Sofia had said: People saw what they expected to see. As long as she took care, her clothes and hair and her boy's name told a story no one thought to question. The dread of discovery, which had made her first weeks in Ferraldi's workshop an excruciating trial of nerves, was only a shadow now—always there behind her thoughts, but rarely consciously called to mind.

Venice, so huge and alien, had overwhelmed her at first. With no access to a boat unless she paid to hire a gondola, her only option was to go about on foot—and in this too Sofia had spoken true: For pedestrians, the city was a labyrinth. There were no long, continuous thoroughfares as in Padua—only a spiderweb of narrow streets and alleys, carried by slantwise bridges over dark canals, intersecting at strange angles and dead-ending unexpectedly on campi and *rii*, so that finding one's way could be as much a matter of retreating as of moving forward.

Ferraldi allowed her to accompany the other apprentices on errands, and this had helped her begin to orient herself—in spite of the efforts of Stefano and Marin, who thought it hilarious to give her invented street names and imaginary addresses. Cautiously, on Sundays and in the occasional hours she had free, she began to venture out on solo sketching expeditions, learning the city not just by walking it but through the alchemy of eye and charcoal. She used scrap paper from the workshop, filling the sheets fully on both sides, sometimes drawing over earlier work. She had a growing stack of these sheets in her little sleeping area in Ferraldi's storeroom.

She was confident enough now to go exploring on her own. She'd found her way to the church of San Giobbe, and spent a rapturous hour before Giovanni Bellini's magnificent altarpiece, so masterfully painted that its illusion of a chamber just off the church, in which the Virgin sat surrounded by saints, seemed like a window onto a living world. She had visited the Piazza San Marco and gaped at the golden domes of the Basilica and the great brick pile of the Doge's Palace. She'd explored the busy docks and markets of the Rialto, where hundreds of shops and stalls and warehouses offered every good or service she had ever imagined, and many she had not. It was on the Rialto too that she glimpsed the dark truth beneath Venice's glittering abundance: the mean back alleys stinking of sewage and refuse, the tenements and the brothels, the beggars and the prostitutes.

She was still an outsider—in the city, whose shape and rhythms she was only just beginning to understand; in the workshop, where everyone, from the artists to the apprentices to Ferraldi's maidservant, knew her as a charity case Ferraldi had taken on for reasons he had not cared to explain. There were still moments when disbelief rocked her like a slap to the face: *What am I doing here? All alone? Disguised as a boy?* But with every day that passed, she gained a little more assurance, the mask of Girolamo a better fit over her own true face.

Now and then she found herself missing Santa Marta—not the changes she'd fled after Humilità's death, but the things she'd loved while her teacher was still alive: the peace and order, the friendships, the certainty of a known future. She wondered sometimes whether it would be risking too much to send Angela a letter, just to let her friend know she was safe. Surely, if she gave no details of her situation . . .

But then she would remember Matteo Moretti. She would think of Domenica and Madre Magdalena. She would feel the presence of the little pouch at her neck, with its weight of secrets. And it would seem too much like tempting fate to remind anyone in Padua that she was still alive.

—

With her errand to the color seller completed, Giulia set out for Cannaregio and the palazzo of the Cesca family, where Ferraldi had his fresco commission.

The Rialto bustled year-round, but midwinter, when the trade vessels began returning from the East, was among its most hectic seasons. Giulia pushed her way through the busy streets, heading for the Riva del Vin, the quay along the Grand Canal where the wine warehouses stood. Boats and barges packed the canal; the quay teemed with workmen unloading goods, merchants in their long black robes, and an occasional cluster of dandies already masked for Carnival, cloakless in the cold to display their fine clothing.

The Rialto Bridge rose at the end of the Riva del Vin. Giulia crossed it and entered the Merceria, the twisting commercial avenue that linked the Rialto with the Piazza San Marco. Here too she had to fight the crowds, but once she turned north toward Cannaregio, the traffic diminished, and she was soon walking through streets and campi nearly deserted in the cold.

Snow had begun to sift down by the time she reached Palazzo Cesca. The servant on guard at the street door waved her into a courtyard, where a marble stair led up to the *pòrtego*, the long central hallway that was a feature of the *piani nobili* of all large Venetian dwellings. Like much of the rest of the palazzo, the pòrtego was under renovation. Holding her breath against the dust, Giulia slipped into the room where Ferraldi and his assistants were working.

Ferraldi ran a very different kind of workshop from Humilità's—necessarily, for though Humilità's workshop had brought in money for the convent, it had not primarily been a commercial concern. Ferraldi did not have the luxury of picking and choosing his commissions as Humilità had; he took on any work that came his way, from portraits, to commissions from churches and civic organizations, to Madonna and Child panels for private homes. He was also in demand as a frescoist. There was not much call for fresco in Venice, with its damp, salty air that ate away at plaster. But Ferraldi, who had trained in Padua, was known as a specialist.

The fresco he was completing now occupied the wall of a bedchamber: a biblical scene, King David spying on Bathsheba as she bathed. The contract for the commission had been very unbiblical about Bathsheba's endowments and the way she should be displaying them, causing much sniggering among the apprentices—though not when Ferraldi could hear them.

Canvas had been spread across the floor to protect it, and lanterns supplemented the daylight admitted by the windows. Ferraldi, his silver hair tied away from his face and a painter's smock covering his clothes, stood over Alvise, who was stirring up the limewater that would be combined with pigments to make fresco paint.

"Did you remember the chalk?" Ferraldi was a kind master, but when deeply involved in his work he could be impatient, even harsh.

"Yes, Maestro," Giulia said.

"Good." He gestured toward a trestle table, where Stefano was working at the grinding stone. "Start with the red ochre. I need it first."

"Took you long enough to get here." Stefano eyed Giulia as she shrugged off her mantle and began to unpack the color seller's bundle.

"There was a cart overturned on the Riva del Vin. I had to wait to get past."

"Or perhaps you were lying late abed and only dreaming of a cart."

As you would do, given half the chance. Giulia swallowed the retort. Stefano was a bit of a bully, and could be vengeful if crossed. Giulia got on with him fairly well, but only because she was careful not to provoke him.

"I didn't oversleep," she said mildly.

"So you say." Stefano tossed his long blond hair, about which he was as vain as a girl. "Pass me that ochre."

Over by the fresco, Ferraldi's cousin, Eugenio, had completed the *intonaco*, the smooth layer of wet plaster on which the painting would be done. Alvise, finished with the limewater, had begun to unroll the template for today's work: part of a full-scale drawing of the fresco that had been made on glued sheets of paper, then cut into pieces corresponding to each day's work. Today's section was the figure of King David, peering out from behind a column.

"Now, Uncle?" Alvise asked, his voice tentative.

"Don't always ask direction, Alvise. Take the initiative."

Alvise swiped his sleeve under his perpetually running nose and held the template to the intonaco, orienting it to the finished sections of the fresco and the underdrawing that had been made on the first plaster layer, which still showed in the areas that had not yet been painted. But, forgetful as usual, he'd neglected to fetch hammer and nails to tack it in place. Glancing nervously at his uncle, who was watching with folded arms and frowning brows, he laid down the template and went to get the tools.

This time he managed to fix the template properly to the wall. But when he began incising the lines of the drawing into the soft surface of the plaster, to give Ferraldi a reference from which to paint, his hand was too heavy. With a ripping sound that carried through the room, his stylus tore through the paper.

"Stop!" Ferraldi stepped forward to examine the mistake. "Clumsy boy, you haven't just torn the template; you've cut all the way through the intonaco."

"I'm sorry, Uncle," Alvise muttered.

"Well, take it down. Eugenio, repair it."

Eugenio smoothed the disturbed plaster, and Alvise positioned the template yet again. He was breathing heavily through his mouth now—Giulia could hear him all the way from where she stood. He took up the stylus; but as he set it to the paper he lost his grip, and it clattered to the floor.

"Enough," Ferraldi snapped. "Stefano! Clean your hands and come over here."

"I can do it, Uncle." Alvise was on his knees, scrabbling for the stylus. "Let me try again."

"No. You are grinding pigments now." Ferraldi jerked the stylus from Alvise's fingers. "Stefano!"

Stefano uttered a long-suffering sigh—though not loud enough that Ferraldi could hear. Before he could do more, Giulia spoke up.

"Maestro. Might I try?"

Ferraldi trained his blue-green gaze on her. "Have you any experience with plaster?"

"No, Maestro. But I've been watching. And my hands are already clean."

"Very well, then. You can hardly do worse."

"That's not fair, Uncle." Alvise's face had turned red. "He's not even a real apprentice."

"Do not argue, Alvise. Go assist Stefano, and try not to drop anything. Girolamo, come here."

Alvise shot Giulia a scalding look of fury and humiliation, then put his head down and obeyed.

Ferraldi handed Giulia the stylus. She was aware of his scrutiny as she stepped toward the wall, inhaling the sharp scent of the wet plaster. Her hand was steady as she began to trace, mindful of the need to keep her touch light. The template did not reproduce the careful shading and modeling of the original drawing, only the principal lines of King David's figure. It did not take long for her to finish.

She eased the template off its nails and stepped back. Ferraldi examined what she'd done.

"Good. Roll up the template now and get back to work."

Through the morning and into the afternoon, the apprentices ground pigments, mixing them as Ferraldi required with limewater, which would bond with the plaster as it dried and fix the paints to the wall. For all his faults, Stefano was an efficient manager; he ordered Giulia and Alvise about as if he were the workshop's master, amusing himself by tormenting Alvise at Giulia's expense. "Oh wait, I think *Girolamo* wants to do that," he'd say each time Alvise tried to begin a new task, directing him instead to some other job. Or as Alvise picked up something breakable: "Let *Girolamo* do that. He doesn't *drop* things."

Immersed in the fresco, Ferraldi noticed none of this. Alvise, who feared Stefano, did not protest, contenting himself with scowls and muttered oaths. Giulia too kept her mouth shut. She felt sorry for Alvise and regretted her part in his humiliation today, but it was not worth antagonizing Stefano to defend him.

Instead, she concentrated on the pigments she was grinding, and on the pleasure of hearing their voices rise. Humilità had never had the chance to teach her the techniques of fresco; Giulia was fascinated by the way the limewater shifted the colors' voices, giving them a harsher edge—different from oil, which made them slower and more languorous, or egg tempera, which made them brighter and harder.

By midafternoon King David was finished. Ferraldi departed, leaving the apprentices to clean up. It was dark when at last they doused the fire. Stefano, holding aloft one of the lanterns, led the way through the courtyard and out into the street. Shadowed by day, the streets of Venice became wells of darkness at night, only a little relieved by the light escaping from shuttered windows. Even the full moon, silvering the rooftops, could not always reach so far down. If not for Stefano's lantern, they would have had to find their way by touch, like the blind.

After a few moments Giulia fell back to walk beside Alvise. He ignored her, stomping along in his loose-limbed way, sniffling every now and then. He was fifteen, the youngest son of

Ferraldi's sister—taken for apprenticeship, Giulia suspected, only out of obligation, for though he had a little talent and was eager to learn, he was the most awkward person she had ever met. He forgot instructions, dropped tools and spilled paint, said the wrong things and laughed at inappropriate moments. Stefano treated him with contempt, as did young Marin, who imitated Stefano in everything. Ferraldi often was not much kinder.

"I'm sorry about this morning," she said, keeping her voice low so Stefano wouldn't hear.

"You're not sorry." Alvise sniffled loudly. "You got what you wanted, didn't you? To make me look even worse than I already do and stick your nose up my uncle's ass while you were at it."

Giulia held on to her temper. "I didn't intend to do any of that."

"Yes, you did. Do you think I'm stupid? I know what you're really after."

"What are you talking about?"

"You want my place." He turned on her. He'd never liked her; but now, in the small light that filtered back from Stefano's lantern, what she saw on his face looked more like hatred. "My uncle has no use for me. You know it, I know it, everyone knows it. Doesn't matter what I do or say. He'll boot me in an eye-blink if a better prospect comes along. So do me a favor and don't pretend."

"You're wrong, Alvise. I do want a place, but I don't want *your* place."

"Same bloody difference, isn't it? Since he can only afford to pay three apprentices."

"Stefano will be leaving soon."

"Oh, *Stefano*." He spat the name. "He talks and talks, but it's just words. He'll never get the artists' guild to accept him. He'll be an apprentice for the rest of his life."

For Alvise, this was unusually perceptive. "You're family," Giulia said. "I'm nothing. Your uncle would never choose me over you."

"*You can draw!* Blood's nothing to him beside that."

His words silenced her. Ahead, Stefano's lantern struck diamonds from the snow that had fallen earlier.

"You could go anywhere and get a place," Alvise said. "But the only place I can ever have is with him. Since we're being straight with each other, you may as well know I mean to get rid of you. I don't know how I'll do it. But I'll figure a way. I swear I will."

"Alvise, this is ridiculous. We don't have to be enemies."

"Yes, we do."

He quickened his pace, leaving her behind. The sting of his anger lingered, like a bad taste in her mouth. She was angry too—angry at his hatred, which she did not deserve, angry that he'd made her see something she hadn't seen before. She wanted Ferraldi to choose her—but could she accept an apprenticeship if it came at another's expense?

They reached a small campo. In the open space of the little square, moonlight illuminated the snow-dusted paving and the wellhead at the center. The surrounding houses were ramparts of shadow, broken here and there by the glow of candles through the seams of shutters.

Giulia tipped back her head. Stars showed in the sky above, glinting through gaps in the clouds. What would they tell her if, like Maestro Bruni, she could read them? She was overwhelmed suddenly with a sense of her own smallness. The bricks below her feet felt unstable, as if they might crack apart and plunge her into the salt water that ran like blood through the body of this strange city.

The light of Stefano's lantern, a small terrestrial star, was already receding down the black throat of the street. She ran to catch up, leaving the moonlight behind.

CHAPTER 15

❖ Bernardo ❖

On the day Bernardo left her in the Campo San Lio, Giulia had put him out of her mind. She'd been certain she would never see him again—or Sofia either, for she did not plan ever to call upon the aid Sofia had promised her.

I'm starting a new life, she had told herself. *A life where no one in the world knows who or what I am. From this moment, the old Giulia does not exist.*

But four days after she'd become part of the workshop, she had answered a knock at the door and found Bernardo standing on the threshold. She'd been so astonished that for a moment she could not speak.

"Good day," he said, unsmiling. Then, in his dry way, "Close your mouth, you look like a fish."

"What are you doing here?" she blurted out.

"That's a pleasant greeting."

"I'm sorry. I didn't . . . I'm just . . . surprised."

He shrugged. "Thank my mother. She wants to be sure you are well settled."

"Oh." Giulia hated how flustered she felt. But the response that had jolted her in the Campo San Lio—the sudden, surprising current of physical attraction—had overwhelmed her again the instant she saw his face. "I'm settled very well indeed. How did you find me?"

"I did bring you most of the way, if you remember. I needed only to ask for the house of Ferraldi the painter. Will you let me in?"

Giulia hesitated. "I have work to do."

"You can spare a moment, can you not?"

He brushed past her into the storeroom. Its clutter was more starkly visible than usual, for she'd been carrying slop buckets downstairs to empty into the rio and had left the water door open.

"This is the workshop?" There was distaste in his voice.

"The workshop is upstairs. This is the storeroom."

He glanced at the buckets, which she'd set down when he knocked. "Don't let me interrupt you."

He poked around the storeroom as she emptied the buckets, inspecting supplies, kicking at the rubbish on the floor. She went upstairs for more slops, taking her time, hoping that when she came down again he would be gone. But as she descended, she saw he was still there.

"Someone sleeps down here?" He pointed to her sleeping area—still makeshift, but thanks to Sofia's purse, better furnished than on the first night, with a straw mattress, a pillow, and a privacy curtain rigged from lengths of linen.

"I do."

"In the *storeroom*?" His eyebrows flew up so high they nearly disappeared into his bangs. "This is how your master treats his apprentices?"

"It's quite comfortable." The involuntary thrill of his presence had vanished; all Giulia felt now was annoyance.

"Comfortable? You're practically on the water. The air is noxious. I wouldn't keep my scullion in such conditions."

"It's not so bad." Giulia wanted to smack him for his arrogance. "It's temporary, in any case, just until there's space upstairs. And now I really should get back to work. Please thank clarissima Sofia for me, and tell her I am well. She needn't trouble herself further."

She closed the door firmly behind him, hoping he would not return. She did not want Sofia's eye on her, no matter how kindly meant—the eye of someone who knew her secret. She didn't want Bernardo poking his haughty nose into her affairs.

A few days later, she was scrubbing one of the worktables, and half listening to the bickering of Zuane and Antonio, when young Marin came running up from the storeroom to announce at the top of his voice that there was a well-dressed gentleman downstairs asking for Girolamo.

She felt a stab of real anger. Why on earth had he come back? But her heart, as if it belonged to someone else, had already begun to race.

"Go," Lauro told her in his gravelly voice. "But be quick about it."

"I thought you said you didn't have friends in Venice." Stefano, at another table trimming brushes, paused to watch her with his sharp blue eyes as she dried her hands on her tunic.

"He's not a friend. He's . . . a patron."

"Ho! Patrons already? Aren't you getting a little ahead of yourself?"

She ignored him and went down to the storeroom, where Bernardo was pacing restlessly about. With his dark hair and clothes, he melted into the dimness, except for the pale blur of his face and the glint of his silver-handled dagger.

"Here," he said, holding something toward her. "From my mother."

She took it, careful not to let her hands touch his: a beautiful blanket of soft wool, rolled up around a feather pillow.

"I'm very grateful. But your mother doesn't need to give me gifts. I have everything I need, truly."

He pointed at her sleeping area. "I see you haven't moved upstairs yet."

"Not yet." She carried Sofia's gift over to her bed. "I'm thinking I may not. I like being on my own."

It was true. Her little curtained area was a godsend for the privacy she needed to manage the more intimate aspects of her disguise.

"Well, if I hear you've died of an ague, I suppose I will know why."

She put down the bedding and faced him. "Truly, you don't need to be concerned."

"It's my mother who is concerned."

"Well, she needn't be concerned either. And you don't have to come back every week to inspect my living conditions."

He looked affronted. "What makes you think I intend to come back every week?"

"I'm just saying it's not necessary." Giulia drew a breath. "I don't mean to be ungrateful. I am well aware of how much I owe clarissima Sofia, and I mean to pay my debt, every penny.

But I have a place now. I have a master. No one needs to be concerned for me. No one at all."

"Well." He swung around, an abrupt motion that made the hem of his mantle flare, and paced toward the water door. "That is not why I came, in any case. I came to ask you to draw my portrait."

"Your portrait?" Giulia said, surprised.

"I'll pay you. I don't expect you to work for nothing."

"What sort of portrait? Is it for your mother?"

"No. For my betrothed."

Giulia felt a small, unwelcome jolt of surprise. Carefully, she said, "I didn't know you were betrothed."

"It hasn't been formalized." He reached the storeroom's far wall and pivoted to pace back toward her. "My mother's friend, the one whose lying-in we were attending, was a courtesan too, but she caught herself a husband. My betrothed is his daughter by his first marriage. I met her while we were in Vicenza." His expression tightened. "A suitable match for one such as me, who does not bear his father's name."

"I hope you'll be happy," Giulia said awkwardly.

"I will be settled. That's good enough for most people." He halted a little distance away, staring past her into the shadowy corners of the storeroom. "This is my mother's wish. Not mine."

"The portrait?"

"The marriage."

"You don't . . . want to marry?"

His dark eyes snapped to hers. There was a pause. "Will you make the portrait, then?"

A dozen reasons to refuse flashed through Giulia's mind. But she heard herself saying, "Yes."

"When shall we begin?"

"I've work to do today. But Sunday I'll be free."

"I must accompany my mother to Mass. I'll come after." He looked at her from beneath his brows. "I do know who he is, you know. My father. If you were wondering."

"I wasn't wondering," Giulia said, though it was not true.

"For a little while he was my mother's only patron. She thought—" He stopped, clamped his lips together. "But then she fell pregnant, and he cast her aside. He knows about me. But he has never chosen to acknowledge me."

He said it matter-of-factly, but something in his voice betrayed a deeper feeling. Giulia remembered the moment when his arrogant shell had cracked on the Campo San Lio, and she had glimpsed a different self beneath.

"My father didn't acknowledge me either," she said.

"You're illegitimate?" She heard the surprise in his voice.

"My father was a nobleman. My mother was his seam-stress. She died when I was seven. He favored her, so for her sake he kept me under his roof, but he never acknowledged me. I grew up among the servants. I was trained as a servant myself, as . . . as a scullion. When my father died in his turn, his wife lost no time getting rid of me."

"So." The whites of Bernardo's eyes caught what little light there was, gleaming like ice, the irises as black as inkblots. "We have something in common."

And for just a moment Giulia felt that it was true.

It wasn't long after he departed that she began to regret agreeing to the portrait, and to remember all the reasons why it was better to cut him—and Sofia—out of her life. Should she send him away on Sunday, telling him she'd changed her mind? But that meant inventing an explanation. And he would certainly be angry.

It's only a portrait, she told herself. *An afternoon of sketching, a week of composing. I'll give it to him, and that will be that.*

She attended Mass on Sunday at the church of San Lio and returned to Ferraldi's house to find Bernardo already waiting. He had brought paper for her to use—thick, fine-quality sheets, far better than she could have afforded on her own.

The day was overcast but bright, so though it was cold, she brought him onto the wide *fondamenta* outside the water door, posing him on a tarpaulin-covered load of lumber that had been delivered a few days earlier. He was as good at immobility as his mother, seeming barely to blink as he stared across the rio at the houses on the other side. Perched on a stool, her drawing board balanced on her knee, Giulia sketched him from different angles, preliminary studies that she would later consider in planning the perspective and approach of the final portrait.

At first they were silent. Then a gondola glided by, its oar dipping, its wake slapping against the foundations of the houses, and Bernardo said softly, "For me, that is the sound of Venice. Water, imprisoned between walls."

"I hear it at night." Giulia kept her voice low, mindful of the open window arcade of the workshop one floor above. Lauro and Zuane and Antonio did not come in on Sundays, and the apprentices went home to their families on Saturday night; but Ferraldi often worked alone when everyone was absent. "It makes me dream of drowning."

"You're as likely to die of cold or filth if you fall into the canals. Are you learning your way about the city?"

"A little. It's easy to get lost."

"There was once a man who disembarked on the Molo on a fine spring day. He set out for Cannaregio and was never seen again. They say his spirit still wanders the streets, trying to find its way."

"Is that really a story people tell?" Giulia looked up from her drawing board. "Or did you make it up this minute?"

His lips lifted a little. "It's really a story. Have you gotten lost, then?"

Giulia described the nightmare experience of being abandoned by Stefano when she went with him to deliver a finished commission. Bernardo confessed that though he'd lived in the city for every one of his nineteen years, he still occasionally made a wrong turn when he traveled on foot.

He went on to speak of his childhood in one of the poorer sections of the Rialto, where Sofia had lived before she reached the height of her success, and of how, thanks to her canny financial management and her shrewd acquisition of ever more noble and generous clients, they had moved to the house in Cannaregio when he was eight. In return, Giulia told him about growing up in her father's household, about her friendship with Maestro Bruni and all he had taught her. It was surprisingly easy to recast her own real history as Girolamo's. For the first time it struck her that in some ways she had really never lived a girl's life at all.

At last the light began to fail.

"I think I have enough now." She put down her charcoal, realizing that she was actually reluctant for the afternoon to end. Bernardo hadn't been haughty or condescending; he had not mocked or interrogated her. They had simply . . . talked. Not since Santa Marta, and her nighttime conversations with Angela, had she really talked with anyone. Every day she responded to instructions or answered questions or fended off Stefano's jibes. But that was not the same.

Bernardo got to his feet and stretched. "How long do you need to complete it?"

"Come back next Sunday. I'll have it done by then."

She worked on the portrait at night by candlelight, using ink bought with Sofia's money, a quill she'd cut herself, and chips of white and red chalk she'd salvaged from the rubbish of the storeroom. She drew him from the waist up: His body shifted slightly away from the picture plane, his face unsmiling, his black hair like a fall of night and his obsidian eyes challenging the viewer's. It was a harsher likeness than she'd originally intended. She considered softening it for the sake of the girl who would receive it—but as many untruths as she had told with her mouth, her hand could not lie.

This is how he is. Better his betrothed should see him true.

Despite herself, she felt a fluttering anxiety when she gave him the portrait on the following Sunday. Men were not like women; they did not examine themselves in mirrors or seek their reflections in still water. Would he recognize himself? Would he deny the likeness? She could read nothing in his expression as he examined the portrait, angling the paper toward the candle she had set on a chest so he could see.

"It's strange," he said, "seeing one's own face like this."

"Is it what you wanted? If you don't like it, I can make another."

"No. No, this will do very well." He rolled up the paper and thrust it inside his doublet. From the pouch at his belt, he took a coin. "Here's what I owe you."

Beyond the silver scudi Sofia had given her, Giulia had little experience of Venetian currency. But this coin shone gold. A ducat.

"That's far too much."

"Take it."

Giulia shook her head. "I don't want charity."

"Not charity. Payment."

He laid the ducat by the candle and left.

The coin gleamed dully against the dark wood. Giulia stared at it a moment before picking it up and stowing it in her belt pouch with the remainder of Sofia's money. She felt ridiculously disappointed. But what had she expected? Praise? Gratitude? It had been a business transaction, that was all.

She carried the candle to her curtained sleeping area, where the sheets of paper she'd filled last Sunday lay stacked on the floor. She picked them up and spread them on her mattress, examining them in the unsteady light: His face turned toward her, his face in profile. His long-fingered hands clasped together on his knee. Details of his sleeves, his cap, the collar of his shirt above the high neck of his doublet. The curve of his eyelid.

A sudden anger took her. *What's wrong with me, mooning over these drawings? It doesn't matter that he makes my pulse leap. It doesn't matter that I've begun to like him a little. Nothing can come of it.*

Sweeping the drawings into a pile, she brought them outside onto the fondamenta, where, although she never destroyed her own work, she tore them into pieces and fed them to the canal.

This time, she thought, he might really be gone for good. She knew it was for the best, despite the small, stubborn part of her that refused to stop hoping he would return. She could hardly have said what she felt when, the following Sunday, he did.

"Get your mantle," he commanded. As before, he'd arrived just after noon. "If you're to live in Venice, you must know her. It's time you started properly learning your way about."

"I have work." With Ferraldi's permission, she had begun to put the warehouse into better order, and she'd planned to spend this day inventorying supplies.

"What work? This is the day of rest."

"Do you not have something better to do?"

"Very likely." He glanced away. "But I don't wish to do it."

He would not allow her to say no, and in truth—and against her better judgment—she did not want to refuse. He'd brought the gondola, which he piloted expertly himself, as well as wine to drink and sweets to share. She was tense at first—far too aware of his physical presence, of her own true self beneath the shell of her boy's clothes. But as they navigated the canals, gliding beneath shuttered windows, eeling past other watercraft, skimming under bridges so low that Bernardo had to crouch, she began to relax.

Standing at his oar, his cap and mantle tossed aside and his normally sleek hair tangled by the wind, Bernardo was at ease in a way she'd never seen before, his handsome face alight with enthusiasm as he pointed out landmarks and shared bits of Venetian history and legend. His love for his city, in all its glorious uniqueness, was clear—the first real passion, other than anger or pride, she'd known him to show. By the end of the afternoon, she could almost feel that passion too.

He returned her to their starting point, at the landing near Campo San Lio. She stood watching as he steered the gondola away, turning to leave only when she realized she was waiting for him to look back.

There was never an agreement or a stated intent. But the Sunday visits became a regular arrangement. He accompanied her on sketching excursions, reading one of the books he always seemed to carry with him while she drew. He brought her to the western seawall to watch the sun set over the lagoon in a blaze of rose and gold. He piloted the gondola to the gates of the Arsenal, Venice's famous shipping yard, closed to all but those who worked there, for what went on inside was a state secret. On one of the city's many feast days, he brought her to see the doge and the Great Council in procession: a line of black- and red-clad nobles so long it snaked all the way around the Piazza San Marco.

He insisted that she witness one of Venice's famous *battagliole*, the mock battles fought by laborers from adjoining parishes for possession of a bridge, and laughed when she could not hide her distaste at the spectacle of men trampling each other, beating each other bloody with sticks, and shoving each other into the filthy, freezing waters of the canal, all accompanied by howls of approval from a huge crowd of spectators.

"You're as delicate as a girl sometimes, Girolamo," he told her. "The way you turn up your nose at things! Have you never seen a good fistfight before?"

"I've seen fights," Giulia replied, pretending affront to conceal the shock his remark had given her. "I just don't see the point of fighting over a bridge that doesn't belong to anyone."

"It's tradition," Bernardo said. "Tradition is its own point."

They were not becoming friends, exactly. It was more as if Bernardo had decided to adopt her—as if, like his mother, he was given to taking stray creatures under his wing, though this was not something she would have suspected lay in his character. He treated her like a younger brother: someone to be instructed, sometimes teased, occasionally confided in.

Why? Giulia could not quite make up her mind. He had no siblings of his own—perhaps he had always wanted one. Maybe the Sundays were an opportunity to escape his responsibilities—collecting rents, overseeing Sofia's household, managing her schedule for the few patrons she still entertained—duties Giulia knew, from the tight-lipped way he spoke of them, that he did not enjoy.

Or . . . could he simply be lonely? From the hints he'd let drop about his life, Giulia had the impression that he did not have close companions, apart from Sofia. He never spoke of friends; the names he mentioned were all of business associates or his mother's tenants. Partly, she thought, this must be temperament. Even before they'd reached Venice, she had seen that he was solitary, prone to silence and dark moods. But his ambiguous social status, so much like her own when she was growing up, must also play a part, with the additional element of scandal from his mother's profession.

She picked at these questions, rolling them around in her mind like beads, wondering if she was foolish to surrender to this friendship, or whatever it was. For if she was honest, she could not deny that from liking him a little, she was growing to like him much too much—a far more troubling feeling than the quick burn of physical attraction, rooted in the time they were spending together and the bits and pieces of himself he'd allowed her—or as he thought, Girolamo—to glimpse beneath the arrogance he wore like armor.

Nothing can come of it. On the day Giulia had torn up her sketches, this thought had made her angry. Now it seemed like reassurance. If nothing could come of this odd companion-ship—if she assumed nothing, expected nothing—surely there was no harm in letting Bernardo be Girolamo's friend.

CHAPTER 16

❖ A Theme of Music ❖

As Giulia had predicted to the color seller, the fresco was finished by the end of the week. Each morning, Ferraldi called her to position the template for the day's work and to incise its lines into the intonaco.

Over the past three months she had worked hard to establish herself in the workshop: obeying orders without complaint, volunteering for unpleasant jobs, keeping herself in Stefano's good graces by deference and flattery. She seized every chance to prove herself at the grinding stone, where her ability to judge her paint mixes by ear as well as by hand and eye gave her an advantage over the other apprentices. Lately, Zuane and Antonio had begun to call on her, especially when they needed one of the more valuable colors. Even taciturn

Lauro sometimes singled her out. Ferraldi, however, had never summoned her to assist him—until now.

On Friday, the last day, he allowed her to stand by him as he applied paint to the wet plaster. In his workshop, as in Humilità's, many paintings were collaborative, with Ferraldi creating the principal figures and his assistants completing secondary figures and backgrounds; but for fresco he preferred to paint alone. He worked at speed, racing the drying of the intonaco, using broad brushstrokes and, except for a few areas of very bright or very dark, only a single layer of color.

Giulia stood spellbound as the rosy nude figure of Bathsheba bloomed beneath his expert hand. The voices of the paints dwindled almost as soon as they were laid on, swallowed by the water-hungry plaster. Never at Santa Marta would she have been permitted to view such a scene; except for the sacred body of Christ, it was considered sinful for a nun or novice to look upon the human form unclothed. She held her own hands behind her back, her fingers burning as they did when she longed to grip the brush. She was aware of Alvise's sullen glare—and also, occasionally, of Stefano's sharp blue gaze. She knew he would do something to humiliate her later, to remind her of her place at the bottom of the apprentice hierarchy. But it would be worth it, for this chance to stand by Ferraldi as she'd once stood by Humilità—learning, always learning.

—

Bernardo arrived on Sunday just past noon, as usual. He was dressed with his customary sober elegance, his fur-trimmed mantle the single touch of luxury. When he threw it back, he winced, and Giulia saw that he was holding his left arm close against his side.

"What happened?" she asked.

Bernardo shrugged, which made him wince again. "I went walking the other evening. I met with a man who was unwilling to let me pass."

He'd told her how he sometimes ventured out alone late at night, a lantern in one hand and the other on the pommel of his dagger. He liked the solitude, he said, the empty streets and deserted campi. Giulia suspected that he also liked daring the attention of thugs and footpads, the breath of danger in the dark.

"And did you persuade him?"

"Oh yes. He's nursing more bruises than I."

"One day you'll get more than bruises, wandering about alone at night."

"I can take care of myself."

"They can chisel that on your gravestone."

"You sound like my mother."

He turned irritably away and began to pace, while Giulia loaded drawing supplies into a leather satchel. There was more space for him to move than the first time he'd come, for Giulia had finished her reorganization of the storeroom. The shelves were dust-free, the supplies well-ordered. The piles of rubbish she had either salvaged or dumped into the rio, and there was now a large, clear area in the center of the floor where deliveries could be received and paintings set to dry. Giulia had managed all the work herself—when she'd tried to enlist Stefano to help with the heavier items, he had rolled his eyes and told her not to bother. "It's always been this way. If you think the Maestro will thank you, you're mistaken." He'd been visibly displeased when Ferraldi praised her.

"I'm ready," she said, slinging the satchel over her shoulder and tucking her drawing board under her arm. "Are you sure you want to come with me today?"

"I'm here, am I not?"

The sky was overcast, the air raw with that penetrating Venetian cold. They headed for the Rialto on foot, then followed the twisting course of the Merceria. Usually they talked as they went, but today Bernardo was silent, preoccupied perhaps by the need to guard his injured ribs against the jostling crowds. Even on a Sunday the Merceria bustled, some shops shuttered but others open, the many taverns doing good business.

They passed through the arched gateway at the Merceria's end, emerging from the cramped confines of the street into an enormity of light and air: the Piazza San Marco, the vast plaza on Venice's southern waterfront. Here were no leaning housefronts, no crowding walls—only open space and soaring sky. To Giulia's left rose the glorious bulk of the Basilica, with its shimmering mosaics and golden domes. Ahead of her lay the long loggia'd façade of the Doge's Palace, and the twin columns that rose at the edge of the Molo, the great quayside that was the main point of arrival for trade vessels from overseas. Opposite the palace, the thrusting pillar of the Campanile, Venice's tallest bell-tower, challenged the clouds.

As he always did when he accompanied her on these expeditions, Bernardo fell back, leaving Giulia to go on alone. The piazza heaved with activity: butchers and produce sellers and bakers at their stalls, money changers in their booths, porters lugging bales and bundles from the waterfront, beggars and black-robed nobles and young men in bright attire going about their business, with every now and then a glimpse of more exotic folk: turbaned Saracens, dark-skinned Africans, bearded Jews. Pigeons congregated on the paving, and gulls wheeled overhead, their cries audible even above the great noise of this place. With every step Giulia breathed in a different odor, fair or foul—and beneath them all, unmistakable, the tang of the sea.

She chose a spot well away from the one she'd picked the last time, near a man who was doing a brisk business selling roasted pears from a brazier. From the satchel at her shoulder she drew a finished portrait: the face of a stranger she'd glimpsed on the street. Drawing a breath, she added her voice to the din of commerce that echoed from the ancient stones of the piazza.

"Portraits! Portraits! Drawn to the life upon the page! Buy a portrait for your wife or your mother, your sweetheart or your sister! Only a scudo!"

Three months ago, she could not have imagined herself doing what she was doing now. But from the night she had arrived in Ferraldi's workshop, she'd known she must find a way to earn money. The coins Sofia had given her would not last forever. Selling portraits, as she had in Padua on the day of her escape, had been the only thing she could think of.

It had taken her weeks to pluck up the courage to try. The first time, she did not sell a single drawing. She forced herself to return, to shout her wares as brazenly as the vendors and stallholders did. Just as she was about to give up, a pair of tipsy youths tossed a scudo at her and demanded she draw them both for the price of one. After that a nearby meat seller offered half a dozen sausages in trade for a portrait of his young son. She'd cooked the sausages that night over her brazier in the storeroom, encouraged but knowing she must do better.

The third time, Bernardo had come with her. And that had made all the difference.

He strolled toward her now, just another well-dressed young man taking leisure on a Sunday, pretending interest in the goods displayed on the stalls nearby. His eyes slid over her as if he did not know her. Then he paused, as though his interest had suddenly been caught.

"A scudo for a portrait?" he said loudly.

"Yes, signor. Drawn to the life. Look." Giulia held up the stranger's face. "My uncle, a likeness so exact you might expect to hear him speak."

"Hmmm." Bernardo pretended to consider. "Well, why not? If it's good, I'll make a present of it to my sister. If it's bad, you will get nothing. Understand?"

"Yes, signor." From her satchel Giulia drew a charcoal stick and a clean sheet of paper, purchased with the proceeds of other expeditions like this one, and fixed it to her drawing board. "Stand just there, if you please, signor. Look a little to your right. A little more. That's it."

The charade had been Bernardo's idea. "You must show them that they want what you are selling," he'd said when she had told him what she was doing and the difficulty of it. "Men want what they think others want. Business draws business."

And it was so. The first time he'd accompanied her, she had sold five portraits. He played his role with surprising relish, afterward making wicked fun of the fat banker who'd asked her not to draw his double chins, and the young dandy in patterned hose and an absurd feathered cap who had displayed his profile as if expecting to be cast in bronze. She would never have imagined he could take such pleasure in deception; she realized only later that what really pleased him was the opportunity to hoodwink members of Venice's elite.

She roughed in the lines of his face, her hand flying over the paper. Already their exchange had caught the interest

of the nearby vendors, and two of the pear seller's customers had paused to watch as well. Humilità had always insisted
that her pupils think about what they drew, analyzing line and
form, light and shadow, before ever setting charcoal or quill
to paper; this was a very different kind of drawing, a transfer
of image to page almost without thought, a lightning union of
eye and hand. Bernardo's face especially, for by now she had
shaped his features at least a score of times. She imagined she
could do so even if her eyes were closed.

She was finished. She detached the drawing and held it up.

"Is it satisfactory, signor?"

"By the saints!" he cried. "It is my very face, there upon the
paper! Let me see it close."

He reached for it, forgetting his injury, catching his breath
as pain reminded him.

"If you take it, signor," Giulia said, following their usual
wordplay, "you keep it. And if you keep it, you must pay for it."

"Oh, very well." Normally he drew the bargaining out—
to attract more attention and also to demonstrate, by Giulia's
refusal to lower her price, that she was not to be trifled with.
But today his heart clearly wasn't in it. "It's a fair price for so
good a likeness."

He gave her the scudo. Moving with care, he headed as
if by accident toward the men who had paused to watch. As
nearly always happened, one of them, a merchant or a banker
in the long black robe worn by all older Venetian men of substance, called to him. He held the portrait so the man could
see. Some nodding, an exchange of words. Then Bernardo
melted into the crowd, and the merchant approached.

"For my wife," he said.

After the merchant came a young man with long blond
hair who reminded her of Stefano, and after him a baker with

his new bride, and after them several others. Scudo followed scudo—except for the baker, who offered two good loaves in trade.

The afternoon was drawing on, and Giulia's hand was tired. She packed her charcoal and papers into her satchel, which now bulged with the loaves, and went to find Bernardo at their usual meeting spot beneath the gleaming gold mosaics of one of the Basilica's entrance porticoes. He'd brought no book with him today. Instead, he gazed out across the bustle of the piazza, his arm clamped against his side.

"Did you do well today?" he asked.

"Two loaves and six scudi. Here's yours back."

He took the coin and slipped it into his belt pouch. Behind him, the great doors were open on the cathedral's interior, a well of darkness pricked in its depths with candle flames.

"I bought some roasted chestnuts."

He offered them to her, pulling aside the cloth that wrapped them, releasing their delicious odor. Giulia took one and slit its leathery skin with her fingernail.

"I heard something from my mother yesterday," Bernardo said. "There's to be a painting competition, sponsored by Archimedeo Contarini. A single painting, any size or subject, on a theme of music."

Giulia reached for another chestnut. "Music? That's unusual."

"Archimedeo is weary of Madonnas and Crucifixions and the agonies of saints. He wants something modern to put in his new palazzo, which by all accounts is already the very pinnacle of modernity." Bernardo's lips curled. "If not of good taste. There's to be a judging on Giovedi Grasso, the last day of Carnival—it will be held at Palazzo Contarini Nuova, and the judge will be Giovanni Bellini himself. The winner will be crowned with laurel leaves and receive a seat of honor at the banquet table. And a purse of five hundred ducats."

"Five hundred ducats!" It was an astonishing sum. "For a single painting?"

"The only thing Archimedeo Contarini loves more than spending money is making sure that all Venice sees him spending it. It will be the event of the Carnival season, or so my mother says."

"I'll tell my master. He'll surely be tempted by that purse."

Bernardo selected a chestnut and shucked it free of its skin but did not eat it. "Are *you* not tempted by it?"

"Me?" Giulia laughed. "Bernardo, I am only an apprentice. I couldn't enter that competition."

"Ah, there's where you're wrong. Entry is open only to those who are not members of the Venetian artists' guild. The intent, presumably, is to exclude Venetian painters, of whom Archimedeo is apparently as weary as he is of their Madonnas. But nothing has been said about Venetian *apprentices*. Who by definition are not members of the guild."

"That's mad." Giulia shook her head. "It would never be allowed."

Bernardo's ink-dark eyes flicked to her face. "You don't know that."

"Even if it were—I can draw as well as anyone, but I have only a little experience of painting. The size of that purse will attract famous artists. I wouldn't stand a chance."

"Why not? You have a gift, Girolamo. Even I can see it."

It surprised her. He'd never said anything like that before. He had returned his attention to the chestnuts, which he was folding back into their cloth.

"My old teacher used to say that a gift is like a block of marble," Giulia said. "It exists, and it is beautiful, but it cannot shape itself. Only teaching can do that. Teaching and experience."

"Think of being judged by the most illustrious painter in Venice. Think of all those ducats. Enough to live on for a long time, or even to establish your own workshop. Isn't that what you want? To be master of your own workshop one day?"

Giulia looked down at the pavement of the portico. She didn't want to think about that. For if she did, she would have to consider whose name the workshop would bear and the fact that, realistically, it could never be her own. Which meant thinking about becoming Girolamo Landriani forever, leaving Giulia Borromeo permanently behind. She knew the desire that drove her had no other possible conclusion. But she was not yet ready to embrace it.

"You're not afraid, are you?" Bernardo's tone was challenging. "To test your skill?"

She raised her head, angry now. "I'm not afraid."

"Then why not try?"

"What does it matter, Bernardo? What difference does it make to you whether I enter this competition or not?"

His jaw tightened. Once again his eyes slid away from hers. He shifted against his column, turning to stare out at the disorderly bustle of the piazza, the sky above it beginning to darken with the approach of evening. It struck Giulia, suddenly, how reluctant he seemed lately to look her in the face.

"I hate men like Archimedeo Contarini," he said softly. "Men who think their fortunes give them mastery of the world. Who think the rest of us should bow down and worship before the altar of their wealth. Whatever honors will be given to the winner, the true purpose of this competition is to establish Contarini's reputation, so foreign painters will come begging for commissions and people will say of him, 'Ah, Archimedeo

Contarini, the great patron of the arts.' It would tarnish his endeavor more than a little if a mere apprentice were to win the prize, through a loophole in the rules."

"So you want me to enter in order to thumb my nose at Archimedeo Contarini? That doesn't strike me as a good reason."

"I'll give you a better one, then. The competition may be a ruse to build Contarini's reputation, and the odds against you are great. But the chance that's being offered is real. It could change everything for you. You would have money. Even patronage, perhaps. Imagine what that would mean."

Giulia was silent.

"You're only fifteen, Girolamo. You don't yet know what it's like to feel your life closing around you like the mud at the bottom of the canals. You don't yet understand how rare an opportunity like this truly is—a chance to move beyond the place where you stand to somewhere better. If you do not take it, you may look back years from now and wish most bitterly that you had."

He had shifted toward her again. He wore an expression of such bleakness that Giulia's heart turned over. She wanted to go to him, to take his hands and ask him what was wrong— what was really wrong, for she knew it was more than sore ribs and the ugly memory of a fight with a stranger that lay behind what she saw now in his face. But she could not do that, any more than she could tell him that she understood exactly what it was like not only to be trapped, but to risk everything to tear free.

Beyond the portico, a group of black-robed nobles hastened past, sending a clutch of pigeons into clattering flight.

"Well." Bernardo pushed away from the column, grimacing in pain. "You'll make up your own mind, I suppose."

"You should see a physician," Giulia could not stop herself from saying.

"And be bled and cupped and wrapped in some stinking poultice? Thank you, no." He pulled his mantle close. "I'll go on ahead, if you don't mind."

"Of course not." Giulia swallowed a completely unreasonable disappointment.

"Take the chestnuts. I don't want them."

He offered them to her, wrapped in their cloth. She took them, forgetting to be careful. Her hand touched his, warm despite the cold. Startled, she flinched. Strangely, so did he.

"Sorry," she said stupidly—what was she apologizing for? But he was already turning away.

She watched him go, striding off across the piazza, canted slightly to the left to favor his injured ribs. Inside her a familiar question turned, painful yet irresistible: What if she told him the truth? What if she revealed herself? If he knew her, truly knew her . . . what might happen then?

It made her light-headed to imagine it, made her close her eyes and catch her breath, even as she recognized it for the dangerous impulse it was. She knew him well enough to know he would be furious at being deceived—too angry, perhaps, to forgive her. And if not . . . though he adored and admired his mother, a woman with a man's intellect and a man's will to make her own way in the world, was there any reason to think he could accept Giulia's desire to do the same? She had not forgotten Ormanno the thief, who, though a painter himself, had scoffed at her ambition.

And then there were her stars—the implacable prediction of her horoscope, which all but guaranteed she could not have had him, even if she had been herself when she met him.

Girolamo or Giulia: It was the same.

This isn't why I ran away from Santa Marta, she reminded herself. *This isn't why I came to Venice. I am here to paint, not to be distracted by a passing infatuation.*

Though she knew—could no longer deny—that it was more.

On the dimming piazza, torches were being lit. Somewhere a bonfire had been kindled—she could smell the smoke of it. She stepped from the shelter of the Basilica and made her way slowly toward the Merceria, her fingers closed around the chestnuts, which still, faintly, leaked their warmth into her palm.

CHAPTER 17

✤ A Loophole ✤

All through the evening and into the night, Giulia thought about the competition.

Was Bernardo right? Was she afraid to challenge her talent? She didn't think so, though she did fear exposing herself to attention if, by some extraordinary circumstance, she were to win.

It was more the sheer improbability of the idea—that with her limited experience of painting, she should have any chance at all against the professional artists from Padua and Verona and Brescia who would be drawn like ants to the sugar of that purse. That she would be permitted to exploit what was undoubtedly an unconsidered flaw in the rules.

And yet . . . the flaw existed. And while there were true artistic geniuses such as the Bellini brothers and Vittore

Carpaccio and Andrea Mantegna, most painters were like Alvise—entering the profession as a family business, regardless of talent or the lack of it—or else like Stefano, who was good with his hands and had wanted a trade that did not require him to work outside. In such company, was it really so improbable that her painting would shine?

And to be judged by Giovanni Bellini, whose colors are as beautiful as the Maestra's . . . what might come of that? And the purse. Five hundred ducats. A fortune.

Giulia arrived in the workshop the next morning to discover that Ferraldi had hired a man to model for the workshop's next commission, a painting of San Sebastiano. As Ferraldi positioned the model in the saint's agonized pose, pulling at the man's limbs as if he were a jointed doll, Giulia fetched her drawing board and joined Zuane, Antonio, and the three apprentices before the dais where the model stood. Ferraldi encouraged his painters to take the opportunity to sketch whenever he posed a scene like this, but for the apprentices, participation was mandatory.

Ferraldi got the model arranged to his satisfaction at last and took up his own drawing board. The model stood in the light from the windows, as still as a stone in his contorted posture, his naked limbs corded with muscle and the shape of his sex clear beneath the linen of his breechclout. Drawing nudes from life, as she would never have been permitted to do at Santa Marta, was one of the things Giulia had most looked forward to in Venice; she'd been furious at the embarrassment she could not help feeling at first, the shameful blushes she could not control. Now, though she was still not accustomed to such frank nakedness, she had learned to set her discomfort aside—to become, not a disguised girl looking upon the unclad body of a man or a false boy pretending to be familiar with such sights, but simply an artist, her eye entranced by light and form, her mind consumed with the need to reproduce those things as precisely as possible upon the page.

Midway through the session, Ferraldi got up and moved quietly around the semicircle of artists, offering criticism and advice. Though he could sometimes be quick-tempered, he was a generous and perceptive teacher. Giulia valued the counsel he had given her. Today he stood behind her for a while, silently observing, then moved on to Alvise, whose work, as usual, did not please him.

The session ended at noon. The model was paid and dismissed, and the workshop returned to its normal routine. Giulia, sent to fetch a bag of gypsum from the storeroom, brought her drawing down to join her growing store of sketches.

She paused before she put it away, looking critically at what she'd done: the model with his head thrown back and his arms pulled behind him, surrounded by smaller studies of different parts of his body: the knotted muscles of his shoulder, the slight bend at one knee, the curled toes of his foot. No one, she thought with pride, would guess that before three months ago she had never seen—much less drawn—a man's nude body.

She thought of Humilità, who had never had this opportunity, remembering her teacher's furious frustration with the restrictions that denied it to her—restrictions that would have bound Humilità just as firmly outside the convent, for it was scandalous for any woman, nun or not, to look upon the naked human form. *Now here I am, free to do what she longed to do, what no true artist should be prevented from doing—but only because no one knows that I am female.*

Giulia felt it stirring again, the conflict that gripped her whenever she thought deeply about her disguise. Girolamo Landriani could paint whatever he wished; he could go any-where, do anything in pursuit of his art. Giulia Borromeo could only dream of such liberty. Free to be herself, she would always be captive as a painter. Yet freedom as a painter meant perpetual captivity in disguise.

Or not. For at any time, misfortune or circumstance or my own carelessness could betray me, and it will all be over.

A sudden reckless purpose gripped her. Bernardo was right. An opportunity stood before her. If she didn't at least try to seize it, she might indeed look back one day and regret that she had not.

You are the sum of your work. She heard Humilità's voice, words the workshop mistress had spoken many times. *Every stroke you paint, every line you draw. Nothing is wasted.*

She placed the San Sebastiano drawing with her others, fetched the gypsum, and returned upstairs.

—

Ferraldi had retreated to his study. Entering, Giulia found the room in its usual chaos, for Ferraldi never allowed Beata, his maid, to set foot in here. He was standing before his easel, frowning at a recently completed commission: a portrait of a richly dressed elderly man with a huge, warty nose. It was a fine, if unflattering, likeness, with a lively sense of life in the tilt of the subject's head and the humorous twist of his lips. The man's brocade doublet was still wet: Giulia could hear the rasping insect-hum of brown ochre, and also the bright tang of yellow orpiment.

"He said I must let my brush tell the truth," Ferraldi said. "I fear I may have taken him too literally. Ah well."

He crossed to his desk. In contrast to the portrait, he was a study in monochrome: gray clothing, pale skin, silver hair, with only the brilliant blue green of his eyes for color.

"What may I do for you, Girolamo?"

"I wonder if I might ask you a favor, Maestro."

"What sort of favor?"

"There's a painting competition that will be held on the last day of Carnival, sponsored by Archimedeo Contarini. I'd like to enter, with your permission."

"I've heard of that competition," Ferraldi said. "An enormous purse, and open only to foreign painters—a nice insult to the many masters who have contributed to Venice's glory. But though you are not Venetian, Girolamo, you are also not a painter."

"The rules exclude only members of the Venetian artists' guild. They say nothing about anyone else."

"A loophole, eh?" A smile lifted the corners of Ferraldi's mouth. "Do you really think Contarini will honor it?"

"I don't know, Maestro. But I'd like to try."

"You've ambition, Girolamo. And nerve. But have you time? Today is the fourteenth of January, and Giovedi Grasso falls on March third this year. Your oils will barely be dry."

"I think I can do it, Maestro."

"Well, I fear you are pursuing phantoms, but you don't need my permission to make a painting of your own. Just be sure it does not interfere with your other work."

"It won't, Maestro, I promise. Thank you."

"One more moment, Girolamo, if you please. I have a matter to discuss with you."

Giulia felt a pulse of apprehension.

"You did fine work today. For a boy with so little training, you have extraordinary natural skill."

"Thank you, Maestro."

"You have proved yourself these past months. You are not only skillful, but diligent and obedient. You do all you are asked and more—I would not have thought to bid you to organize the storeroom, but you undertook it on your own. And you are eager always to learn, something I wish could be said of others in my charge. Stefano will be leaving soon, for his master painting is near complete. All in all, I think it is time I offered you a true apprenticeship. With all the privileges it entails, including a wage."

Joy flooded Giulia, pure and absolute, with not a shred of conflict in it. "Thank you, Maestro. Thank you! You won't regret it."

"I don't expect to." Ferraldi smiled. "I'll have a contract drawn up. You'll get the same wage as Marin. And once Stefano is gone, you may move upstairs."

"Maestro . . . if it's acceptable . . . I'd rather stay where I am."

"But why? Surely you'd prefer the light and air of the upper floor."

Giulia felt herself starting to flush. "I like being on my own. I like being private."

"Yes, you do, don't you?" His vivid gaze enclosed her. She forced herself to meet it, like someone with nothing to hide. "Well, suit yourself. But you'll take meals with us."

"Thank you, Maestro."

"And if by some astonishing chance you should win that competition"—Ferraldi pointed a finger at Giulia's chest—"you are still bound to me and to your contract. Understood?"

"Yes, Maestro."

"Good. You may tell Lauro I've given you the rest of the afternoon off. I imagine you'll want to begin planning your painting."

—

In the concealment of her bed curtain, Giulia pulled the waxed canvas pouch from beneath her clothes and extracted the recipe for Passion blue.

She had known immediately that she would use it. In her mind she heard its ice-on-crystal voice . . . what would it be like to hear it in truth, rising not from the completed paint, as she'd always experienced it before, but from the grinding stone, as her own hands brought it into being? The moment she imagined it, there was nothing she wanted more. There was surely no risk. Matteo, Domenica, Madre Magdalena—all were in Padua and would never know. She even had the money she needed: Bernardo's ducat, which would buy a quantity of Passion blue's costly main ingredient.

She had memorized the recipe at Santa Marta. Now she read it through again, her eyes lingering on the familiar loops and slashes of Humilità's hand. To follow this formula was, in some sense, to bring Humilità back to life. She wanted to be certain she did it right.

She returned the recipe to the pouch. In a corner of the big room, she'd chipped away loose mortar and made a hiding place behind a brick for the money she earned from portrait selling. Bernardo's ducat flashed in the light of her candle as she drew it out. She placed it and ten scudi in her belt pouch, then set out for the Rialto and the color seller's shop.

"Lapis lazuli!" the color seller exclaimed when she told him what she needed. "Your master is making ultramarine blue, is he?"

"He is," Giulia lied.

"Well, he's in luck. I've some fine samples on hand. I also have a quantity prepared and ground, if he'd prefer it ready-made. Of course, the cost is greater. But if he needs it quickly—"

"No," Giulia said. "Just the stones, if you please."

"Now, as to price. Your master is an honored customer, but as I'm sure you know, lapis is among the rarest of materials, for it can only be mined in Persia. Your master will understand, therefore . . ." The color seller paused delicately. "Why I cannot put this on account."

"Of course, signor." Giulia withdrew the golden ducat from her belt pouch and held it up. "He has given me this to give to you." She pulled back her hand as the color seller, his eyes lighting up, reached for the gleaming coin. "He also wishes me to say that he knows well the value and quality of lapis lazuli. And that he is pleased with the business you and he have done together these past years, and hopes to be pleased with it equally today."

"Of course, of course. He may rely on me."

Giulia put the ducat in his hand. While she had no doubt that Ferraldi knew the value of lapis lazuli, she herself had only the vaguest idea. But the color seller had been honest in the past, and she could only trust that he would be honest this time also.

A ducat, it turned out, bought four lapis lazuli nuggets, each about the size of the first knuckle of Giulia's thumb. The color seller first tried to give her three; taking a chance, she demanded the ducat back, threatening to go to one of his rivals a few streets over, causing him reluctantly to produce the fourth. To his credit, they were of excellent quality: very blue, and less adulterated with other minerals than some of the stones she'd seen in Humilità's workshop.

With her remaining money she bought pine resin, gum mastic, beeswax, linseed oil, and lye, as well as the four other ingredients called for in Humilità's recipe. Heading back to Ferraldi's with the bundle under her mantle, she felt more vulnerable than she had with the ducat in her belt. The ducat was just a ducat, but the bundle was Passion blue.

She sat that night at Ferraldi's supper table on the third floor with Ferraldi and the apprentices. Prepared by Beata the maid, it was a better meal than those she'd bought from nearby taverns to eat in her storeroom hideaway.

Even so, she would have preferred to dine alone. Stefano, she could tell, was annoyed by her promotion; she had the feeling that she was in for a rough few days until he satisfied himself that she'd been put in her place. Alvise, of course, was furious—to him this must seem like confirmation of all his fears. Only Marin seemed unconcerned, wolfing down his food with scarcely a breath between bites—and Ferraldi, who had a pile of drawings by his plate and was in a world of his own.

Supper over, Giulia descended to the darkened workshop, where she took a covered mortar from a chest and brought it down to the storeroom. She lit her candle and set to work pounding the nuggets of lapis lazuli into coarse powder in the mortar. Returning to the workshop, she began to grind the mineral fine on a marble grinding slab, using the short, rounded hand tool called a muller. With the braziers extinguished for the night, the workshop was frigid. She could see her breath, pluming out into the little circle of light cast by her candle. But the work warmed her—hard, monotonous labor, eased by all the color grinding she'd done at Santa Marta, which had padded her palms with calluses and made her arms and shoulders as strong as if she really were a boy. The muller crunched and squeaked on the slab, and she thought someone might come down from upstairs to investigate, but no one did.

Her shoulders were on fire when she woke in the morning. The day that followed was as tedious as she'd feared, between Stefano finding inconsequential things for her to do and Alvise fixing her with hateful looks. Not until evening did she manage a minute for herself.

Last night's grinding had yielded a good half-pipkin of lapis powder. Following the recipe's proportions, Giulia melted pine resin, gum mastic, and beeswax over her brazier in a beaker, and strained the liquid through coarse linen into a bowl. Holding her breath—for once the lapis was added, it could not be taken out, and if she'd made an error, all her effort and expense would be for nothing—she poured in the precious blue powder, tilting the bowl this way and that to blend it.

The mixture thickened rapidly. When it was cool enough to handle, she coated her hands with linseed oil and began to knead it as if it were bread. The result was a waxy blue lump the size of her two clenched fists. She covered the bowl and hid it in her sleeping area.

For the next four nights she warmed and kneaded the lapis mixture, thoroughly integrating the mineral with the other materials. At last, on Sunday, she was ready to extract the color, a lengthy process that would require the entire day.

She had the house to herself, for even Ferraldi was away, at work on another portrait commission. She'd completed one extraction and was preparing a second when Bernardo arrived.

"I can't go out today," she told him. "I am making paint."

"Your master has you working on a Sunday?"

"It's not for him, it's for me. You were right about taking chances, Bernardo. I've decided to enter the competition. Or try anyway."

"Ah. Well, good. I'm glad to hear it."

She'd thought he would be more pleased. She felt the rise of the same sharp, foolish disappointment that had gripped her last week when he'd left her to walk home alone. Swallowing it down, she returned to the brazier, where she had just finished heating a porringer of lye.

"Are your ribs mended?" she asked as she prepared to pour the porringer's contents over the lapis mixture in its bowl—carefully, for the caustic lye would burn if it touched her skin.

"Oh," he said dismissively. "I've already forgotten about that. What is that you're pouring? It smells foul."

"I'm making ultramarine blue from lapis lazuli." She saw no harm in telling him this; it was only a small part of the secret. "Lapis is full of impurities, so you can't just mix the ground stone with oil or egg to make paint, as you can with other pigments. You have to combine it with wax and other materials, and work it in a bath of lye to pull up the color."

He followed as she carried the bowl outside. On the pavement by the canal, she had set out eight clear glass beakers, one of which was already full of dark-blue liquid, the hue of a sapphire in shadow. Kneeling, she set down the bowl and began to push and prod the lump of lapis with a pair of wooden dowels.

"This extracts the blue." The sun was shining, warm on her shoulders even though it was January; she squinted against the flashes it called from the liquid lye. "I'll do this eight times, and each time the color will be paler. Then I'll mix the second beaker with the first and the fourth with the third and so on, to get four grades of blue."

Bernardo crouched down for a closer look. "How do you get the color out of the lye?"

"It's heavier than the lye, so it will settle to the bottom of the beakers. Then I'll pour off the lye, wash the pigment in several waters, dry it, and regrind it. Then it will be ready to make into paint."

"It sounds a terrible labor. Could you not buy it ready-made?"

"No. Not prepared this way, at any rate. It's a labor, true, but the quality is worth it."

"What will you paint with your blue?"

"A Muse of song." Inspired by her San Sebastiano sketch, Giulia had thought first of Apollo with his lyre, or Orpheus casting his fatal look back into the darkness. But it seemed too likely that other painters might choose those subjects—and anyway, drawing and painting were not alike, and she feared that to paint a man's body would show her inexperience too clearly. She'd turned instead to other myths, delving into her memory of Ovid's *Metamorphoses,* one of the most precious of the books in Maestro Bruni's library. "She'll be holding her instrument but looking up, startled, interrupted in her playing by the whisper of a greater music: the music of the spheres."

"Well. If Contarini is hoping for something unusual, that should certainly suit his taste."

He rose and began to pace, back and forth along the fondamenta. Giulia finished kneading and poured the second extract into its beaker—less intense than the first, the color of a sapphire pierced by light—and returned to the storeroom to prepare more lye.

Bernardo was still pacing when she came out again. His restlessness was like a fingernail scraping against slate; almost, she wished he would go.

"My marriage agreement will be finalized soon," he said abruptly.

Giulia had nearly forgotten about this. Since she'd given him his portrait, he had not once mentioned his betrothal. She felt her heart contract, a reaction that, she knew, was as foolish as her earlier disappointment.

"We had a letter two weeks ago. Her father and brother want the wedding to take place in September. They are traveling from Vicenza to discuss the arrangements."

If he'd said "funeral" instead of "wedding," he could not have sounded grimmer. He'd stopped pacing and was standing at the fondamenta's edge, staring down at the sun-sparked water of the rio.

"Of course, there are still matters to be decided. Where we are to live, for instance. She—my betrothed—doesn't wish to leave her family. Her father has offered to take me into his business in Vicenza."

"You'll be leaving Venice?"

It popped out before Giulia could catch it back. Her face was suddenly on fire—not so much at the words as at the completely inappropriate tone of dismay in which she'd spoken them. But Bernardo, who now was as still as he'd earlier been restless, did not seem to notice.

"Of course not. I've no interest in the banking trade. My inheritance is in Venice—it's absurd to expect me to manage it from a distance. Nor will I desert my mother." He sighed. "But as far as my father-in-law is concerned, he has already made the greatest possible concession by giving permission for his daughter to wed a courtesan's bastard, and now my mother and I must do our part by yielding to all his demands. Never mind that his present wife was also a courtesan—and never famous, as my mother was. Never mind that marrying his daughter off to me gives him an excuse to provide a dowry that is only just short of an insult. But if I must do this thing"— his stance was no longer merely still, but rigid—"I *will not* also give up my city."

Giulia saw, now, how things fit together: the marriage he did not want, his dark mood last week, and his bleak words about change and chances. Even his bruised ribs—for in his frustration, perhaps he had not merely happened upon but sought out a violent confrontation with a stranger.

"Bernardo, if you don't want this marriage, why did you agree to it?"

"It's what my mother wants. For me to have an ordinary life. A wife. Children. Security. Everything she lacked for so long."

"Does she know that *you* don't want it?"

"She believes I will come to want it. And who's to say she's wrong?" He shook his head. "It's too late for second thoughts, in any case."

"But if the agreement isn't signed—"

"It would be an insult to withdraw now. She's a pleasant enough girl, my betrothed. Pretty enough too. I shall have nothing to complain of."

The third extract was finished. Giulia put down her dowels and poured the lye, the color of a cloudless summer sky at noon, into its beaker. All the while words pressed at her lips, words she knew it might be wiser not to say.

She rose to her feet, the bowl of lapis mixture in both hands. Bernardo stood against the flooding sunlight, dark in his dark clothes, gazing down at the water, where reflections fragmented, reassembled, broke apart again. Something rose in her, a strange melding of sympathy and anger. She ached for his distress, but even more she burned at his passive surrender to it.

"You told me once," she said, the words coming easier because she did not have to look him in the face, "that you couldn't ask your mother to release you to go to Padua, to the university, because you were afraid you might hate her if she refused. I think it's the same now with this marriage. You're doing what you think she wants, at the cost of what *you* want. But have you ever thought that in the end it may be *that* that will bring you to hate her? All the choices you are making to place her wishes above your own?"

He turned, and in his expression she saw the affront she had expected.

"You know nothing about it," he said. "You've had hard luck in your life, I'll grant you, but you've never been responsible for someone else's welfare."

Giulia thought of Sofia, amber eyed and cool. "I don't think she needs you to be responsible for her."

"Who are you to judge? You traveled with her for a week. I've lived with her my whole life. She could have abandoned me when I was born. Many in her profession do, for what patron wants his lover's brat underfoot? But she never did. There were nights, before she became famous, when she ate nothing so that I might have a meal. She gave her favors to a scholar in exchange for my education—for years she serviced that old man, all so I might learn to read Latin and Greek and figure with numbers. The wealth she has built, the property, the house in Cannaregio—it is all for me. I owe her everything, do you understand? And now it's my turn. I can never repay her for all she has done for me, all she has given up, but I can at least try. I can at least do what I can to make her happy."

His voice shook. His fists were clenched at his sides.

"Perhaps she doesn't want you to repay her," Giulia said. "Perhaps she'd rather *you* be happy."

His mouth opened, but no words came. Their eyes held— the full, direct gaze he'd lately made such efforts to avoid.

"You're just a boy," he said. "Why am I listening to you?"

He swung his mantle into place and strode past her without another glance. She heard the sound of his boots as he crossed the storeroom, the thump of the street door falling closed.

She stood on the fondamenta for a time, the bowl of blue in her hands. She was aware of the sun on her face, the slap of water against stone, the call of gulls from the rooftops. At last, slowly, she returned to the shadows of the workshop, to mix another batch of lye and begin the fourth extraction.

CHAPTER 18

❖ Tangled Lives ❖

Through the rest of the afternoon, Giulia's mind turned and turned, like a dream in which she ran with all her might yet got nowhere. How angry had she made him? What if she'd offended him so much he never returned?

Well, what if I did? Would it be harder than being with him? Than playing the friend, or the little brother, or whatever it is that Girolamo is to him, knowing I can never show him who I really am?

Would it be harder than watching him marry?

She shook her head, even though there was no one to see. She didn't want these thoughts. She didn't want these feelings, this stupid, useless, dangerous infatuation. She wished she'd never met him. She wished it had been he and not Sofia who had prevailed that night on the Vicenza road.

She forced herself to concentrate on her work. She had worried she wouldn't manage to complete the extractions before Ferraldi and the apprentices came back, but she finished in good time and was sweeping the storeroom floor when Ferraldi returned. He nodded to her and disappeared upstairs. The apprentices arrived a little later, all wearing Carnival masks. Marin raced up the stairs, followed by Alvise. Stefano paused, pushing up his mask and sniffing the air like a hound.

"What's that I smell? Lye?"

"I don't smell anything." Giulia did not pause in her sweeping. "You'd better get rid of the mask. The Maestro is upstairs."

Ferraldi, who disapproved of Venice's long Carnival season, forbade his apprentices mask themselves before Giovedi Grasso. Stefano snatched off his mask and shoved it under his mantle, then tossed back his hair and followed the others.

Beata the maid had Sundays off, so there was no supper gathering that night. Giulia went out to buy a meal, retreating behind her curtain to eat it by candlelight. Then she brought out her studies for the Muse and resumed work on her final drawing, which was nearly complete. The light was poor, but she was used to making do. She welcomed the absorption of the task, which spared her thoughts of Bernardo.

When enough time had passed for Ferraldi and the apprentices to be abed, she fetched out the beakers of blue, which she'd hidden behind a stack of lumber, and combined their contents as she'd described to Bernardo—a task she had not had time to carry out before. Then she took her candle and climbed upstairs, for she needed the covered mortar again.

The mortar was not in its usual place. After some searching, she spotted it on one of the worktables. Whoever had used it had been crushing lead white and hadn't bothered to wipe away the residue. She found a rag and began to clean it.

"What are you doing?"

Stefano's voice came from behind her. She jumped around. He was standing one table over, dressed only in his shirt, a curious expression on his face.

"Nothing." Her heart was pounding. He had crept up on her as quietly as a cat; she hadn't heard a thing. Thank the saints she hadn't cried out or screamed, as a girl might have done. "What are *you* doing?"

"I heard a noise." He pointed to the rag, clutched in her hand. "That doesn't look like nothing."

"I need to borrow it. The mortar, I mean."

"Hm." He eyed her. "You were up here last week too, grinding something in the middle of the night. I heard you through the floor, and I know it was you because everyone else was in bed. And I did smell lye today, even if you tried to pretend otherwise. What are you up to that you don't want anyone to know about? You had better tell me. I'll find out whether you do or not."

Giulia sighed. Passion blue was a secret, but there was no reason why her painting had to be. "I'm making paint. I'm going to enter Archimedeo Contarini's competition. The Maestro has given me permission."

"The competition with the five-hundred-ducat prize?" Stefano frowned. "You can't. It's closed to Venetians. Anyway, you're just an apprentice. Barely an apprentice, at that."

"It's only closed to Venetians who are members of the artists' guild. Nothing has been said about closing it to apprentices."

Stefano laughed. "You really think you can use that to cheat your way in?"

Giulia shrugged. "I can try."

"Five hundred ducats. That's a lot of money." Stefano folded his arms, looking thoughtful. "I wonder . . . My master painting is well under way. If I finished it in time . . ."

"There must be a theme of music," Giulia said sharply.

He shrugged. "I can add some angels playing instruments. What are *you* painting?"

"I haven't decided yet," Giulia lied.

"And yet here you are, already making paint." Stefano's narrow blue eyes glinted in the yellow candlelight. "You're an odd one, Girolamo, with your bed curtains and your dainty ways. Always going off by yourself, never joining in. It's enough to make a man wonder, if he was the wondering type. But no one can say you aren't clever. Talking your way into the workshop, showing up poor old Alvise as you did a couple of weeks ago—" He nodded. "Oh yes. I see the path you're walking."

Giulia stared at him, cold with sudden dread. She felt the skin of her disguise as she rarely did these days, and her own true self beneath it, hiding in plain sight.

"Don't fear. I don't care a whit what you're up to. I'm away from here the minute I get my guild membership—go ahead and scheme, and good fortune to you. In the meantime, though"—he grinned—"I'm going to try my hand at that five hundred ducats. 'Night, Girolamo."

Giulia went back to cleaning the mortar. She was furious—both at the way he'd made her feel and his theft of her idea. *Bernardo's idea*, she corrected herself. Now she could expect to have her free time curtailed, for while Stefano might not actually try to stop her, he'd surely throw every possible obstacle in her way.

Ah well, she thought as she returned downstairs, the heavy mortar cradled in her arms, *it's not as if whatever he produces will actually be competition.* As a painter, Stefano was no better than adequate, doing well enough with the Madonna and Child panels the workshop turned out in endless succession but faltering with anything more ambitious. *I have nothing to fear from him.*

—

As Giulia had expected, Stefano did his best to keep her busy in the week that followed, and she was hard put to snatch any free time at all. Even so, she managed to wash the lapis extracts clean of lye, burnish the final layer of gesso on the small panel she had prepared, and, working by candlelight in the evening, complete the transfer of her final drawing of the Muse.

She also paid another visit to the color seller, where she used the rest of her portrait earnings to buy the additional pigments she needed. The bill came to more money than she had; reluctantly, she set aside the cinnabar she'd been planning to use to make vermilion and asked for madder lake instead. The color seller, however, inquisitive as always, had deduced that she was buying for herself rather than for her master. He winked and put the cinnabar back.

"Pay me when you can," he told her. "Don't think I won't forget you owe it, though."

On Sunday morning Giulia woke thinking about Bernardo. Would he come today? She tried to banish him from her mind as she began work on the painting, concentrating on the voices of her paints as she laid in a monochrome ground of shadows and highlights over which she would later build up color. But every sound from outside made her jump. It was not until well after noon, when she could no longer pretend he might arrive, that she was able to give herself fully to creation, her brush flying across the smooth surface of the gesso, the disappointment and the hurt forgotten for a little while.

A week later, on the first Sunday of February, Giulia climbed to the workshop to mix pigments. Once again she had the house to herself; the apprentices were with their families as usual, and Ferraldi was spending the day at the home of a friend.

Today she would be painting flesh: the Muse's face and neck, her bare arms and shoulders. She ground the colors to paste with walnut oil, their voices rising one after the next: the thrumming growl of bone black, the velvet purr of lead white, raw umber rasping like a locust, and lead tin yellow trilling bright and tart, like the taste of lemon peel. Vermilion she needed also, a sizzling cadence as if hot oil could sing, and green earth, its mossy hum rising and falling like the breath of secret growing things. The paints told her when they were ground fine enough, though she could not have put into words how she knew. Each one, completed, joined its voice to the rest, a rising, unearthly harmony.

The familiar joy of creation filled her. She was thinking only of painting as she returned downstairs, carrying the pigment pots on a tray. She bundled herself in an extra tunic and put on her fingerless gloves, then went outside, where she'd set up her easel by the rio. The sky was overcast but the clouds were high, and the bright, shadowless light was perfect for working.

She was kneeling on the fondamenta, scooping dollops of paint onto her palette, when she heard the street door open. She got to her feet just as Bernardo came striding through the storeroom.

She saw the change in him at once. The darkness of two weeks ago was gone. He blazed with energy and purpose.

"I have news," he said.

"News?" All week Giulia had hoped for his return. But for most of the morning, her eyes color-saturated and her mind filled with the singing of the paints, she hadn't thought of him at all. His presence now seemed unreal, as if she'd called him out of her imagination.

"Yes!" The word burst from him, exultant. "I've broken my betrothal. I'm free."

"Bernardo! But . . . how? What changed?"

"I was angry, Girolamo." He began to pace, unable to keep still. "About what you said. But I couldn't get it out of my head, and when my anger began to pass I saw that you were right. Last week I spoke to my mother. I explained everything. She'd guessed I was reluctant for this marriage, but she never realized how much I dreaded it. I never told her, you see. It was just as you said—I was so determined to do what I believed she wanted for me, what I believed she needed from me, that I never thought that she might wish for me only what I wished for myself."

"So she agreed to call it off?"

"Yes. The family will be angry, but no contract was signed and no announcement was made, so my betrothed will not be shamed, nor will my mother and I be liable for broken promises. I'll stay through the summer to make sure that all here is in order, and to hire a reliable man to oversee our properties. Then, in August—" His face shone with joy. "Girolamo, I am going to Padua!"

"To the university?"

"Yes! My mother has given me her blessing—and she didn't hesitate, Girolamo; she gave it gladly. I cannot believe I waited so long or feared so much."

"I'm glad for you, Bernardo," Giulia said. And she was, though it was a strange, regretful kind of gladness.

"She will miss me, of course, and I her. But Padua isn't far. I can come back when I'm needed. And I won't stay forever. Venice is my home—one day I will return for good, and marry and have children and fulfill all the things she wishes for me. But not yet. Not yet!"

He came toward her, alight with jubilation, as if the sun had come out to shine on him alone. Giulia, dazzled, could not look away.

"How tangled in our lives we are," he said. "All of us, wrapped up so tight we can't see clearly. Sometimes it requires a stranger to perceive the knot. To understand where to cut. This is all because of you, Girolamo, and what you said to me that I did not wish to hear. Thank you."

He placed his hands on Giulia's arms, gripping them strongly, then pulled her into an embrace. She was sure, when she thought about it later, that he meant it to be the kind of embrace men exchanged: rough, quick, accompanied by back-slapping and shoulder pummeling. But the change in him, or the singing of the colors, or the certainty of farewell—she would never afterward be sure—had temporarily breached the guard that caused her to flinch or stiffen at any contact between them. Without thinking, she softened against his chest, leaning into him. She thought, for just an instant—for just the flickering space of a breath—that he responded, pulling her more tightly against him.

But then her hands touched him.

He jerked back, shoving her away with enough force to make her stagger. Their eyes met. She saw the confusion in his face. Horror at her mistake rolled over her like icy water. *He's guessed.* She had pressed herself against him, and he had guessed.

But then disgust clamped like a Carnival mask across his features. And she realized, with a different kind of horror, that he'd guessed something else entirely.

Without a word, he left her. She heard his hurried footsteps, the slam of the street door—exactly as she had two weeks ago, except that this time there was no doubt in her mind that he was gone for good.

CHAPTER 19

✧ Passion Blue ✧

Well. That's it, then.

A strange calm had settled over Giulia. It was actually better this way, she thought: a quick, sudden severing, a door closed and locked. *Now I can forget about him. I can give myself to work and learning without distraction. I should be relieved.*

Should be.

She looked at the easel, where the Muse awaited her brush. At her feet, the color songs wove unceasing harmonies. All at once their voices were not enough. She wanted—she needed— to hear the voice she had been waiting for, the voice she longed for: the icy, silvery, secret voice of Passion blue.

She returned to the storeroom. From their hiding place, she took the beaker that held the first two lapis extractions, fully dry now at the bottom of the glass, and the four other ingredients she had prepared.

Upstairs in the workshop, she measured out the brilliant blue powder, placing half on a grinding slab, returning the other half to the beaker. The little heap on the slab seemed tiny; she wasn't sure it would be enough even to finish the Muse's gown. But if she made a mistake today, she wanted to have some pigment in reserve.

She set out the bowls that held the additional materials, then closed her eyes for a moment, visualizing Humilità's recipe, reviewing the proportions to make sure she'd calculated the amounts correctly.

Carefully she began adding ingredients to the slab, arranging them in smaller heaps around the blue: an eighth part lead white, to bind with the oil she would add last. A pinch of powdered gold leaf, to add subtle warmth to the blue. An eighth part pearlescent powdered alabaster, to absorb the light. And to give the light back, to lend Passion blue its extraordinary luster: a sixth part water-clear Murano glass, from a roundel crushed flour-fine in the mortar, scintillating like star stuff even in the gray light of the day.

Ordinary ingredients, unremarkable on their own. But if she'd followed the recipe as carefully as she believed she had, joining them together would produce an alchemical transformation, creating something greater than the melding of individual parts.

With the muller, she gently swirled the powders together. She added a measure of walnut oil, and took up the muller once more.

The song began to rise the instant she started to grind— faint at first, a shimmering bell-like music drifting up through the silence of the workshop—just as she had heard it more than a year ago, standing at Humilità's side in the windswept courtyard at Santa Marta. She rolled the muller around the slab, spreading the color over the marble, scraping it back to the center, starting again. All blues chimed—azurite like a silver cymbal, smalt brittle and off-key, natural ultramarine pure and resonant—but not like this. Nothing on earth was like this. With each repetition the song intensified, drawing closer, growing clearer, as if she were opening the substance of the world and summoning something incomparably beautiful from underneath.

How could I ever have thought such a thing was sinful? How could I ever have imagined that hearing this music was anything but a gift from God?

Humilità's recipe cautioned against overgrinding. Giulia had feared she would not know when to stop. But the instinct for *rightness* that was part of her strange sixth sense was as sure now as ever. Between one breath and the next the song achieved its peak. She rolled the muller a final time and set it aside.

She scraped the paint into a pot, gathering every speck. The song was unmuffled by the clay that held it; unconsciously, as she descended to the storeroom, she matched her footsteps to its cadences.

She added the blue to her palette. Its voice rose above the voices of the colors already arrayed there but did not obscure them, like a principal singer surrounded by a choir. Stepping to the easel, she dipped her brush. For a moment she held back, letting the tension build. Then, with a rush of release that felt like flying, she set brush to panel.

Working quickly, she laid the color over the area of the Muse's gown, which she had previously prepared according to Humilità's instructions—for that was also part of Passion blue, that it must be supported by a dark ground rather than the more conventional light one. Then she began to incorporate darks and pales to model the folds of the fabric, referring often to her master drawing, which she'd laid out on the pavement at her feet. These shadings deepened or brightened the timbre of the song but did not alter its glorious, crystal essence.

This is what matters. Not passing infatuations. Not false names or disguises. Not cruel, stupid stars. This. This is what I was born to do.

She promised herself she would not forget again.

Only when the last smear of blue had been used, and the muscles of her painting arm were quivering with exhaustion, did she step away from the easel to inspect what she had done.

The Muse's gown was complete. Against the monochrome of the underpainting, it shone brighter than a peacock's plumage, singing sapphire harmonies.

Did I make that? Giulia felt as if she were waking from a dream. Wonder swept her, tinged with sadness, because Humilità, who had given her this—all of it, not just the priceless color, but painting itself—was not here to see it.

"That's a lovely blue."

Giulia jumped, startled. Ferraldi was standing in the doorway. How long had he been there?

"Thank you, Maestro," she said, then added, "They're my own materials. I didn't borrow them."

Ferraldi stepped closer. "This is your competition painting?"

"Yes."

"Hm. You'll want to rework some of the modeling. The folds there look a little stiff." He pointed. "Do you see?"

Giulia's exalted mood was slipping away. She saw that he was right. "Yes, Maestro, I do."

"Try blending the shadow a little more, there and there."
He pointed, indicating, then leaned toward the singing blue.
Giulia tensed, though of course he could not guess its secret
just by looking. "That really is an extraordinary blue. Natural
ultramarine, yes?"

"Yes, Maestro."

"It's unusually pure. You must tell me where you obtained
it."

"I made it, Maestro."

"You? On your own? Not from raw lapis lazuli, surely?"

"Yes, Maestro. I've been working on it for the past two
weeks."

"Hm. Impressive." He stepped away. "Well, when I need
more ultramarine, be very sure I will call on you to prepare it."

"Yes, Maestro." She would make blue for him if he wanted,
but not Passion blue. She thought of Domenica, and Matteo,
and all the others who had coveted the transcendent color. She
hoped Ferraldi was not like them.

After he departed, she stood for a while before her work,
trying to recapture the euphoria of creation. But it had left her,
and doubt was seeping into the space where it had been, heavy
and unwelcome. She could see her mistakes now, not just the
flaw Ferraldi had pointed out but others: errors of execution,
born of inexperience.

She could address them, or try to. But the blue, the shining, singing blue . . . that could not be changed. And though it
was brilliant, though it was beautiful, was it *Passion* blue? She
had followed the recipe to the letter. She'd been sure she recognized its unearthly voice, its sapphire luster; but it had been
months since she had heard or seen Passion blue—not since
before Humilità had taken to her bed. Could she be certain

that the bell-like tones that filled her senses now were exactly the same?

It's only the lateness of the day, she thought. *And that I am so tired. It does no good to question anyway. What's done is done.*

For the first time in several hours, she thought of Bernardo—Bernardo, who would never come back.

She scraped her palette and cleaned her brushes and returned them and the painting to their hiding place. She climbed wearily to the workshop to clean up there as well. At last, too exhausted to be hungry, she lay down on her bed and fell into dreamless sleep.

CHAPTER 20

❖ Unmasking ❖

February wore on, its gray skies and raw cold pierced now and then with bursts of sun, making all of Venice shine and hinting at the possibility of spring. Giulia filled every moment with work, in the workshop when she was needed and at her easel when she was not. She had a painting to finish, and Bernardo to forget.

With each new day she saw her foolishness more clearly. He'd never been her friend, for the boy he thought he knew was a figment. He could never have been her lover. All he'd been was a distraction and a threat—to her self-control, to her disguise, to her passion to paint. By allowing their companionship to continue, she had put at risk everything she'd come so far to gain.

I should never have let it go on so long. I should have sent him away when he asked me to make his portrait.

But if her intellect understood this, her heart did not. There was a hole in the world where he had been. On Sunday afternoons, she found herself listening for his knock at the door, for his footsteps in the storeroom. Only when she was painting could she forget him for a little while.

It will change, she told herself. *It's only a matter of time.*

During a free hour on the last Saturday in February, she set up her easel inside the water door, out of reach of the rain sluicing down outside. She still hid the Muse when not working on the painting, but she no longer troubled to work in secret. The entire workshop knew what she and Stefano were doing. Even Alvise had sneaked down to spy, though he'd jumped back into the shadows the moment she noticed him.

As for Ferraldi, he had been a regular visitor, and she knew the painting was better for his advice.

"It's a remarkable effort for one so young," he'd told her as she was brushing in the final details. "I am almost tempted to attend the banquet, just to see you show it."

"I'd be honored if you would, Maestro."

Ferraldi shook his head. "Contarini has invited every Venetian painter of note, but only so they may experience their exclusion anew. I will not acknowledge so childish a provocation."

The painting was finished. The Muse sat on a stool, her face and upper body lit to incandescence by the candles at her side, the chamber around her veiled in shadow. She had lowered her lyre, her attention caught by something else; her lips were parted, her eyes wide with wonder. Above the dusk-dimmed landscape beyond her window, a tide of stars swept the night-blue sky. Within those twilight depths lay the suggestion of great crystal rings: the ever-turning spheres of the cosmos, whose aetheric music the Muse had just perceived.

At the bottom left, near the Muse's bare foot, Giulia had painted a small half-unrolled scroll, marked with black letters: *Gamma Me Fecit*. Gamma—the Greek letter for *G*, which seemed a better attribution than the simple Latin *G* with which she'd marked Sofia's and Bernardo's portraits—Made Me.

She felt a fierce pride. This was far beyond any of the practice paintings she had done at Santa Marta, even the Annunciation she'd shown Humilità, which she had considered her best. She did not think it was too much like hubris to imagine it could stand beside the work of any professional painter.

Yet, honest in her recognition of her strengths, she could not deny that there were also weaknesses, which even Ferraldi's astute critiques hadn't enabled her to eliminate entirely: a slight shallowness to the perspective framed by the window, a ropiness to the Muse's twining tresses. The Muse's hands, painted and repainted a dozen times and still not quite right.

And the blue—the glowing cobalt of the Muse's gown, the deeper sapphire of the star-strewn sky . . . it was beautiful, unquestionably superior to the ready-made ultramarine the painters upstairs used for the cloaks of their Madonnas. But Giulia was certain now that she'd been correct the day she'd first laid on the color. It was not Passion blue. It lacked the radiance she remembered from Humilità's paintings, the near-magical quality of seeming to shine from within. For all her care, even with the assistance of the color song, she had not been capable of duplicating Humilità's achievement.

This was not the perfect work that had existed in her mind. It was only the imperfect rendering that was the best her skill could manage. Yet Giulia was not dismayed. For she knew that she would try again—and again, and again, for as long as it took to gain the experience, the judgment, the understanding to get it right. And perhaps she never would get it right. Perhaps she would never attain that flawless blue, never create that perfect image, never find the ultimate point of balance between what she could accomplish and what she could dream. Yet wasn't that the point? To be drawn onward, ever onward, in pursuit of your deepest passion? To look back at the end of the race and know that you had never done less than the most you could do?

Gamma blue, she thought. *Giulia blue.* She shook her head, embarrassed by her own vanity. How absurd, to imagine that her blue might deserve a name.

She moved to stand by the water door, wrapping her arms around herself against the cold. Rain streamed from the eaves, pouring off the pavement and pimpling the surface of the canal. *Just three days until Giovedi Grasso.* Three days until she would make her way to Palazzo Contarini Nuova and test the loophole in Archimedeo Contarini's rules.

If she were allowed to enter . . . could she win? It didn't seem entirely impossible, though it was surely highly unlikely. But winning was no longer what drove her. To test herself; to stand with other painters beneath the eye of the great master, Giovanni Bellini, and be acknowledged as one of them, woman though she was—though, of course, none would know the truth of that. To prove, if only to herself, that all she'd done—the choices she'd made, the lies she'd told, the risks she'd taken—had been worthwhile. That was what she wanted now. That was what mattered.

"Girolamo!" Lauro's gravelly shout jolted Giulia from her daydreams. "Where in blazes has the boy got to? Girolamo!"

Giulia removed the Muse from the easel and returned her to her hiding place. Most of the color songs had sunk to silence as they dried; but blues slowed the hardening of the oils with which they were mixed, and the Muse's gown was still a little soft, though it was the first color Giulia had laid on. As she headed for the stairs to answer Lauro's call, she could hear its bell-like tones, faint but still perceptible, whispering from concealment.

—

Lauro put Giulia to work with Stefano at the grinding slabs, displacing Alvise, who was sent to scrub the worktables.

"You done with your painting?"

Stefano's tone was casual, but Giulia wasn't fooled. He'd been keeping track of her progress—appearing at odd moments, justifying his presence with dismissive or mocking comments. Of course he pretended to be unconcerned, but the fact that he came as often as he did told its own story. His own painting was an Annunciation of the most conventional sort, to which, as he'd promised, he had added a troop of instrument-playing angels, crammed awkwardly into a corner of the room where the Archangel Gabriel knelt before the Virgin.

"Yes." Giulia began to break up a block of ready-made lead white in a mortar. "You?"

"I'm putting in a fifth angel, with a viol. I've got practically an entire orchestra now." He grinned. "Maybe you should think about adding an angel or two. Your lyre-playing lady could use company."

"The paintings are supposed to be *about* music," Giulia said. "Not simply to include musicians."

"Musicians make music, don't they?" He paused in his grinding to look at her. "How is yours better, anyway? A girl with a lyre, looking startled?"

"A Muse of song, her attention captured by the music of the spheres."

"How will anyone know that just by looking at her?"

"I'll tell them. While *you'll* have to explain why the Archangel Gabriel needed to bring an orchestra to the Annunciation."

For a moment Giulia thought she saw uncertainty in his face. Then he shrugged and turned back to the grinding slab.

"I suppose we'll just have to see."

They continued working. Giulia dumped the lead white out onto her grinding stone and added oil, making the color purr. Beside her, Stefano's red ochre sounded just as it should; he might be an indifferent artist, but he was a competent paint maker. The rain still drummed down outside, a counterpoint to the singing of the paints and the voices of Zuane and Antonio, bickering over a girl they both fancied. Then—

Boom! Boomboomboomboom! A ferocious pounding on the street door echoed up the stairs.

"Christ's blood!" exclaimed Lauro. "Alvise, go see who's in such a lather."

Alvise dropped his scrubbing brush into his bucket and slouched from the workshop, wearing his usual put-upon scowl. Giulia heard him thumping down to the storeroom, heard the creak of the door and the sound of conversation. Then Alvise's voice, raised—"Wait! You can't go up there!"— and then footsteps on the stairs.

Something flashed in Giulia's mind, an explosion of black light. Recognition? Premonition? She would never afterward be sure. The muller slipped from her hands. She turned—

Matteo Moretti stood in the doorway.

It was like being struck blind, for she could not believe the evidence of her eyes. It was impossible. He could not be here. She was dreaming. She'd gone mad.

He was looking past her, toward the far end of the workshop. If she'd spun around right then, he might not have recognized her. But shock held her frozen. As if in a nightmare, she watched his head turn, watched his eyes sweep the room, watched them find her. Amazement blanked his face, followed at once by triumph. His mouth opened, shaping words that to her disbelieving ears sounded as if they were issuing from underwater:

"Giulia Borromeo!"

It catapulted her from her immobility. Her frozen wits leaped forward. Escape, she had to escape, right now, this instant. Not the door—he was blocking it—but the window arcade, she was closer to it than she was to him—if she sprinted, she might reach it before he caught her—if she leaped with all her might, she might clear the fondamenta and land in the canal—

She flung herself forward, shoving Stefano aside.

"Seize her!" she heard Matteo cry. "Don't let her get away!"

She almost succeeded. But inches from the sill, hands closed on the loose fabric of her painter's smock and yanked her backward. She felt her arms crushed in someone's grip—Lauro, his hands like iron.

"Girolamo! What's possessed you, boy?"

"Let me go." She fought against his hold. "He means me harm. Let me go!"

"Be still! Signor, what is your business here?"

"*She* is my business." Matteo pointed. His gray curls were dark with rain, his heavy mantle soaked. "That girl you hold."

"There is no girl here, signor. This is Girolamo Landriani, an apprentice in Maestro Ferraldi's workshop."

Matteo stepped forward, leaving the man he had brought with him waiting in the doorway. Giulia's heart felt as if it would tear from her chest. Alvise peered around the henchman's back, goggle-eyed. Antonio and Zuane stared openmouthed over the tops of their easels. Stefano still leaned against his grinding slab; he'd caught himself on it when Giulia pushed him, and his palms were covered in red ochre.

"What is all this shouting?"

It was Ferraldi, emerging from his study, a quill in one hand and a sheet of paper in the other. Matteo halted.

"Gianfranco."

"Matteo!" Surprise spread across Ferraldi's face. There was no pleasure in it. "This is unexpected. Why didn't you let me know you were coming?"

"My business is not with you, Gianfranco. It's with your . . . apprentice . . . over there."

"With Girolamo?" Ferraldi turned. "Lauro, what is this? Has the boy done something?"

"That is no *boy*," Matteo said. "That is Giulia Borromeo, a runaway novice from the Convent of Santa Marta in Padua."

"No, no, Matteo," Ferraldi said. "I don't know how you conceived such a notion. Girolamo is Giulia Borromeo's *cousin*. Giulia Borromeo is dead."

"Very far from dead, in fact. She stands before you now, having disguised herself, betrayed her vows, and stolen a valuable secret in the bargain. I have come to Venice to retrieve her."

Of course. Giulia felt a sickening despair. *Of course he found me. How could I ever have thought he wouldn't?*

Ferraldi stepped toward her. The quill and paper had slipped from his fingers. "Girolamo, is this true?"

"It's easily proved," Matteo said. "Order her to remove her doublet and shirt."

Ferraldi ignored him. *"Is it true?"*

She thought of denying it. But all Matteo had to do was rip away her clothing. And in Ferraldi's face she saw unwilling comprehension, and knew that all the odd things he'd noticed about her were falling into place inside his mind. He believed Matteo already, even if he hadn't yet admitted it. She closed her eyes.

"I'm Giulia Borromeo. That's true."

"Humilità's pupil," he whispered.

"I did run away from Santa Marta." She opened her eyes, though she could not meet his blue-green gaze. "But it isn't true that I'm a thief. I've stolen nothing."

"She lies," Matteo said. "She fled Padua to keep from revealing a secret to which she has no right."

"That's not so! The secret was mine; she gave it to me of her own free will!"

"What secret?" Ferraldi demanded. "What are you talking about?"

"Passion blue," Giulia said. "The recipe for Passion blue."

Once again she saw comprehension in Ferraldi's face. "Humilità's famous color."

"My daughter was not in her right mind before she died," Matteo said. "This girl, coveting the color for herself, took advantage of that to obtain the recipe. Then when my daughter's successor quite rightly demanded that the secret be shared with her, this girl betrayed her vows and fled. She is a viper, Gianfranco. See how she has already tricked you. She would have taken your secrets too."

"It's not true. None of it is true." Giulia realized that Lauro's hands had fallen away. She was free—but where was there to go? "He wants the color for himself. He has always wanted it. You know that, Maestro—I saw your letters, I know she wrote to you about how he coveted the recipe, how he pushed her and pushed her to give him Passion blue, though she never would. She knew what she was doing when she gave it to me. To her last breath, she knew."

Ferraldi understood. She could see him struggling with it. She felt a desperate hope.

"Please, Maestro, don't let him take me." She held out her hands, pleading. "I'll go away—you'll never see me again. Just don't let him take me."

"Listen to me, Gianfranco." Matteo's voice was quiet. "Whether you believe me or the girl, Santa Marta has a claim on her. She is pledged and promised to it by vows made before the altar. I advise you to consider well the . . . distress . . . it will cause if she is not returned. Venice may wink at the authority of Rome, but I promise you, Rome's hand can reach as far as your workshop."

Ferraldi stood motionless. He was looking neither at Giulia nor Matteo, but staring down at the paint-stained floor. His silver hair had fallen across his face.

"I know your feelings for my daughter. Would you wish her reputation to be tarnished by such shameful intrigue if this scandal were to become known? Not to mention the damage to your own reputation if it were revealed that you have harbored, even unwittingly, a fugitive novice in illegal disguise."

Matteo's voice fell even further. His face might have been carved from stone but for the living jewels of his eyes. "Don't oppose me in this, Gianfranco. Truly, it will not serve you."

Slowly, Ferraldi turned to Matteo.

"If you carry . . . her . . . back to Santa Marta, will she be taken into the workshop again?"

Giulia knew then that she was lost.

"Certainly." Matteo did not lose a beat. "She owes her labor to the convent, and the workshop is where she labors best. It is another reason they want her back."

"Her talent will not go to waste, then. That is good."

"Don't believe him," Giulia said, though she had no hope it would make a difference. "If I go back there, I'll never hold a brush again."

"I'm sorry, Girolamo." Ferraldi shook his head. "Giulia, I mean. For Humilità's sake, I would help you if I could. But what he says is true. I have no choice."

"Maestro, please—"

"I have no choice." This time it was he who could not look her in the eyes.

"Good man." Matteo clapped his hands. "Dario!"

Matteo's henchman came to take hold of Giulia's arm. His grip was like a manacle; she knew it would be useless to resist.

"Farewell, Gianfranco," Matteo said. "You have my gratitude for your assistance. God grant that we may see each other soon in better circumstances."

Ferraldi folded his arms. He did not reply.

Dario urged Giulia forward. She went, stumbling, her eyes cast down, for she could not bear to see how the other members of the workshop would be watching her. She nearly fell as Dario pushed her onto the stairs; as he caught her, her head flew up, and for an instant she glimpsed the shocked face of Alvise, who was still standing in the doorway.

Then they were in the storeroom, twilight-dark with the water door closed, and then in the street, where the rain still poured down. It soaked her instantly, streaming from her hair and clothes, running into her nose and mouth until she thought she would drown. And indeed, she half hoped she would, for to die in the freezing rain in the streets of Venice might well be better than what she would face now.

CHAPTER 21

✤ Surrender ✤

A gondola was waiting, the gondolier standing like a statue in the downpour. Matteo took the seat under shelter of the felze. Dario shoved Giulia down in the bow, keeping a hold on her all the while.

The gondolier pushed smoothly away from the landing. Giulia paid no attention to where they were going. What did it matter? It was over. Her escape, her deception, her dream of painting. What kind of fool had she been to imagine it could end any other way?

The rain had stopped by the time they drew up before the water steps of a palazzo—not as large as the great palazzi along the Grand Canal, but very grand all the same. Lanterns lit the alcoves by the water door, haloed by the mist that had begun to rise off the rio.

Matteo disembarked and pounded on the door, which was opened after a few moments by a servant with a candle. Matteo beckoned; Dario hauled Giulia onto the slippery landing and hustled her up the steps. They followed Matteo along a dim passage, into a courtyard, and up the stairs to the *piano nobile*. There Matteo turned aside. Dario pushed Giulia up another flight of stairs. He shoved her into a room and locked her in.

The room was small, with no furnishings at all. Giulia stood dripping on the floor like laundry hung to dry, unable to summon the will to move. At last, slowly, she crossed to the single window, which looked out across an alley onto the side of the house next door. The fog was thickening, blurring the world away. She loosed the catch and pulled the window inward, and leaned out over the sill. There were no balconies. The stuccoed walls were smooth, bare of any ornamentation that might have provided handholds. The alley below was much too far to jump, unless she wanted to break her legs or crush her skull.

Trapped.

She closed the window and rested her forehead against the cold glass. Even now that the first shock had passed, she found it hard to believe what had happened.

How on earth had Matteo found her? He could not have learned from anyone at Santa Marta, for she'd never yielded to temptation and written to Angela. What about Ferraldi? She'd told him that story about being her own cousin; she supposed he might have tried to confirm it and somehow guessed the truth. But he'd been truly shocked by her unmasking. And why would he have told Matteo? She'd seen his displeasure at Matteo's abrupt appearance. No. It could not have been Ferraldi.

Stefano, then, wanting to rid himself of a rival? Alvise, who believed she was a threat to him? Bernardo, who'd been so angry with her, whose mother knew her secret? But she'd never told Sofia her name. And even if the others had guessed her sex, how would they have discovered who she really was, or connected her with Matteo?

In the end it hardly mattered. Once again she was Matteo's prisoner. She knew what he wanted; she knew he would come for it. Her despair was so great that she did not even feel afraid.

She was freezing in her soaking clothes. Stepping away from the window, she twisted her hair to wring out the water, then did the same with her garments. She crouched down in a corner, her teeth chattering, to wait.

—

It was full dark when he arrived.

A line of light appeared beneath the door. The lock rattled and the door swung open. Matteo entered, accompanied by a servant with a lantern and a chair. Matteo seated himself; the servant set down the lantern and departed, closing the door but not turning the lock. Involuntarily, Giulia's eyes followed him.

"He has instructions to wait outside," Matteo said. "If you are thinking of attempting to escape."

She looked at him across her drawn-up legs. He sat easily in the chair, one ankle crossed over the opposite knee, his arms folded on his chest. His mane of gray curls was dry, and he had put on dry clothes; but he hadn't changed his boots. She could still see the marks of water on them.

"Are you aware," he said conversationally, "that in Venice it is forbidden by law for a woman to wear men's clothing? Of

course, that is a rule meant for whores, who costume themselves for the entertainment of their clients. But I imagine it
could be considered to apply to you as well."

"Where am I?" Giulia could hear her own heartbeat.
"Where have you brought me?"

"This is the house of a patron, who has kindly offered hospitality for my stay."

"Does he know how you're using his generosity?"

Matteo smiled. The lantern illuminated him from below
like an image on an altar, casting strange shadows on his face,
hooding his eyes and throwing his cheekbones into sharp
relief.

"I imagine you are curious to know how I found you. It
was the man you hoodwinked. My former pupil, Gianfranco
Ferraldi."

Giulia sucked in her breath. Matteo's smile widened.

"Not deliberately, you understand. You deceived him
most thoroughly; he did not realize what he was telling me.
He wrote to me, you see, with condolences on the death of my
dear daughter, and mentioned also that he was sorry for the
equally untimely *death*"—he paused—"of her most promising
pupil, Giulia Borromeo. And that, by chance, young Giulia's
cousin, a talented artist in his own right, had come to him on
my daughter's recommendation and was now employed in his
workshop."

Giulia closed her eyes. *My fault,* she thought. *It was my
own fault.*

"Well, as you can imagine, I found this curious since I
knew from my daughter that young Giulia had no family
in all the world. Nor was she dead, unless she'd perished in
a ditch after her escape from Santa Marta—of which I was
kindly informed by a very apologetic abbess. And if she hadn't

perished . . . well, I had good cause to recall what an enterprising girl she was. Might she not have disguised herself as a boy, and taken the name Girolamo Landriani, and run off to Venice to pretend to be her own cousin and trick her teacher's dearest friend into apprenticing her?"

He shifted in his chair, reversing the position of his legs.

"Of course, I knew this was the merest speculation. I was quite prepared to reach Venice and discover that young Giulia had a cousin after all. But I thought it worth the chance. And so it proved. I would have come more promptly," he added. "But Ferraldi's letter was delayed."

"I won't give you what you want," Giulia said.

"I have not yet asked you for anything."

"You know what I mean. You can beat me or starve me. You can do anything you like. I won't tell you."

"What sort of man do you think I am?" He sounded genuinely affronted. "I would not beat or starve a young woman, no matter how she vexed me."

She stared up at him. The light of the lantern did not reach the ceiling; the darkness above him seemed infinite, like the vault of the cosmos robbed of stars.

"What I will do," he said, "is offer you a bargain. Give me Passion blue and I will set you free, to live or die as you may. Refuse, and I will return you to Santa Marta, where you will be imprisoned as fast as in any dungeon and never draw so much as a line for the rest of your life. Those are your choices."

"I don't believe you. You came all this way to find me on nothing but a suspicion. You'll never let go of me until you get Passion blue, and if you get it you will never set me free."

"Such mistrust! Think about it, girl. Why would I put myself to the trouble of dragging you back to Padua if I am not forced to do so? I've no doubt those holy virgins would like to sink their claws into you, but I have no interest in serving their purposes, or in putting Passion blue back into their hands. I am a determined man, young Giulia, but I am not a vengeful one. Surrender my daughter's secret, and you have my oath on my own secrets that you will go free."

He leaned down to take the lantern, then got to his feet.

"I will give you time to consider. I'll come again to hear your answer."

He departed, the lantern swinging from his hand. Its light trembled under the door as the lock turned, then dwindled, fading to nothing along with the sound of his footsteps. The dark closed round again, so smothering and complete that there might have been no light left anywhere in the world.

—

Some time later a servant—Giulia couldn't tell if it was the same one—came with a blanket, a bucket, and bread and cheese and a jug of water on a tray. He deposited everything by the door and locked her in again.

Giulia could not bring herself to eat, but she drank from the jug and made use of the bucket. Then she wrapped herself in the blanket and huddled against the wall, staring at the faint gray rectangle of the window.

She felt too many emotions to sort them out—despair, fear, anger—but most of all a kind of numb disbelief. How could she be here again, at the exact same point of choice that had driven her from Santa Marta? She could almost imagine that the nearly five intervening months had never happened.

What an idiot she had been to tell Ferraldi that stupid, complicated story. Yet if she hadn't, would he have invited her to stay? What would she have done if he'd turned her away?

I wouldn't be here now, though. At least I wouldn't be here.

Had Matteo told the truth when he promised to set her free? She had no reason to believe him. But she did not doubt for a moment that he would send her back to Santa Marta if she defied him—a fate she feared more than any physical pain, as she was sure he well knew.

Nor did she doubt that Santa Marta would take her. Perhaps it would not want her—but it would take her, for the sake of the secret she had withheld and to make her pay for her defiance. At Santa Marta she *would* be starved and beaten, punished without mercy until she surrendered Passion blue. And then she would become a *conversa*, a servant nun, scrubbing floors, washing the sisters' laundry, darning their sheets, keeping the Little Silence during the day and the Great Silence at night until, perhaps, she forgot how to speak at all. She would never again set foot in the workshop. She would never again hold a brush. She would never again hear the voices of the colors singing the songs of their creation.

Not just loveless and nameless, but passionless. That's how I will live at Santa Marta. That is how I'll die.

And outside the convent, where the only certainty was that terrible things existed and were bound to happen—how would she live there? She didn't know. But she'd survived before; perhaps she could again. She'd followed her gift before; perhaps she could again. And if she could not . . . to die alone in some back alley, or on the roadside, still seemed a better fate than the living death of Santa Marta.

It came to her, with a shock of recognition colder than the air of the dark little room, that she was thinking of giving Matteo what he wanted.

Horror swept her. *No. I can't betray my promise to the Maestra.* But she could see the high brick walls of Santa Marta, the grim gray stone of the punishment cells. She could feel the emptiness of the life she would live within them, a void into which all the fire that burned in her would fall and be extinguished.

Would Humilità demand that she pay such a price? That she consign her gift, for which Humilità had hoped so much, to certain oblivion just to keep the secret of Passion blue?

She recalled the intensity with which Humilità had demanded her promise. In truth, she did not know.

She buried her face in icy fingers, wretched before the vista of her own cowardice. *But I never asked for this.* She'd wanted Passion blue—of course she had. She'd loved knowing that she held the secret—hers alone, no one else's. But she was tired of running, of hiding, of resisting. Nothing was worth so much. Nothing.

"I'm sorry, Maestra," she whispered. "This was your burden. You had no right to make it mine. I can't carry it any longer."

The blanket was damp, moistened by her still-wet clothes. She was colder than ever. Miserably she huddled against the wall, waiting for the long night to end.

—

In spite of her discomfort, she fell asleep. She woke to light and the sound of church bells. It was Sunday, less than a day since her capture, yet looking back at the day before was like looking across a gulf of years.

The hours dragged by. Matteo did not return. Servants arrived at intervals with food—not just bread and water, but full meals, as if Matteo meant to prove his promise about not starving her. She had no appetite but she ate anyway, and paced back and forth across the floor to try and warm herself. Anticipation was a wire inside her, twisting tighter with every breath. *Come back,* she urged Matteo silently. *Come back, come back, come back. Let me get it over with.*

He came at last on Monday morning, accompanied by a servant carrying paper and an ink pot.

"Well?" he said, after the servant had laid the materials on the floor and left the room. "I've brought you the means to write, if you need it."

"I don't." Standing by the window, Giulia reached into her sleeve and drew out Humilità's recipe, which she'd taken yesterday from the pouch at her neck. She crossed the room, surprised at the steadiness of her footsteps, and placed the paper in Matteo's outstretched hand.

He unfolded it, his rings catching the light. She waited, every muscle tense. She understood the risk of what she'd just done: He might indeed have lied about setting her free. But only by gambling that he'd told the truth did she have any chance at all.

"My daughter's hand." He brushed his fingers across the page, almost a caress. "Good. Now I need not wonder whether you have tried to trick me."

It hadn't occurred to her to trick him. Her face must have showed this, for he smiled.

"Just as well, young Giulia. I'd only have had to find you again." He returned his attention to the recipe. "Hm. Not just ingredients, but a procedure. Ah! Alabaster." He sounded like a man reading a letter from a lover. "And ground glass. Glass! Of course. Yes. Yes, I see."

Giulia had wondered what she would feel in this moment. Now she knew: shame and anger. But also a secret understanding. He believed he had the key. She thought—she hoped—that she knew better.

He looked up. She dropped her eyes.

"I suppose you've memorized it."

She shook her head.

"Don't lie. It's nothing to me—what use can you make of it, a girl like you?"

"I might surprise you," she said, and immediately regretted it.

He laughed. "Don't flatter yourself. Even if the world does not eat you up, you have not a fraction of my daughter's genius."

Carefully he folded the recipe again and placed it in his belt pouch.

"My daughter did you a disservice, young Giulia. She should have known she could not keep this from me." He shook his head. "We shared a heart, she and I, though she forgot that at the end."

Giulia felt a wave of disgust. *You can say such things, now you've conquered her at last. For that's what it was always about, wasn't it? Bringing her to heel.*

She drew a breath, steadied her voice. "I've done what you wanted. Will you let me go now?"

"I will. But your clothes are in a dreadful state. I'll order new garments brought up."

"I don't need new clothes."

"I insist." He looked at her with his deep-set eyes that were so much like Humilità's. "I expect we will never meet again."

"God willing," she could not stop herself from saying.

He smiled. "Farewell, Giulia Borromeo."

247

———

He locked her in again. She waited, her heart racing, terrified he had lied after all and the next thing she would hear was the steps of someone coming to take her back to Santa Marta. But when the door opened at last, it was only a servant—a woman this time, carrying a pile of folded garments.

"These are for you," the servant said.

Giulia looked at what she held. "Those are women's clothes."

The servant shrugged.

"I don't need new clothes. I'll keep what I've got on."

"I'm not to let you out unless you wear them. You're to leave the ones you have."

It was Matteo's final demonstration of his power, stripping her of the last piece of her deception even as he let her go. Giulia struggled to contain her anger. "Can't you just look the other way? No one will know."

The servant said nothing, a refusal as clear as words. In her face was absolute indifference—to Giulia and her desires, and probably to Matteo's orders also, the distinction being that Matteo was the guest of the man who paid her wages.

The garments were plain, probably a servant's, but clean and of decent quality. Giulia peeled off her boy's clothes and pulled on the woolen drawers, the linen chemise, and the loose-sleeved woolen dress. It all fit fairly well, though she had to lace the bodice tight. The servant watched. Who, Giulia wondered, did this woman think she was, locked up in this chamber?

She pushed her feet into her boots again and wound the final item, a thick woolen shawl, around her head and shoulders. The servant opened the door, gesturing Giulia to precede her along the hallway to the stairs at its end. Giulia began to descend, the dress impeding her steps. Over the time of her disguise, it seemed, she'd lost the skill of walking in skirts.

The courtyard was shrouded in mist. The servant pointed Giulia toward the street door. Beyond it lay the alley on which Giulia had looked down from her prison window. When she hesitated on the threshold, the servant pushed her, hard, so that she stumbled out onto the brick paving of the street. The door slammed behind her.

Not until that moment did she truly believe Matteo had let her go.

She stood for a moment, feeling strangely light, as if she might rise up and float away. Then she began to walk. The paving was slippery underfoot; the fog was thick and wet, and with each breath, she drew its cold into her body. She didn't know where she was going or what she meant to do. For the moment it was enough simply to put distance between herself and Matteo Moretti.

Part V

Season of Light

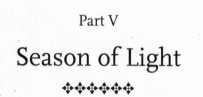

CHAPTER 22

✧ Lost ✧

Venice, Italy
March 2, Anno Domini 1489

Giulia did not know how long she walked, or where her foot-steps took her. The fog made it impossible to tell the time of day or to identify landmarks—even if she'd been able to recognize them, for she had no idea to what part of Venice Matteo had brought her.

She simply moved, making turns at random, striking blind across campi whose boundaries she could not see, crossing bridges that seemed to span smoke rather than canals. The fog smelled of sewage and the sea; it muffled noise, wrapping her in an eerie silence through which the voices of passersby and the slap of water intruded like dreams or fancies. Most people were sensibly indoors; but even in this miserable weather Carnival revelers were abroad, looming through the mist in their nightmare masks, staggering in and out of the candle glow of taverns.

She paused at last to rest on the edge of a wellhead, in a campo so small that the fog did not quite obscure the walls of the surrounding houses or the dark opening of the alley out of which she'd come. A little church huddled among the dwellings, the lanterns by its door making golden gossamer of the mist. She was exhausted, wet, and cold, so cold. She felt as if she had been cold forever.

But she was free. Free of her oath to Humilità. Free of Matteo. Free of her disguise, of her apprenticeship. Free of secrets, free of plans, free of everything except her own body and the borrowed clothes that covered it. She tried to find some emotion in that, anger or resolve or even fear. But all she felt was cold—her blood like ice, her thoughts as slow as sap in winter. Her face was wet with water vapor, but her eyes were dry: She was free even of tears.

She could not sit here forever, waiting for whatever happened next. She must rise and move on. But where? And to what? The thought of starting over—disguising herself again, talking her way into another apprenticeship with a different master, in a different city perhaps—made her feel so weary she could have sunk into the stone on which she rested.

Sofia. She could go to Sofia, who had offered to help her if she ever needed it.

Longing rose in her—for the comfort of Sofia's house, for the refuge of a place she knew, even a little. Yet it would be bitter to return in failure to the one person who had understood not just the nature of her disguise, but the reasons behind it. And Bernardo would be there—Bernardo, who still believed she was a boy and despised her for it. The memory of the disgust she'd seen on his face on that last day made her flinch. How would he look at her when he learned the true depth of her deception?

It can't be worse than what's already happened. What does it matter anyway, what anyone thinks?

The sound of voices stirred the smothering quiet. At the alley's mouth, the fog began to glow. Three men in bone-white masks melted into view, their steps unsteady with drink. They were singing, a loud, off-key song about a shy girl and a clever thief.

On the wellhead, Giulia tensed.

"Hold up, fellows!" The reveler in the lead halted, causing the man at his back to collide with him. "What have we here? A ghost?"

"A shy girl!" The third man lifted the lantern he carried. These were not nobles or young dandies, but working men in rough clothing. "Where's your thief, shy girl? Has he deserted you?"

"No one should be alone at Carnival time," slurred the first man, taking a swig from a bottle.

The little campo was a dead end. There was no way out but past them. Giulia pulled her shawl closer around her face and stood.

"Where are you going, shy girl?" The man with the bottle lurched forward. "Stay and celebrate with us."

"I just want to be on my way, signor," Giulia said as calmly as she could.

"By the saints, she's shy in truth!" cried the lantern holder. "Whoever heard of such a thing?"

"Leave her alone, you two." The second man, the one who'd collided with the drinker, caught his companions' arms.

"I'm sorry, signorina. They are drunk and foolish, but they mean no harm. Go along now. You've nothing to fear from us."

"Thank you, signor." Giulia hesitated. "Could you . . . could you tell me the way to Cannaregio?"

The lantern holder laughed. "The shy girl doesn't know where she is!"

"Quiet, Giorgio." The second man pushed up his mask. Beneath it, his face was middle-aged and homely, with a scruffy growth of beard. "This *is* Cannaregio, signorina."

"Oh!" Had she been in Cannaregio all along? "Can you tell me how to get to the Rio dei Miracoli, then?"

"Easier to show you, as long as you don't mind these two fools following along."

Once before Giulia had made the mistake of trusting men she shouldn't. "I don't want to put you to the trouble."

"You'll be lost again in no time if you try it on your own. And there's worse than us about today." He looked at her. "My name is Rinaldo Favretto. I've a daughter about your age. If she was alone in the fog, I'd want someone to help her get safe home."

Again Giulia hesitated. But she was so tired. She couldn't bear the thought of more blind stumbling down streets she did not know.

"Very well," she said. "Thank you."

—

Rinaldo walked at her side, directing her with authority, certain of his way even in the enveloping fog. He took care to keep a respectful distance between them. The other two trailed behind.

They came at last to a waterway that he said was the Rio dei Miracoli. Much to his companions' annoyance, he refused to leave her, accompanying her along the broad fondamenta that ran above the canal and accosting passersby to ask for the house of La Fiamma.

After several such inquiries, they met a woman who said she knew the way. Rinaldo and his friends rolled off into the mist, singing their song again, while Giulia followed the woman over a bridge and down an alley to another campo, her sodden skirts tangling around her ankles. The woman pointed to a door and was gone almost before Giulia could thank her.

The fog had thinned enough that Giulia could see the wellhead at the campo's center, the houses that ringed it, and the church on the far side, closed and dark. She tucked her tangled hair behind her ears and wrapped her head and shoulders in her shawl again, then stood before the door for several moments, gathering her courage, before she raised her hand and knocked.

A pause, then the sound of footsteps. A key turned in an inside lock. A young woman with rolled-up sleeves and a stained apron pulled the door open a little way.

"Is this the house of La . . . of Sofia Gentileschi?"

"It is." The servant's eyes were wary.

"Please. I need to see her."

"We don't feed beggars." The servant's gaze traveled from Giulia's face to her dirty hem and back again. "If you want alms, knock at the church."

"I'm not a beggar—" But the servant was already stepping back. "Wait!" But the door thumped closed, and the key turned once more. Giulia knocked again, then pounded with her fists and shouted. Somewhere above, a shutter scraped—a neighbor, looking out to see the cause of the noise. That was all.

Giulia found suddenly that she could not stand up. She sank down on the step, its chill biting through the fabric of her gown. *I'll wait.* Someone was bound to come in or go out eventually. Although, she realized, she couldn't stay here, on Sofia's step, where the person who arrived or departed might be Bernardo.

She meant to get up, to cross over to the church and watch from there. But she was weary, so weary. *I'll rest a moment.* She closed her eyes. *Just a moment.*

—

She woke slowly, as if surfacing from deep water. It was full dark; she was lying on her side, her hair across her face, her back against something hard. Somewhere above her, a light was shining.

"You there." A man's voice, familiar. "Wake up. You can't sleep here."

Where am I? Why am I so cold?

"Come now." Something nudged her leg—the toe of a boot. "If you're hungry I can have something brought from the kitchen."

If her mind had been clear, she would have realized that she'd fallen asleep without moving from Sofia's step. She'd have known at once whose voice it was and turned from the light so he would not recognize her. But she was confused and only half awake. She had already pushed her hair back, was already sitting up, before she recognized him.

"Girolamo?" By the light of his lantern, she saw Bernardo's eyes widen. His gaze fell to her skirts, snapped back to her face. "What is this?"

"Not Girolamo." Her tongue felt frozen. The words were thick and slow. "My name is Giulia. Giulia Borromeo."

"What . . . ? What do you . . . ? What are you . . . ?"

He seemed to have lost his breath. His face was blank with shock. Giulia shut her eyes; she didn't want to see the anger that would surely follow. The lantern light moved against her closed lids, as if his hand were shaking; she could hear him breathing, harsh and fast. Then she felt a rush of air, heard the rattle of a key. The door opened, slammed. His rapid footsteps faded to silence.

She leaned her head against the icy stone behind her. Her body was lead, her mind an empty well.

Sometime later—long or short, she did not know—the door scraped open once more. A hand touched her shoulder. She looked up to see Maria, Sofia's dark-skinned maid.

Maria helped her to her feet, drew her across the court-yard and up to the pòrtego and into Sofia's sitting room, where the Bellini portrait hung. Sofia's bedchamber door stood open, the room beyond it gilded with firelight.

"Clarissima," Maria called softly, the first word Giulia had ever heard her speak. A moment, then Sofia swept into the sitting room, clad in her silk wrapper, her hair a copper torrent across her shoulders: her own portrait come to life. Giulia caught her breath. She hadn't wept in Matteo Moretti's house. During her long day of wandering, she hadn't shed a tear. But now she hid her face in her hands, and the sobs burst out of her, harsh and wrenching, uncontrollable.

"Ah," Sofia said as if someone had struck her.

Giulia felt arms go around her shoulders, felt herself guided stumbling into the bedchamber and pressed down on a cushion before the fire. Then Sofia held her as she cried, rocking her like a child. Not since her mother died had Giulia been embraced this way, a nearly forgotten memory that tore open a door to deeper griefs. She wept not just for what she'd given Matteo and what he'd taken from her, but for Humilità, for her mother, for all the losses of her life.

Eventually there were no more tears. She pulled away, drying her wet cheeks with her sleeves.

"I'm sorry," she whispered.

"There's no need to apologize."

"Thank you for letting me in." Giulia's breath hitched. Her throat was raw. "How did you know I was here?"

"Bernardo told me."

"Bernardo?"

"He stormed in and woke me from my sleep. He wanted to know if I knew what you really were. I told him I had guessed."

"He's . . . he must be very angry."

"At me, certainly, for keeping your secret. I suspect he feels something of a fool." Sofia's amber gaze was grave. "But largely, I think, he is relieved."

Relieved. The word slid into Giulia's mind and sat there, like a box she was afraid to open.

"Of course, he kept secrets of his own. I did not know he was visiting you."

"I thought you sent him. He told me you did."

"Did he?" Sofia gave a small, close-lipped smile. "Well, I did not. If I'd realized, I might have forbidden it—not for your sake, but for his. You have caused him great distress, though I don't imagine you intended it."

There was a knock at the door: Maria, with a tray that held a plate of bread and cheese, a withered apple, and a steaming jug of mulled wine. Sofia poured wine for them both, then got the coverlet from her bed and draped it around Giulia's shoulders. She settled back onto the hearth, waiting as Giulia devoured the food.

"Tell me your name," she said when the plate was empty but for the core of the apple.

Giulia folded her hands around her wine cup, breathing its spicy odor. The fire brushed warmth across her face, and the food was warm inside her. Still she was cold, a knot of ice that would not thaw.

"Giulia Borromeo," she said.

"Tell me who you are. Tell me what happened."

"My father was Count Federico di Assulo Borromeo of Milan. My mother was his seamstress . . . "

The story poured out: Santa Marta, the workshop, Passion blue, Humilità's illness, Domenica's ultimatum, Matteo's threats, her own escape and flight. She did not speak of the talisman and Anasurymboriel, nor of the color song; nor could she bear to speak of Ormanno and the shameful part she'd played in Matteo's first betrayal of Humilità. Those secrets she would keep. But everything else she confessed.

Sofia sat silent after she was done, gazing into the fire. The forgiving light erased the lines around her eyes and the creases in her forehead; she looked like a girl, hardly older than Giulia herself.

"Is it really so valuable?" she said at last, softly. "This Passion blue."

Giulia huddled deeper into the coverlet. How could she explain? Could anyone who was not a painter appreciate the worth of a paint that shone like sunlight through stained glass, that never changed or faded as it dried and aged? Could anyone who was not part of the story understand why Passion blue had been so much more than that, something different to all who desired it: for Humilità, a legacy, something that would live on after her; for Matteo, the one thing he could not force the world to give him, and so the thing he wanted most of all; for Madre Magdalena, prestige and income for Santa Marta; for Domenica, ambition and perhaps greed.

And me. Wasn't I greedy for it too? Isn't that at least part of why I refused it to Domenica?

"Yes," she said simply. "It is."

"I guessed you were fleeing something. I wondered if it might be a convent."

"I wasn't a very good liar, was I."

"You were quite a deft liar. It's just that once I pulled the first thread, all the rest unraveled too. You are even braver than I thought, Giulia, but also more foolhardy, to set off on this adventure with no assurance of what lay at the end of it."

"I couldn't stay at Santa Marta. I had to take the chance, no matter where it brought me. You saw that when we were traveling, even though you knew almost nothing about me. I still remember what you said to me when I gave you your portrait."

Sofia shook her head a little. "What did I say?"

"That my gift demanded . . . *everything* . . . of me." Giulia's breath hitched again, but she refused to shed more tears. "And I almost succeeded. I almost did. But *almost* doesn't matter, does it? Oh, if only I hadn't told Maestro Ferraldi so many lies! Signor Moretti never would have found me then. I'd never have had to break my promise to my Maestra."

"You were right to do so. It would have been foolish to resist."

"It was selfish. I did it to save myself from going back to Santa Marta."

"And why is that selfish? You didn't choose to be a nun, and if you had gone back they would have made you a slave. I faced a choice like yours once, Giulia. My mother did what I do, only in the gutter rather than a palace. She died when I was just thirteen. I had no family, no one to take me in. I could have gone to the nuns, to be a *conversa* like you, scrubbing floors and doing penance for my mother's sins, though I had no part in them and was still a virgin then. Or I could become a whore myself." She smiled, with a strange mix of bitterness and pride. "You see what I chose."

"But you are not just . . . that. You have learning, and independence, and . . ." Giulia looked around the shadowy room, with its great bed and painted chests and coffered ceiling. "All this."

"Oh, child. A whore is a whore. The trappings change, but the act does not, nor the abuse, nor the disease, nor the tedium. I have won, perhaps, the best a whore can hope for: the right to be a whore no longer, and not to starve in my retirement. But had I been as foolish as others in my profession and lost it all, I would still rather that than live as I'd have had to live if I'd become a nun. I understand, Giulia, why you chose to break your promise to your teacher. I'm certain she would have understood as well."

"She was proud of how fiercely she resisted him. She would have wanted me to do the same."

"One must be strong to keep a secret. But stronger still, sometimes, to let it go."

Giulia shook her head. "I can only hope I didn't let it go completely."

Sofia tilted her head. "How so?"

"When my Maestra first gave me the recipe, I thought I had it all—the entire secret of Passion blue, just a matter of ingredients and proportions and instructions. I knew I might make a mistake in mixing it, but I thought if I was careful, if I followed the formula without fail, there was no reason why I shouldn't create Passion blue, exactly as my Maestra did. But . . ."

Giulia paused, searching for the words to explain the elusive insight that had come to her during the day and two long nights she'd spent as Matteo's prisoner.

"But I didn't think about the different skills of different hands. Every hand has its own touch, and I think that the work of each hand is different. So it was for me. I did everything precisely as the recipe required, and my blue was beautiful. But it wasn't *Passion* blue. And I don't know if it ever will be, if ever I get the chance to try again. I think . . . well, I hope . . . it'll be the same for Signor Moretti. He will make blue—but not my Maestra's blue." She drew in her breath. "Perhaps the real secret, the one even my Maestra didn't know, is that the secret of Passion blue cannot be given."

They sat in silence for a time. The fire was burning low, and the corners of the chamber were lost in shadow.

"Have you thought what you will do now?" Sofia asked at last.

Giulia looked down at the glossy tiles of the hearth, at the tray with its empty plate. "I don't know."

"You'll want to find another teacher, surely. I can help you, if you wish to disguise yourself again."

"I don't know." Giulia put her hands over her face. "Please don't ask me to decide."

"Ah, Giulia. Poor girl. You need decide nothing until you wish it. You are safe here, and you may stay as long as you like."

"Thank you, clarissima. You've been so kind to me."

"Come." There was a rustle of silk. Gentle hands took Giulia's wrists, pulled her fingers away from her face. "You need to sleep."

Like a child, Giulia let herself be drawn to her feet. She stood while Sofia removed the clothes Matteo had given her and slipped a clean chemise over her head, made of linen almost as fine as silk. The great bed with its pile of feather coverlets was the softest thing she'd ever felt, the sheets smooth and lavender-scented.

She felt the mattress shift as Sofia lay down beside her. She closed her eyes on the red glow of the coals in the grate, feeling the ice inside her beginning, at last, to melt.

CHAPTER 23

❖ A Girl Again ❖

A sound pulled Giulia from sleep. She opened her eyes on an expanse of crimson: a bed-canopy.

Sofia, she thought. *I'm in Sofia's house.*

She sat up, the heavy covers slipping from her shoulders. Through the windows flanking the fireplace she could see sunlight on the wall of the house across the alley. The noise that had roused her was Maria, bending down to replenish the fire.

Maria straightened. Seeing Giulia was awake, she gestured to the tray that had been placed on the hearth. Giulia wondered what the silent woman thought of her transformation.

"Thank you," she said.

Maria inclined her head and departed. Giulia slipped out of bed, pulling the quilt with her, displacing one of Sofia's cats, which had been curled up beside her. She wrapped herself in the quilt and sat down to eat her meal: cold meats, olives, and some sort of pickle, spicy and delicious. The cat sauntered over to join her, with a cat's assurance of its absolute right to whatever place it happened to occupy. Giulia smoothed its silky fur. She felt calm, cleansed of emotion like a street after a hard rain. The events of the past few days were there inside her mind, but for now, in this quiet room with the cat for company, she was at peace.

She'd just finished eating when Sofia entered, in a gown almost the exact color of her hair, which was braided around her head and caught at the back with a veil as translucent as spider-silk.

"Good afternoon, sleepy one!"

Giulia put down her plate and wiped her fingers on the napkin Maria had provided. "I'm sorry. I didn't mean to sleep so long."

"You needed the rest." Sofia knelt at Giulia's side in a swirl of gleaming skirts. "Now, I don't wish to press you. But you must be clothed, and while you are considering what next you will do, will you let me turn you into a girl again?"

That took Giulia by surprise. "I have the clothes I came in."

"Bah. Those are servant's weeds. I will give you something better. Come, indulge me. It would give me pleasure to make you pretty."

Pretty. Giulia hesitated. Yesterday she'd despised her skirts, for they had seemed like Matteo's proclamation of his mastery of her. But now she felt the pull of temptation: to be female again, free of the mask for a little while.

"Yes," she said. "Yes, I'd like that."

Maria was summoned to bring a copper bathing tub, which she filled with hot water and scented with aromatic oils. Giulia sank into the delicious warmth, the chemise, which she still wore for modesty, billowing around her. Sofia unlaced her sleeves and rolled them up, and lathered Giulia's hair with a foaming cake of scented soap, while Giulia washed her body with another. It was the greatest luxury she'd ever experienced. What would it be like to live this way—to grow so used to it, perhaps, that it ceased to seem extraordinary?

Giulia climbed at last from the tub, gloriously clean but for the ingrained ink and charcoal on her hands, which even soap could not remove. She toweled herself dry and slipped on the fresh chemise Sofia gave her.

From the painted chests against the wall Sofia drew an array of elaborate gowns, which she laid out on the bed for Giulia to inspect. Giulia chose the plainest, which was still finer than anything she'd ever imagined she might wear: a sleeveless underdress of russet silk, round necked to display the embroidered band of the chemise, and a high-waisted overdress of bronze brocade, its skirt split at the front so the underdress would show. Sleeves of the same brocade, loosely laced to the shoulders of the overdress, were held along their seams with more laces, leaving gaps through which Sofia teased the fabric of the chemise into decorative puffs.

"This is an outdoor gown," Sofia said. "On me it would be too long, unless I wore chopines. But you are taller than I, so for you it will do for indoors."

"Chopines? What are those?"

"A device with which the ladies of Venice delight in tormenting themselves."

Going to the chests, Sofia drew out the oddest footgear Giulia had ever seen: leather slippers fastened to wooden platforms more than a hand span high.

"How in the world can anyone walk in those?"

Sofia laughed. "It's an art, learned with pain. There are laws to limit how high chopines can be, of course, just as there are laws to say how many yards of material may be used in a lady's gown or a pair of men's sleeves, or how many pearls may be sewn to a bodice. But we Venetians wink at such rules."

She tucked the chopines back into the chest, then settled Giulia once more on the hearth cushion and began to tease the tangles from her hair—exclaiming at the unevenness of it, for Giulia had kept it short by sawing it off with a knife. When it was smooth and nearly dry, Sofia combed it lightly with oil, then did complicated things with braids and pins and golden laces.

"If you remain a girl, we can obtain a hairpiece to fill you out while you grow it again. I know an excellent supplier—he buys only from the convents, clean hair, free of vermin. There." Sofia drew Giulia to her feet and stepped back, examining her handiwork. "You make a striking girl, just as you did a convincing boy." She smiled her close-lipped smile. "In my trade, such flexibility could earn you a fortune."

"May I see?"

"Of course."

Sofia fetched a hand mirror of silver-backed glass. Giulia held it before her face. How long had it been since she'd seen her own reflection? She barely recognized the person looking back at her: a long-necked girl with large dark eyes and smooth olive skin, her black tresses braided away from features too pronounced to be truly feminine: the nose too proud, the mouth too wide. Not the boy she had been until yesterday, with his shaggy hair falling over his cheeks; not the girl she'd been before that, with her simple plait and high-necked che-mise. Someone else. Someone in between.

"What do you think?" Sofia asked.

"I hardly know myself."

"That was the intent. Now come. I have household duties to attend to. You will be more comfortable in my sitting room."

—

The sitting room was just as Giulia remembered, with its attractive arrangement of tables and chairs and its writing desk in the corner. Sunshine flooded through the windows, printing lattices of light upon the floor. Between the sun and the fire, it was warmer than the bedchamber; but Giulia was wearing so much clothing she would not have been cold in any case. She'd thought she might feel like herself again, dressed in woman's attire; but these tight, stiff garments were like noth-ing she had ever worn.

She went to look at Bellini's portrait of Sofia, but its fine details and glowing hues reminded her too sharply of what she had lost. She moved to stand instead before the windows. The cat, which had followed from the bedchamber, sprawled in the sun at her feet.

Today was Tuesday: *Giovedi Grasso*, the last day of Carnival. In Palazzo Contarini Nuova, they would be prepar-ing for the competition. Giulia thought of her painting in its hiding place in Ferraldi's storeroom—the best work she had ever done, saturated with the blue that was not Humilità's blue but instead was her own. It would never fulfill its intended purpose now—would never be placed beside the work of other painters and, perhaps, judged worthy.

She looked down at her hands, at the black graining her fingers and bedded beneath her nails. A painter's hands. Yet she was not a painter now. And if she was not a painter, what was she?

The latch rattled. She turned, expecting Sofia—but it was Bernardo.

She froze. So did he. An endless moment passed: he with his fingers still on the latch, she by the window. Then she gasped. Her hands flew to her face. She whirled away from him, as if that could conceal her.

Silence. Then the door closed. Had he gone? No: She heard his footsteps. Then silence again. She stood rigid, her heart beating wildly, her face still bowed into her hands. *If I wait, if I don't move, surely he'll go away again.*

He did not stir. The situation began to seem ridiculous. She was in his mother's house—she couldn't avoid him forever. Better to get it over with.

She forced her hands to fall. She straightened her shoulders. She turned.

He stood a few paces away, achingly familiar: his strong features, his sleek black hair, his elegant, impeccable clothing. His eyes were nailed to hers. Never in her life had she felt so exposed. The skin above the band of her chemise, where the tops of her breasts swelled over the tight lacing of the underdress, seemed to burn. It took all the will she had not to raise her arms and cover herself.

"My mother guessed the truth about you." His voice was harsh in the silence of the room. "I never did."

"I'm sorry" was all she could think to say.

"I always suspected you were hiding something. But this—" He bit off the words. "I imagine you found my stupidity amusing. Were you laughing at me the entire time?"

"No! No, never!"

"Did you really think you would get away with it? That you'd never be found out?"

"Of course I knew I might be caught. I thought about it every day. But no master painter would apprentice a girl. I *had* to become a boy. You know—I know you know—what it's like to want something more than anything else, to fear you may never have it—"

"What *I* want is reasonable at least." His eyes were like black ice. "And I didn't have to build a tower of lies to achieve it."

"No." Anger flashed through her, sudden as a lightning bolt. "You only kept silent for years on end because you were afraid of what might happen if you spoke. Yes, I deceived you. Why would I not? I don't owe you anything. You have no special claim on the truth. I never sought you out—all I wanted was to be left alone, but you came to me, and you kept coming back, and that was *your* choice, just as it was your choice to tell me it was your mother who sent you when really you were coming on your own. So I'm not the only liar, am I? And why *did* you lie? Why did you need an excuse to see me? Why would you even want to have anything to do with someone like me, with the person you thought I was? You have no right to be angry. None at all."

She stopped, breathing hard. He was staring at her, his lips a little parted. She waited for him to respond, to flash back. But he said nothing.

"I wanted to tell you," she went on, more quietly. "I did. But I was afraid you'd be angry or . . . or disgusted if you knew the truth. So I said nothing. And with every day that passed it became more impossible to speak."

"Why did you come here, then?" He gestured to the clothes she wore. "Without . . . your disguise?"

"I was discovered. Didn't your mother tell you?"

Bernardo looked down at the cat, which had woken from its sunny nap and was twining around his ankles. "She said I must ask you."

He'd inquired about her, then. There was no way to know what that meant, or if it meant anything.

"I told you the truth about my childhood," she said. "About my father and my mother and how I grew up. But I was a seamstress, not a scullion. And I'm eighteen." She felt a blush rising to her cheeks. "I thought it would better explain my voice and my lack of beard if I pretended to be younger. My father's wife did banish me from the household after my father died, and I did apprentice in a painter's workshop—except the workshop was in Padua, in the Convent of Santa Marta."

"A painter's workshop?" His eyes flicked up, then down again. "In a convent?"

"Yes. Perhaps the only one of its kind in all the world. My teacher was Maestra Humiltà Moretti, and she was a genius . . . "

She told him what she'd told Sofia, leaving out the same details. She hadn't realized until she began to speak how much of her story he already knew, though she'd reshaped its bones to fit inside the skin of her disguise. Only Santa Marta was new to him, and Matteo, and Passion blue. She expected him to interrupt, to ask questions, but he heard her out in silence, standing very still. The sun inched across the shining marble of the floor; the cat tired of Bernardo's ankles and curled up to sleep again. Outside, life went on, but in this room the world had narrowed to the two of them.

At last Giulia was finished. She could not read Bernardo's expression. But at least he had listened.

"I would have left you by the side of the road," he said. "The night you found us. I would have sent you off into the dark."

"I know."

"What would you have done if I had? If my mother hadn't taken pity on you?"

"I would have gotten to Venice. Somehow."

He moved closer to the windows, gazing across the canal at the houses opposite.

"I hardly know what to say to you. What you did—running away, disguising yourself . . ." He touched the glass, tracing the lattice that held it. "It's like one of the tales my mother made up for me when I was a child." He paused. "I don't know if I could have done as much."

It surprised her that he would say such a thing.

"What if he hadn't found you? This Matteo Moretti. How long would you have continued in disguise?"

"For as long as I could."

"Truly? To be . . . what you are not? For months or years, perhaps for all your life? Could you have borne that?"

"I'm not certain," Giulia said honestly. "But I would have tried."

He turned his head. He'd looked at her now and then while she spoke—brief, wary glances that skated swiftly across her face and then away. This time he did not drop his eyes. They moved on her mouth, her neck and bosom, slipped down to her waist and up again. Heat rose through her body, kindling her skin. Did he find her pleasing? Wasn't this what she'd wished for—for him to see her, finally, as a man sees a woman?

Yet all she wanted now was to twist away, to hide from that dark, searching gaze.

He turned away at last, back to the vista beyond the window. "Will you try again?"

"I don't know." The words were heavy in her mouth. "Your mother says I may stay here for a little while. I . . . I hope you don't mind."

A pause. Then: "No."

One word, quietly spoken. Giulia felt something loosen inside her.

"Did you ever finish your competition painting?"

"I did. It's still at Maestro Ferraldi's." Giulia thought of the painting, of her sketches and the small amount of blue pigment she had not used. "I'd like to have it back."

"My mother can send one of the servants to fetch it."

"That would be kind." Giulia sighed. "I'm not sorry I painted it, even if it can't be part of the competition now."

"Why not? You've time. It's only midafternoon."

Giulia shook her head. "Please don't make fun of me."

"I am not making fun of you. The painting is finished, and it is by your hand. Why should you not enter it?"

"My disguise is lost."

"The rules don't exclude women."

"They don't include them either, which is as good as the same thing."

"Now you sound like my mother."

"I'd never be allowed to present it." Giulia felt disbelief; were they really discussing this? "No one would even believe I'd painted it."

"I'll vouch for you."

She turned on him. "Why? Why would you do that?"

He met her gaze. The corners of his lips lifted in what was almost a smile. "To see the scandal it will cause."

"That's truly your reason?"

He opened his mouth, closed it again. "It is part of the reason."

She stared at him. It was impossible. Or was it? She felt the idea taking hold of her, like the forbidden thing to which one cannot help but yield.

"I don't know if I can go back there. To Maestro Ferraldi's."

"I'll go with you."

It's mad. Absurd. With complete clarity, Giulia saw all the reasons she must fail: Ferraldi would turn her away. Palazzo Contarini Nuova would deny her entry. Even if she were allowed in, what could possibly come of attempting to present her work as if it—as if *she*—were worthy of consideration alongside the other painters gathered there? Professional painters. *Male* painters. At best she'd be treated as a curiosity. At worst she'd be ridiculed and censured. Bernardo might really get the scandal he wished for.

And yet . . . isn't it at least possible that if my work draws Giovanni Bellini's eye, it will speak for itself?

"You know they may not even admit me," she said.

"Then that," Bernardo said, "will be that."

Giulia felt as if she were balanced on a ledge, with air on both sides. She could fall either way.

Do I really have anything to lose?

"The competition begins at dusk," she said. "If we are to go, we must go now."

Bernardo smiled—a real smile, quick and fierce. "You'll need a mantle. I know where my mother keeps them."

He went into Sofia's bedchamber and returned with a cloak of grass-green wool, its hood lined with ermine. It was a garment any noblewoman might have envied, and Giulia felt like an imposter as she put it on.

Her breath came quick with fear as they left the sunny sitting room. But as on the night she had run away from Santa Marta, she could no more have turned back than she could have stopped her heart from beating.

CHAPTER 24

❖ A Sound of Bells ❖

Getting into the gondola was a challenge, for Giulia had to manage four layers of clothing—chemise, underdress, over-dress, and mantle. She felt a sharp nostalgia for the ease of hose and boots, for a boy's long, unencumbered stride. Bernardo, already on the pilot's platform, made no move to assist her.

It was the last day of celebration before the prayer and fasting of Lent, and the city had gone mad. The Grand Canal teemed with gondolas ferrying Carnival revelers of all classes. On the quays of the Rialto, masked men and women danced to the music of horns and drums; and at the highest point of the Rialto Bridge, a gang of boys leaned down to toss objects at the boats below: eggs, Giulia realized as Bernardo steered toward the bridge's pilings, filled with scented water.

They reached the Campo San Lio, where a whole pig was being roasted and the entire neighborhood had turned out to celebrate. In the Salizzada San Lio, the shops were closed but the taverns were jammed, the noise of merriment spilling from open doors as Giulia and Bernardo passed. The Calle del Fruttariol, however, was deserted. They made their way to its end, Giulia holding her skirts off the grimy paving.

"Go on," Bernardo said when she did not raise her hand at once to knock at Ferraldi's door.

She looked up at the plaque of the Lion of San Marco. How many times had she seen it over the past months, going in and out on Ferraldi's business and her own? Yet in this moment it seemed completely unfamiliar. What had seemed possible in Sofia's sitting room suddenly felt as unlikely as flying to the moon. The thought of coming face-to-face with Ferraldi made her feel sick.

She might have stepped away. She might have turned to Bernardo and said, "I've changed my mind." But before she could do either, he leaned past her and knocked, three hard blows with the side of his fist.

Almost at once there were footsteps. The door opened to reveal the skinny form of Alvise. Expressions chased rapidly across his face when he saw Giulia: puzzlement, suspicion, shocked recognition, hardening into the familiar hostility.

"You've got a nerve," he said. "Coming back here after what happened."

"She has come for her possessions." The pronoun left Bernardo's lips without the slightest awkwardness. "Let her in."

Alvise scowled. "None of that's here anymore. We got rid of it."

Giulia found her voice. "You won't have found my drawings or my painting. It's those I've come for."

Something flickered in Alvise's face. He hesitated, then stepped back and let the door swing wide.

Giulia's sleeping area had been dismantled. The mattress, the makeshift curtain, her brazier—all were gone. Rolls of canvas were bundled haphazardly into the place where they had been—the disarray that Ferraldi seemed naturally to create around himself, already beginning to undo the order Giulia had made.

She crossed to the stacked planks behind which she'd made a hiding place for the things she had wanted to keep safe. Her sketches were there, neatly tied with cord, and the blue pigment. But the painting—

"It isn't here," she said, breathless. "My painting. It isn't here."

"Are you certain this is where you left it?" Bernardo asked.

"Yes. Yes. I had it out last Saturday, the day Signor Moretti came, but I put it back."

She tossed Sofia's mantle aside and knelt, careless of the rich fabric of her borrowed gown, pushing at the heavy bags. Bernardo came to help. It was no use. The painting was gone.

"Someone's taken it." Giulia stood. Her heart was pounding. The warehouse was empty: Alvise had vanished. She thought of the flicker she'd seen in his face just before he let them in. "That little snake. He must have seen me hide it."

"Who, Alvise? You think it was him?"

"Oh saints—what if he's done something to it?"

She lifted her skirts and ran to the stairs. Bernardo followed. The workshop was deserted—Alvise must have fled to the third floor. Giulia rounded the landing, ready to rush after him. But then something brushed the edge of her awareness— faint, almost imperceptible, like the touch of cobwebs.

She checked, holding her breath. And there it was, trembling ever so faintly at the limits of her perception: a sound of bells.

She felt her heart stop.

"What?" Bernardo said from behind her. "What is it?"

Ignoring him, she advanced into the workshop. There she paused, closing her eyes and stilling her thoughts, reaching out with the strange sixth sense that once had terrified her but now seemed as natural as touch or taste. Step by step, her eyes open just enough to see where she was going, she followed the color song, her gown dragging unheeded in the sawdust and other debris that littered the floor.

She found herself at the far wall, by the door to Ferraldi's study. There, as in Humilità's workshop, the apprentices had a separate area in which to store their materials and sketches and the smocks they wore while working. Giulia had never been given a space, even after Ferraldi had made her an apprentice. But Alvise, Marin, and Stefano each had his own shelf.

Wherever her painting was, it wasn't on these shelves. That had been obvious even from a distance. Yet she could hear the glass-clear singing of her blue, faint as a memory but, to her altered senses, utterly distinct. Not knowing what she expected to find, she began to rummage among the jumble of objects on Alvise's shelf, lifting papers, knocking brushes to the floor.

"What are you doing?" Bernardo had followed her.

She opened her mouth to reply. And then she saw it: a smear of blue on the rolled-up sleeve of a painting smock. She would have recognized its pure intensity even if it had had no voice. But the smock was not Alvise's.

She drew in her breath, disbelieving.

A door creaked. She turned. Ferraldi stood in the entrance to his study, wearing his painting clothes, his silver hair bound back with a cord.

"Ah," he said. In his face she saw none of the confusion Alvise had shown; he recognized her at once. "I had not thought ever to see you again."

"Signor Moretti let me go."

"Let you go?"

"He wanted Passion blue. I gave it to him. He had no more use for me after that."

"What about Santa Marta?"

"They know nothing. He was never sent to bring me back—he came because you wrote to him and mentioned me, or who I made you think I was, and he guessed the truth."

"It was my letter that brought him? My letter of condolence?"

"Yes."

Ferraldi dropped his eyes. "Ah," he said again.

"I'm sorry I deceived you." The words came in a rush. "But the new Maestra didn't want me after my Maestra died, and there was no one else to teach me. She left me your letters—Maestra Humilità did; that's how I knew to come to you. But a girl can't be a painter's apprentice—I *had* to disguise myself or you wouldn't have taken me. It was never my intent to bring trouble to your workshop, I swear it. I'd never have stolen your secrets, no matter what Signor Moretti said."

Ferraldi did not reply at once. "Well. It is done now." He surveyed her gown, her gold-laced hair, Bernardo standing by her. "You seem to have found a comfortable refuge."

Giulia flushed. "I've been fortunate."

"Why have you come here?"

"There are things I left behind, my sketches and my competition painting. They were hidden downstairs. But my painting has been stolen."

"Stolen?" Ferraldi looked skeptical.

"I thought it was Alvise. But—" Giulia turned to pull the smock off its shelf, holding up the sleeve with its telltale smudge of blue. "This is my blue. I'd know it anywhere. It wasn't quite dry, he must not have realized that when he took it—Stefano, I mean. This is Stefano's smock."

"Stefano? Why would Stefano take your painting?"

"To enter it in the Contarini competition."

The three of them turned at the sound of a new voice. Alvise stood just inside the doorway.

"What?" All at once Giulia could not get her breath. "But he has his own painting."

"Yes, but it's rubbish, isn't it? And yours is better. Any fool could see it, even Stefano. He wants that five hundred ducats, so he took your painting to pass off as his."

"But . . . but he can't do that! It is mine! It has my signature!"

"He painted over your name and put his own name on top."

Giulia couldn't speak. She could hardly credit that Stefano, with his overweening vanity, could be capable of perceiving the superiority of someone else's work. But she remembered how he'd come to watch her, how he'd frowned when she mocked his angel orchestra. Alvise had no reason to tell the truth, yet she found that she believed him.

"This is a serious accusation, Alvise." Ferraldi's voice held the end-of-patience tone he reserved for his nephew. "Have you grounds for making it, or is it merely something you suppose?"

"I caught him doing it. The night after they took *that one* away." Alvise pointed at Giulia, as he might have to an animal in a menagerie. "I know you think I'm an idiot, Uncle. But I saw what I saw. When I asked how he thought he'd get away with it, he said you and Lauro were the only other ones who knew who'd really painted it, but neither of you were going to be at the competition, and even if you were you wouldn't say anything because then he'd tell everyone that the workshop had harbored a runaway convent girl in man's disguise."

"God's death," Ferraldi swore. "And you are only informing me of this now?"

"He said he'd beat me senseless every day for a month if I told. I wasn't going to say anything, especially not to *that one*." Alvise's eyes flicked to Giulia's face. "But you've already figured most of it out, haven't you? Stefano is a shit, Uncle. He manages things so you and Lauro don't notice, but Marin will tell you the same if you ask him, and I'll bet *that one* will too. I know he'll hurt me, whatever you decide to do. But it'll be worth it if he gets what he deserves."

"He cannot do this. *He cannot.*" All Giulia's fear and uncertainty were gone, swallowed by a high, clear rage. She turned to Bernardo. "You said you'd vouch for me before Contarini and the others. Will you still?"

Bernardo's gaze was steady. "I will."

"What do you plan to do, storm Palazzo Contarini Nuova?" Ferraldi said. "You have neither a painting nor an invitation— you'll be turned away, and not kindly. I will deal with Stefano myself when he returns. I will get you your painting back."

"No! It is my work. It is *my* hand, *my* eye, *my* colors that I mixed myself. It is . . ." Giulia heard Humilità's voice: *You are the sum of your work.* "It is the sum of me. I know I am merely a girl. I know it will cause a scandal. But I have to stop him. I cannot let him take what I have made and claim it's his. *I will not!*"

The words rang through the quiet room. Ferraldi regarded her. She met his eyes, challenging that vivid gaze.

"You will not gain admittance on your own," Ferraldi said. "But I have an invitation—which, fortunately for you, I did not discard."

Giulia caught her breath. "You will help me?"

"Against my better judgment—yes, I will."

"Thank you, Maestro. I swear I will say nothing about you or my time here."

"If I were a gambler, I'd wager you won't get far enough to say anything at all."

He returned to his study. Giulia could hear him rummaging among his papers. He emerged after several moments with his mantle over his arm and the invitation rolled up in his hand.

They headed for the stairs. When Alvise would have followed, Ferraldi gestured him back.

"You'll remain here, Alvise. The city will be wild tonight. Someone needs to watch the house."

"But, Uncle—"

"Do as I say." Then, in a kinder tone: "You did right to speak up. I'll make sure Stefano doesn't touch you."

"It won't matter," Alvise muttered. "He'll get me anyway."

They left him standing at the head of the stairs. Giulia looked back once; he scowled when he saw her turn, but not quickly enough to hide the misery in his face.

CHAPTER 25

✤ Gamma Me Fecit ✤

On the Grand Canal, Bernardo turned the gondola north,
toward the Rialto Bridge.

The afternoon was waning. In the west, the falling sun had
set the sky on fire. Lanterns swung from gondola prows and
shone from felze enclosures, and all along the quays bonfires
had been kindled, their smoke hazing the dimming air. In the
black water, a mirror-world of light stirred and shimmered,
mocking the solidity of the world above.

The bridge was a bright necklace across the throat of
the canal, with torches for jewels. Giulia barely saw it as they
passed beneath, was barely aware of Ferraldi beside her or of
Bernardo on the gondolier's platform, deftly manipulating the
oar. She willed the gondola to move faster, her hands closed
on the edge of the seat, her fingernails digging into the wood.

"There it is, ahead," Bernardo said. "The one that looks as if it's on fire."

Giulia saw it at once, climbing three stories above the canal's right bank. Every window blazed, as if an entire city's worth of candles had been set alight inside. An army of torches flared along the water floor; more torches lit the water of the canal itself, raised up on long stakes. In the gathering dusk, it really did look as if Palazzo Contarini Nuova were burning— both the high house above and the reflection-house below.

Mooring poles bristled before the water steps, already crowded with gondolas. As Bernardo steered toward them, Giulia gazed up at the palazzo's vast façade, each story faced in a different kind of marble and densely embellished with balconied arcades and decorative stonework. *Am I really here—I, Giulia Borromeo, nobleman's bastard, convent runaway, preparing to steal into the palace of one of the richest men in the richest city in the world?* Like so much else in these past days—these past months—it seemed to be happening to someone else, someone larger and braver and more determined, while the real Giulia, small and frightened, crouched in a corner and looked on.

Bernardo found an empty mooring post. They crossed from boat to boat to reach the palazzo's broad landing, Giulia holding up her skirts so she would not stumble.

"If anyone asks, I'll say you are my niece and nephew," Ferraldi said as they approached the liveried servant who was inspecting invitations. Giulia nodded. Her heart beat high and fast. She could feel the heat of all those torches licking at her skin.

The servant waved them into an immense entrance foyer, where more servants waited to receive the guests' cloaks. An imposing flight of stairs led up to the pòrtego. Emerging into it, Giulia could not help gasping. But for the churches she had visited, it was the vastest interior space she had ever seen, the ceiling soaring so high she thought a forest might fit under it, the walls enclosing an area the size of a small campo. On the patterned marble floor, more than a hundred of Venice's high nobility paraded in all their finery: older men in long black or crimson robes; young men in daringly short doublets; women in gowns of every color, their throats and hair wound with jewels, tottering on their high chopines. The air rang with conversation and with the music of the chamber orchestra seated opposite the stairs.

Giulia felt Ferraldi's hand on her arm. She allowed him to guide her to the side, out of the way of the entering guests.

"I have no taste for such events," he said, leaning close so she could hear him over the noise. "It's a long walk home, but I know my way."

Please stay and vouch for me. The words pressed behind Giulia's lips. But she knew she had no right to ask.

"Thank you, Maestro, for helping me."

"Good luck." Ferraldi's fingers tightened on her arm. "Whatever happens here tonight, be certain that Stefano and I will have a reckoning."

He turned and headed for the stairs.

"They say Contarini spent twenty thousand ducats on the interior alone." Bernardo was surveying the walls, which were paneled in alternating slabs of green and yellow marble and inset with gilded plaques. "I wonder if it cost more to make it so vulgar. Well. What now?"

Yes, what now? Giulia looked out at the milling crowd. Even growing up in her father's palace, where she and the other servant children had spied on banquets and receptions, she had never seen such a display of wealth. The candles burning in the Murano glass chandeliers could have lit an ordinary household for a year. She reached for the anger she had felt in Ferraldi's workshop, for the courage that belonged to the larger part of herself, the self that had run away to Venice in disguise.

"Find the paintings, I suppose," she said.

They began to walk, imitating the slow pace of the other guests. None were masked: Archimedeo Contarini had forbidden it. "After all, how can he boast of the caliber of his guest list if his guests' identities are in doubt?" Bernardo had remarked. Younger than most of those present, they attracted curious glances. Giulia's skin prickled with self-consciousness; at any moment, surely, someone would look past her borrowed finery and know her for an imposter. She wished for her mantle back, far too aware of her bare neck and bosom, though some of the women wore bodices cut much lower than hers.

By contrast, Bernardo seemed perfectly at ease, inclining his head politely to those they passed. His expression of bland courtesy was as impenetrable as any mask; no one would guess the resentment that burned behind it. Giulia wondered if there were men present whose faces he knew from their visits to Sofia.

Why is he here with me? What does it mean that he is—or does it mean anything?

They walked the length of the pòrtego and saw no paintings.

"Perhaps they're in another room," Bernardo suggested.

Giulia looked around the cavernous space. There were doors, but all were closed.

Boom! Boom! Boom!

The sound echoed over the noise of the crowd: servants in livery striking staffs on the floor. The clamor of conversation subsided. The music fell to silence.

"Noble and esteemed guests." A deep voice rang out. "I welcome you to my home, and thank you humbly for your presence."

"*Humbly?*" muttered Bernardo. "Does he imagine anyone actually believes that?"

The guests had all turned toward the voice. Giulia craned her neck; but there were too many people in front of her, and she could see nothing.

"Tonight, for your entertainment and delight, I present to you thirteen esteemed painters from afar, and a fourteenth from our own city. Each has created a work of art whose worthiness will be judged by Venice's greatest master, Maestro Giovanni Bellini."

A fourteenth from our own city. Stefano. Giulia's heart had begun to race. She stepped forward, wanting to get closer, but the brocaded and velveted backs in front of her were like a wall.

"I have decreed the subject of these works, which is music, but I have permitted the artists to interpret it in the manner of their choosing. As you will see, their inventiveness knows no bounds. There is music here in all its forms, all its history, all its meaning—music made in paint, one art embodying another. Accept this twofold gift of beauty, dear guests. Allow your eyes to sing."

A warm hand seized Giulia's own. Bernardo pulled her forward, maneuvering between the guests as neatly as he'd earlier guided the gondola between the boats on the Grand Canal, keeping up a stream of murmured comments: "Your pardon. Your indulgence. My apologies."

They reached the front of the throng. The musicians who had been seated opposite the head of the stairs were gone, and a semicircle of easels had been set up in their place. Two men stood nearby. One was tall and bony, with pale skin and red-blond hair, clad in a black robe of sumptuous figured silk. The other was long-nosed and thin-lipped, his hair a mix of brown and gray. His black robe was not as fine as that of the man beside him, though he wore a heavy chain of gold upon his shoulders. His hands were clasped before him, the thumb and fingers of the right darkened to the knuckles with a lifetime of ink and charcoal.

Giulia closed her own hands, similarly stained. *Giovanni Bellini.*

One at a time, the artists mounted the stairs to the pòrtego and bowed to their host, then positioned their paintings on the easels and took a place beside them. Some had brought apprentices or servants to carry their work. There were panels and canvases, small works and large ones; there were celestial choirs, musicians with their instruments, images from myth and Scripture. Giulia, her body shaking with the force of her heartbeat, barely noted the brilliant colors, the intricate compositions. She was counting: six painters. Eight. Ten. Where was Stefano?

Then she saw him, rising into view at the top of the stairs: the fourteenth entrant, last to appear. He wore clothes Giulia hadn't seen before, a short green doublet and striped hose tied up so taut he could scarcely bend his legs. And in his hands . . .

Giulia hissed. She wasn't aware she had moved until Bernardo caught her arm.

"Wait," he whispered. "Let him take his place."

She allowed Bernardo to hold her back as Stefano paced stiffly past. *Look at me,* she willed him. She wanted to see recognition in his face, wanted to see him understand that his lie was known. But he was staring straight ahead, as if the final empty easel were a rock and he a man lost at sea. He bowed to Contarini and Bellini, then set Giulia's painting on the easel and stood aside.

"Painters!" called Archimedeo Contarini. "Name yourselves and your work!"

The painters spoke in the order of their entrance. Later, Giulia would remember that she had recognized some of the names, famous masters from Vicenza and Padua of whom Humilità had spoken with admiration. Now, though, her attention was all for Stefano, ill at ease in his uncomfortable clothes, his eyes darting back and forth as if anticipating discovery.

His turn to speak came at last. "I am Stefano Scarpazza," he said in a stilted tone quite unlike his usual easy drawl, "of the workshop of Gianfranco Ferraldi. I am of Venice, and I'm only an apprentice, but Maestro Bellini has judged me worthy to stand here even so. I have painted a Muse of song, her attention captured by the music of the spheres."

Giulia's words—her own exact words, stolen like the painting itself because he had no understanding of what she had made and no care for it except as a means to an end. Rage sucked her down; for an instant she was blind. She threw off Bernardo's hold and stepped forward.

"You lie," she said, lifting her arm, pointing square at Stefano's chest. "That painting is not by your hand."

A ripple ran through the crowd: astonishment, disapproval, excitement. A hundred heads turned Giulia's way. Stefano stared at her openmouthed, as if she were an apparition.

"Young woman." Contarini's voice was colder than the marble floor of his hall. Behind him, Bellini and the other painters looked on. "What is the meaning of this?"

"*Clarissimo.*" Lifting her heavy skirts, Giulia sank into a curtsy, a skill learned long ago in her father's household. "My name is Giulia Borromeo. Stefano Scarpazza is a thief and a liar. He did not paint that panel. He stole it from me."

"You are its owner?" Contarini said, his red-blond brows drawing together over deep-set eyes.

"I am its author, clarissimo." A fierce and entirely unexpected exultation shook her: to declare herself without disguise, to stand before all these people with her own true face, her own true name, and claim what she had made. "It is my work, by my own hand."

Exclamations from the crowd: some scandalized, some disgusted, some delighted at the unfolding of this unanticipated entertainment, a tale they would tell tomorrow to those who had not been there. The painters exchanged uneasy looks. An expression of distaste spread across Contarini's face.

"Clarissimo, I know this girl." Stefano spoke up. "Poor creature, she is mad. She dabbles her fingers in ink and believes she paints. I don't know why she has followed me here. Her delusion must be deeper than I thought. But I beg you, clarissimo, forgive her interruption and do not treat her harshly. She doesn't understand what she does."

Fury robbed Giulia momentarily of breath. Bernardo moved to stand beside her.

"She is neither mad nor a liar," he declared in a ringing voice. "The painting is her work, stolen by Scarpazza as a fraud on you who are gathered here. I vouch for all she has said."

He used no title of respect in addressing Contarini, did not bow or cast down his eyes. Giulia could see that this was not lost on the nobleman. "And who are you?" Contarini demanded.

"I am Bernardo Gentileschi, a citizen of Venice."

Murmurs from the crowd. Giulia, clearly, heard someone say, "La Fiamma's son."

"Clarissimo—" Stefano began, but Contarini raised a hand, his long, black sleeve expanding like a crow's wing, his eyes never moving from Bernardo's. Stefano flinched and was silent.

"Is this girl in your care?" Contarini said to Bernardo.

"She is a guest of my family."

"And it is your assertion"—Contarini's tone made clear his disbelief—"that her claim is true? That *she* made this painting?"

Bernardo began to reply, but it was not his voice that spoke.

"*I* assert it."

Giulia felt a shock of recognition. She turned, the faces of the guests wheeling before her. Ferraldi stood at the head of the stairs in his plain mantle and paint-marked hose, his silver hair half out of the cord that tied it: a clay mug among glass goblets. But his back was as straight, his gaze as self-possessed, as any of the nobles'.

He changed his mind. He stayed to vouch for me after all.

"And who might you be, signor?" Contarini's exasperation was plain.

"I am Gianfranco Ferraldi, clarissimo, a painter of this city, whom you invited here tonight as you did other masters of my art." Ferraldi advanced across the floor. "Stefano Scarpazza is my apprentice, though after this night he shall not set foot in my workshop again—nor, I venture, in any other workshop in Venice. The girl tells the truth. She is the true author of the work he claims as his."

"You have evidence of this?"

"My own eyes, which saw her paint it." Ferraldi halted at Giulia's side. "She has been my pupil for some months now."

"*Your pupil?*" Stefano's face was scarlet. "She wasn't your *pupil*! You didn't even know she was a girl! Clarissimo, she is an imposter, a runaway novice. She disguised herself as a boy and took a false name and tricked her way into my master's workshop, and he never knew it, never even suspected it, till someone came looking for her to get back what she stole from her convent in Padua."

A hum of comment and exclamation arose.

"Ah, Stefano. Have you not told lies enough?" Ferraldi raised his voice to carry above the rest, looking directly into his apprentice's eyes. "Let it end here. Admit that you were envious of this girl's gifts. Admit that in your greed for the reward that will be won tonight, you took advantage of her absence to steal her work and present it as your own."

"I signed it. Look!" Forgetting himself entirely, Stefano snatched the painting from the easel and thrust it toward Contarini. "Do you see, there is my signature, plain as day!"

"He painted his name over mine," Giulia said. "Not three days ago. The paint will still be soft."

Until that moment, Giovanni Bellini had watched in silence. Now he stepped forward. Giulia saw Stefano's face change as he realized his mistake. He tried to pull back the painting. Bellini caught it, twitched it from his hands.

The great master tipped the panel to the light of the candelabrum overhead. Blue flashed—Gamma blue, Giulia's blue, as ravishing as a sapphire's dream. With his blackened thumb, Bellini rubbed at the little scroll below the Muse's foot, where Stefano had obscured Giulia's signature with his own.

"She tells the truth," he said. "Another signature lies beneath."

"'Gamma' for Giulia," Giulia said in a voice that seemed to arrive from somewhere very far away. "*Gamma Me Fecit.*"

The master's eyes rose to hers. "It is so."

A sound like wind rushed through the pòrtego: a hundred people, drawing in their breaths. Contarini's face was thunderous. He clapped his hands. A pair of servants came forward.

"Remove him," he ordered, gesturing to Stefano.

Giulia thought that Stefano, even knowing himself beaten, might struggle or protest. Instead, to her surprise, he mustered some semblance of dignity, lifting his chin and squaring his shoulders. He did not resist as the servants took his arms and urged him forward. Giulia turned to watch him pass, no more than an arm's length away. His eyes were fixed ahead, his face rigid. His escorts pushed him onto the stairs. A few steps and he was gone.

"Young woman."

Giulia turned. Bellini was approaching.

"This is yours." He held out her painting, smiling kindly. "A little turpentine will clean the rest of his forgery away."

Giulia took it. At last she felt the awe she had not been able to experience before: Venice's greatest painter, whose magnificent altarpiece in the church of San Giobbe had stolen hours from her life, standing before her in the flesh. He'd judged her painting worthy to be shown. Now he had acknowledged her as its author. Her heart was racing again—not with fear or anger, but with hope.

"It is a creditable effort," he said. "No doubt that owes much to your teacher"—he nodded at Ferraldi—"whose skill I know."

"He has helped me, Maestro. But the work is my own."

"And now you have it back." Bellini smiled again. "Good fortune to you, my dear."

He turned to go.

Giulia did not believe it at first. *That can't be all. Surely he has more to say to me.* But he was moving away, toward Contarini and the painters, where another servant was folding up the fourteenth easel.

"Maestro." Giulia stepped after him. "Maestro Bellini."

He wheeled around, his eyebrows rising in surprise.

"Maestro, my painting is here, and there is an easel for it. May I not stand with the others and be judged?"

"With the others?" Behind Bellini the contestants stirred, some frowning or shaking their heads, others bending toward one another in whispered comment. "No, no. That is not possible."

"Maestro, you judged it worthy to be shown when you believed Stefano painted it. Why not now?"

"My dear, you are a lovely young girl, and very brave to do as you have done, though some might judge your actions less kindly. It is clear you have some talent for the brush. But you are not a painter, nor will you ever be. You cannot stand among the masters gathered here."

Giulia clutched the Muse. A huge and crushing disappointment was unfolding inside her, all the worse because she had allowed herself to believe it was not inevitable.

"Why not, Giovanni?" Ferraldi said. "The work is fine. I only counseled her—she conceived it entire, and the whole of it is by her hand, even that marvelous blue, which she made herself. She has a natural skill I have rarely seen equaled, certainly never in any of the male apprentices I have taught. Let her stand."

"To what purpose, Gianfranco? Even if she is as gifted as you say, what can come of it? Your liberal views are all very well, but that is not the way of the world, and you know it."

"Then perhaps the world should change."

"Perhaps," Bellini said. "But nothing we do tonight will make it so."

Ferraldi might have said more. But Contarini, his patience clearly at an end, intervened.

"Maestro Bellini has spoken," he said. "Maestro Ferraldi, accept my thanks for preventing the perpetration of a fraud. Honored guests, my apologies for these distractions that have taken us far from our true course tonight. Master painters—" He turned toward the contestants. "You have my gratitude for your patience, which will be tested no further. We will now begin the judging." He extended an imperious hand toward Bellini. "Maestro."

Bellini glanced once more at Ferraldi. Then he turned away. The crowd, sensing that the drama was at an end, began removing its attention, though some still watched in hope of more to come.

Giulia was trembling. Whatever had sustained her till now had gone out of her all at once, like sand from a shattered hourglass.

"Please," she whispered. She didn't want to fall to the floor or burst into tears before all these people. "I want to go."

Ferraldi reached to take the Muse. Bernardo gripped her arm. She let him lead her down the stairs, the noise of the crowd falling away as they stepped out into the Venetian night.

CHAPTER 26

✤ The World Will Change ✤

Carnival was in its final hours. The city blazed with celebration. Behind candle-gilded windows, on streets and quays, in rooms rich beyond dreams of avarice and campi as mean as any in the world, the people of Venice drained the last dregs of the season of excess.

Above the Piazza San Marco, fireworks split the night, flowers of light unfurling in an instant and fading in a breath. Giulia tipped back her head to watch them as the gondola slipped through the black waters of the Grand Canal. In her mind, over and over, she heard Bellini's voice: *You are not a painter, nor will you ever be.*

I didn't fail, she told herself. *I exposed Stefano. I claimed my work.* She held the Muse in her lap; in between the fireworks' echoing concussions, she could just hear the crystal bell-song of her blue, whispering from the not-quite-dry paint that had betrayed Stefano's treachery. Perhaps she hadn't been allowed to stand with her painting, but at least no one else could claim it as his own.

What if I'd waited to speak until the judging was finished? Might the Muse have won?

But there was no purpose in such thoughts. And she knew now that the ultimate outcome would have been the same.

Celebration was still in full swing in the Campo San Lio. The noise of revelry came out to meet them as Bernardo guided the gondola up to the water steps. Beside Giulia, Ferraldi turned.

"You have courage," he said.

His face was a dark blot against the light of the fires and torches from the campo.

"I don't feel very courageous," she said.

"But you are. Never doubt it. I saw in you tonight the same bravery Humilità had, to stand against the scorn of the world and refuse to yield. I think she would have been proud."

Giulia felt something turn in her, a mix of hope and pain. "Do you really think so?"

"I know it. The world *will* change, Giulia. It must."

He rose and ducked out from beneath the felze, nodding to Bernardo. Giulia looked back as they pulled away. Ferraldi stood against the fire glow, gazing after them.

The world will change.

You are not a painter.

Ferraldi's words, Bellini's. A promise; a refusal. Which should she believe?

Like the Grand Canal, the Rio dei Miracoli was crowded with illuminated boats. Revelers made their way along the fondamenta, bearing torches and lanterns. Venice, Giulia thought, was surely the brightest city in the world tonight.

Bernardo moored the gondola at Sofia's landing, then leaped out and reached back to assist Giulia. She set the Muse on the floor of the boat and gripped his fingers, remembering how he'd made no move to help her when she embarked that afternoon. Once on the landing, she would have stooped to retrieve her painting, but he held on to her hand.

"I'm sorry they wouldn't let you offer your painting to be judged."

They were the first words he'd spoken since they left Palazzo Contarini Nuova. Giulia looked away from him, down at the damp marble under her feet, glistening faintly in the light of the lanterns burning by the door. She hadn't realized until now how exhausted she was. The memory of the evening turned inside her, a tangle of hope and disappointment—and also, obscured for a little while but as inevitable as the dark days of Lent that came after this season of light, the questions she must face: What to do next? Where to go?

"Thank you," she said. "For accompanying me. For speaking for me."

"Giovanni Bellini is a fool."

"He's a great master."

"And a fool. I'll tell my mother to turn that portrait to the wall."

Giulia had to smile. "It's not the painting's fault."

"Stefano is ruined, isn't he?"

"I should think so. In Venice, at any rate."

"Good."

He was still holding her hand. It was beginning to feel uncomfortable. She was too aware of his closeness, of the warmth of his fingers twined with hers. Yet she did not wish to pull away.

"What you did tonight," he said. His face was in shadow, but his eyes caught the lantern light, glinting. "It was . . . quite something."

"You got your scandal, I suppose."

"You won't be able to disguise yourself again. Not in Venice."

It was true. She hadn't considered that. Yet if she had, she did not think she would have acted differently.

"This afternoon . . . in my mother's sitting room . . ." Bernardo paused, then went on in a rush. "I told you that I never guessed. About you, who you—*what* you really are. But I think that's not wholly true. Somewhere in myself I must have known. Otherwise, how could I—"

He bit off the words. He'd dropped his eyes, fixing them on their clasped hands. Giulia held her breath. Her heart had begun to race.

"I thought I must be unnatural. Or that you must be. I told myself I had to overcome it. I told myself that was why I kept returning, to prove to myself that I didn't—" Again he stopped himself. "And then I learned the truth, that there was nothing unnatural after all. But I'd been telling myself for so long that there was . . . I didn't know what to feel, about you or about myself. And so I was angry." He raised his eyes to hers. "But you were right in what you said to me. You did not owe me the truth. I see now . . . I see now that I was angry not at you, but at myself."

It shook Giulia to the core to hear him admit so much. She would never have expected it. She wanted to tell him she understood, that she bore no grudge, but she could not find the words.

"Giulia." He had never spoken her real name before. The sound of it thrilled her. "I want to offer you something. A home."

"A . . . home?" she repeated, not sure she had understood.

"With my mother and me. A true home, one you will never have to leave."

She looked up at him, disbelieving. "You are asking me to . . . to live . . . *here*?"

"Yes. You are all alone in the world. You have nowhere to go." He shook his head. "I'm sorry, that was badly spoken. But it's true. You need a place to rest. A place where you can be safe. We could give you that."

"Bernardo . . . I have nothing. No money, no family, not even the clothes I'm wearing. I've just made a spectacle of myself in front of the highest nobility of Venice, and before that . . . well, you know my story. You know what I come from."

"My mother came from less. And if you think either she or I care about such things, you very much mistake our characters."

Giulia felt longing sweep her. *To have a home. Not to make my way alone again . . . not to disguise myself or lie . . . and if he is offering this to me, does it mean . . . could it mean . . .*

"Your mother. Does she . . . is this her wish too?"

"I haven't asked her yet. But I know she'll welcome you." All this time Bernardo had not let go of her hand. Now his fingers tightened, until his grip was almost painful. "Say you will stay. Say yes."

"Yes," Giulia said. Her eyes, suddenly, were full of tears. "If your mother agrees, I'll stay."

He did not move. His searching gaze did not shift. But something had changed—Giulia sensed it, a tightening of the air, a tingling on her skin. The night leaned in around them, alive with anticipation.

When he drew her toward him, it felt inevitable. And then she was in his arms and his mouth was on hers, just as she had sometimes dreamed but never allowed herself to hope. A lightness burst inside her head, a swirling dizziness that threatened to sweep her away. She rose into the kiss, sealing herself against him, feeling his heart pounding like a hammer, beat for beat with her own; and then they were spinning, spinning, and the great city of stone and black water spun with them, wheeling like the celestial spheres around the Earth; and the night embraced them, the gorgeous glittering mad Venetian night, so urgent with life that it seemed, for just these moments, life could never end.

When she heard applause and laughter, it seemed to her at first that Venice itself must be speaking. But then Bernardo lifted his head and Giulia, returning abruptly to Earth, realized that it was only a group of revelers who'd paused on the fondamenta across the canal to watch.

"I'll wager you won't be giving *that* up for Lent!" one of them yelled.

"Mind your business," Bernardo called back, producing more laughter.

The men moved on. Bernardo's arms had loosened, and like a door cracking open to the cold, Giulia wondered if he was regretting what they had just done. But then he looked down at her. In what she saw in his face, she knew he felt no regret.

"Giulia Borromeo," he said softly. He reached up to smooth back a tendril of her hair that had escaped its braid, his fingers lingering on her skin. "The girl who was a boy. I think I fell in love with you tonight."

Joy filled Giulia so full that for a moment she could not speak. "And I with you," she said, her voice unsteady. "Though much longer ago than that."

"When?"

"I don't know exactly. One day I looked, and there it was. I never thought—I never dreamed—that anything would come of it."

"Then perhaps we owe Matteo Moretti a debt of thanks."

He kissed her again, less urgently than before but all the sweeter for that. When he pulled away, his face was grave.

"Understand, Giulia, I can promise you nothing. Not now. I must go to Padua, and it may be years before I can return."

"I understand." She had not expected promises. She had not expected even so much as this.

"But I will return, be certain of it. Venice is my home. One day I will come back for good."

It *was* a promise of a sort—if only of the possibility of a different promise. She looked into his shadowed face, into his glinting eyes.

"I can promise nothing either, Bernardo," she said. "I don't know yet what I will do—even what I *can* do, after tonight. But I do know—" She caught her breath. Something surged in her, like the fireworks exploding over the Piazza San Marco, a pure, hot radiance that lit up everything inside her. "I do know that I will paint."

"Yes," Bernardo said, as if it were completely to be expected.

"And I will do more . . . I will do more than simply use a brush. I will *be* a painter. As my profession." In her mind she heard Ferraldi's voice: *The world will change. That* was what she must hope. *That* was what she must believe. "Maestro Bellini told me it was impossible, but I will prove him wrong. I don't know yet how I'll accomplish it. I don't know what I'll have to do or where I may have to go. I only know that I will be a painter, and I will do anything, *everything*, to make that so."

He watched her. "Even disguise yourself again?"

"If I must."

A silence. Then he nodded. "But you will have a home. And if you leave it, you can return. As I will."

"Yes."

Not a promise. The possibility of a promise.

"Come." He stepped away. The cold night air rushed into the space between them, but his hand was still folded around hers, warm and firm. "Let's go in and see my mother."

"Wait! My painting."

She stooped to the gondola to retrieve it. He bent with her, for he would not let her go. Hand in hand, they crossed to the door, where the servant who had been drowsing in the passage held a candle to light their way.

As she passed inside, Giulia looked back, her eyes rising to the distant, circling stars, fully visible tonight in a sky that was icy-clear. The words of her horoscope fragment returned to her: the prophecy that had dogged her life. But now, for the very first time, she understood it differently. It barred her from family and children. It denied her name. But it did not forbid her to love, or to be loved in return.

CHAPTER 27

✤ Rebirth ✤

Giulia woke from dreamless sleep to gray light and the sound of church bells.

Cocooned in the comfort of feather quilts, she lay looking up at the ceiling of the cabinet-bed where she'd slept on her first night in Venice, the events of the day before taking shape in her mind like ships emerging from fog. Almost, it seemed a dream—a long, complicated dream of many parts.

Bernardo. The warmth that unfolded in her was no dream, nor the shiver of delight that ran through her, transporting her back to last night: his body against hers, his arms so tight around her she could hardly breathe. *I think I fell in love with you tonight.* She closed her eyes, hearing it again. *The girl who was a boy . . .*

He'd held her hand all the way into the house, all along the pòrtego, releasing her only as they reached the fan of fire glow that spread from the open door of Sofia's sitting room. When they'd entered, they had been separate. From her chair by the fire, Sofia had smiled in welcome, enclosing them in her tawny gaze. Giulia sensed that she knew exactly what had just happened, outside on the landing.

Bernardo pulled up a chair for Giulia and seated himself on the hearth. Giulia sat silent as he told the story of the evening, while Sofia listened and exclaimed.

"It will be the talk of the city!" Sofia said when he had finished. "One of the contestants at Contarini's splendid event exposed as a fraud by a mere girl, who then had the audacity to demand a place among the men! And her accomplice, the son of a famous whore!" She laughed, a ripple of delighted amusement. "Oh, it is delicious!"

"It's certainly not what Contarini hoped," Bernardo said with satisfaction.

"You are famous now, Giulia. Or perhaps notorious would be a fitter word."

"I take no delight in that," Giulia said, a little stiffly.

"Ah, Giulia, I am sorry. You must excuse the pleasure such scandals give my son and me." Sofia's smile became mischievous. "But you might take a *little* delight. Notoriety has its benefits. I'll wager you could get patronage from this, if you wished it."

This had not occurred to Giulia. "Do you really think so?"

"The lovely girl painter whose beautiful blue caught the eye of Giovanni Bellini himself?" Sofia gestured to the Muse, propped against Giulia's chair. "Venice loves novelty, the more shocking the better. If you are careful and clever, you could

turn this to your advantage." Her eyes gleamed. "I can advise
you, if you wish."

"Mother." Bernardo shifted on the hearth. "There's something I wish to ask you."

"Indeed?" Sofia turned to him. "And what might that be?"

"I have offered—that is, I would like to offer Giulia a home
here, with us. Not a temporary refuge, but a true home that she
will not have to leave. The benefit won't be to her alone. She
can be a companion to you while I'm gone."

"And to you?" Sofia looked into her son's upturned face.
"What will she be to you?"

"A friend," he said, his eyes sliding away from hers. "And
one day, perhaps, something more."

"I see." Sofia turned her amber regard on Giulia. "What do
you say, Giulia? Is this what you wish? To live with me?"

"Yes, clarissima, if you'd allow it."

"Consider well. This is not an ordinary house. For one
who does not delight in notoriety, the household of a courtesan might not be the wisest choice of residence."

"You know everything I've done, and you don't condemn
me for it. You know all I want to do, and you don't condemn
me for that either. And there is freedom here."

"A kind of freedom, yes. But I wonder if it is the kind you
seek."

"I seek only the freedom not to be judged. Never again
to be told I cannot paint. Clarissima, you have been so kind
to me. You had no reason at all to help me and yet you did,
and I'm already in your debt more than I can ever repay. You
know my history—you know I have nothing. What Bernardo
is asking is too much—I know that. But I would like more than
anything to call your house my home. If you consent, I swear

that I will never take advantage of your generosity. I swear I'll find a way to pay you back."

"Then it is settled. This shall be your home, for as long as you wish it." Sofia held out her hands. "Come. Kiss me to seal the bargain."

"You see?" Bernardo was smiling as Giulia settled back into her chair. "I told you she would welcome you."

"My presumptuous beast." Sofia looked at him with affection. "One day you'll presume too much, and then what will you do?"

"Persuade you it was your own idea."

Sofia laughed. "Go now, Bernardo. I would like a word with Giulia alone."

Bernardo departed, with a kiss for his mother and a lingering look for Giulia. She could not help turning to watch him out of sight. He glanced back when he reached the door, and their eyes met. Then he was gone.

Giulia turned back to the fire, and to Sofia's knowing gaze.

"There is something I must ask you, Giulia. Is there an understanding between you and my son?"

"No, clarissima. That is . . . he has promised me nothing. But we . . . I . . ."

Giulia trailed off. Her cheeks were aflame.

"I understand," Sofia said. "I suspected as much."

"I would never presume, clarissima. I know . . . I know you wish him to make a good marriage."

"What I *wish* is that he be happy. If he were happy with you, it would be no presumption."

"Clarissima, I don't know what will become of me." Giulia looked down at her hands, clasped together on her knees. "There's nothing in the world I'm certain of, except that I will paint. Also—" She hesitated. "When I was a baby, my mother had a horoscope cast for me. It said—" She raised her eyes. "That I would never marry."

Sofia made a dismissive gesture. "I set no store by horoscopes. The stars are the stars. We make our own fates."

"I believed that too when I was younger. But everything I've done to fight my stars has only brought me back to the prediction."

"Well, perhaps that is so and perhaps it is not. Either way, it is certain that your path will be a difficult one."

"I know that, clarissima."

"Know this also, Giulia. I welcome you as my companion, and I would welcome you also as my daughter, if things between you and Bernardo were to come to that. But I would not have him suffer for your ambitions. He does not love easily, and when he does, he loves too well. If your journey carries you where he cannot follow, do not hold him. Do not trifle with his affections. It is the only thing I will not bear."

The fire had dwindled as they spoke, and Sofia's skin gleamed pale in the dusky light. She had shown Giulia many aspects of herself in the time they'd known each other: compassion, warmth, amusement, interest. But the woman Giulia saw before her now did not wear any of those faces. This, Giulia understood, was the face of the woman who had chosen whoredom over slavery, who by force of will had carved for herself a place in the world, and made certain she could keep it.

"I would never hurt him, clarissima. I swear it."

"Then you and I will do very well together." Sofia smiled. The fierce woman, the hard woman, faded back behind the lovely mask—which was also the true Sofia, but only because the fierce woman had made it possible. "I'll tell you a secret. I like to let Bernardo think he gets his way more often than he does, for it lends force when I must refuse him. But I would have invited you to remain even if he had not asked it. I've come to care for you, though we know each other only a little. And I would be pleased to help you in the struggle that lies ahead of you."

"Thank you, clarissima." Giulia's eyes stung with tears. "I'm truly grateful."

"I think it's high time you stopped addressing me as 'clarissima.' Call me by my name."

"Thank you . . . Sofia."

Sofia had taken Giulia by the hand then and brought her to her room, and helped her remove her complicated clothes and take down her hair. She'd kissed Giulia and held her in an embrace, and then departed. Exhausted, Giulia had crawled into bed. Sleep had received her instantly.

Now, in the pearly light of the overcast morning, she felt as if a lifetime had passed since she'd woken yesterday under the crimson canopy of Sofia's bed. She had claimed her painting and exposed Stefano. She had claimed her name, standing before the assembled nobility of Venice. She'd gained a home: a place to rest, a place where she need keep no secrets. And whatever fragile thing there was between herself and Bernardo—she had gained that too.

She thought of what he had offered her: not a promise but only the possibility of one, years into the future. *And if he had offered more. Would I have wanted it?*

Her eyes went to her painting, propped across the room on the lid of a chest. Her own beautiful blue shone from it, jewellike even on this clouded day. She felt the presence of her plan, the idea that had come to her deep in the night, after the midnight bells had rung the clamor of Carnival away.

She pushed back the covers and swung her feet to the chilly floor. She had things to do.

—

Venice was a city transformed. The memory of Carnival lingered: discarded masks, broken eggshells, a reveler sleeping off his drunkenness in a doorway. But the color and the gaiety, the mad dance of life, were gone as if they had never been. The streets and canals were crowded, for commerce never ceased; but there was a new soberness to the way people went about their business, their foreheads marked with ashes for the first day of Lent.

Giulia hurried along, her shawl pulled around her head and shoulders against the cold. No one cast her a second glance, for she was dressed not in the rich gown she had worn yesterday, but in the plain servant's garments Matteo Moretti had given her, her hair pulled back from her face with a cord. It still felt strange to walk in skirts, but she was far more at ease in these clothes, which were similar in quality to those she'd worn when she'd lived in her father's household.

She had to ask directions to the Rialto Bridge, but once there, she was on familiar ground. In Campo San Lio, the spit that had held the pig still stood above the remains of the fire, and the paving was littered with refuse that had not yet been cleared away.

Ferraldi's door was opened, as Giulia knew it would be, by Alvise.

"Hello, Alvise. Is your uncle in?"

He eyed her as he might have eyed a snake, and for a moment she thought he would slam the door in her face. But then he stepped back and let her pass.

The painters, busy at their work, did not notice her at once. Lauro, at the drafting table, saw her first: He went still, his quill poised above his ink pot. Then Zuane and Antonio looked up, their bickering falling quiet, and Marin dropped his muller with a sound of ringing glass, his mouth making an O of astonishment. Giulia raised her chin and pressed on through the sudden quiet, looking neither to the left nor right.

"I'm working." Ferraldi's reply to her knock was sharp with impatience. "Can it wait?"

She pushed open the door. He was standing at his easel, palette in hand. His brush held malachite green; she could hear its acid trill. He turned, frowning, but whatever angry thing he meant to say died when he saw her.

"Giulia Borromeo," he said in a tone that held no surprise at all.

Giulia had had a speech planned. Now as on the very first time she'd seen him, all the words flew out of her head.

"Maestro," she blurted, "I've come to ask you to teach me."

Ferraldi stood a moment without moving. Then he set aside his tools and went to sit down.

"You cannot be Girolamo again," he said, folding his hands on the mess of rags and papers and broken quills that heaped his desk.

"I don't want to be."

"What are you proposing, then?"

"Maestro, I realize now that even if Signor Moretti hadn't found me, I would have been discovered in the end. Stefano suspected—I think even you suspected—and if it hadn't been you or him it would have been someone else. I don't want to spend my life waiting for discovery, fearing that a single mistake could destroy anything I manage to build. Last night"—the memory thrilled through her—"I stood up before all those people and claimed my painting—myself, as I am, without subterfuge or disguise. I never imagined I would do such a thing. I thought that outside the convent, I would always have to lie in order to paint. But last night I told the truth."

"And precisely because you did, your painting was turned away."

"Yes. But those who were there heard me, and some of them will remember. And if I stand up again, and again, perhaps one day I *won't* be turned away."

He looked at her. "Do you think you have the strength for that?"

"I don't know. But I want to try. You said the world must change, Maestro. I don't imagine I'll be the one to change it. But I want to learn—not as a false boy, but as myself. As Giulia Borromeo."

"What makes you think I would be willing to teach you?"

"Because you spoke for me last night when you did not have to." Giulia's heart was racing now. "Because you believe a woman can paint as well as a man. Because you're a fine teacher. Because you know I have a gift, and *I* know that I still have so much to learn." From her sleeve she pulled the paper she'd written earlier, borrowing materials from Sofia's writing desk. "I don't have money to pay you with. But I have this."

She stepped forward and laid the paper before him. He looked at it a moment.

"Passion blue," he said.

"That's the recipe exactly as my Maestra wrote it. I memorized it."

"You made it too, didn't you. I should have realized. The Muse's blue gown."

"I followed the recipe. But I am not my Maestra. I don't have her hands or her experience, and what I made wasn't

Passion blue. If you make it, it will be your blue, not hers. But it will be beautiful."

He did not answer at once. At last he looked up, his blue-green gaze capturing her own.

"If I am to consider this, there must be no untruth between us. I know a little of your history from Humilità, but you must tell me the rest. All of it, without exception."

And so for the third time in as many days she told her story, standing before Ferraldi's desk with her hands wound into the fabric of her shawl, while the gray Lenten light crept in through the window and the sounds of the workshop rose and fell outside the door. She told him everything, even the things that shamed her: her purchase of the talisman, her part in Matteo's first betrayal. As she'd suspected, he had not known about the plot to steal Humilità's book of secrets. He was horrified and angry—and also wounded, that Humilità had not trusted him with the truth.

Her tale was nearly done. She hesitated, her resolve faltering, then steeled herself and plunged on.

"There's one more thing you need to know, Maestro. It is . . . very strange, and I fear you won't believe me. But I swear to you it's the truth, and that I am neither mad nor bewitched."

And she told him about the color song. It was even harder than she had imagined, for she had never thought to share her strange ability with another soul, and she knew how much she was risking by doing so. But if he was to be her teacher, there could be no lies between them, not even of omission. To him, of all the people in the world, she would give the whole truth about herself. From him alone she would keep no secrets.

He was silent when she finished. She waited, her pulse sounding in her ears.

"I do not know what to think of this," he said. "If I knew nothing else about you, I would indeed think your mind diseased. Or that you were lying, though I cannot imagine why anyone would construct such a falsehood."

"It's the truth, Maestro," Giulia said again.

"Whether it is or not, I can see that you believe it. Did Humilità know?"

"No." Giulia swallowed against the sudden tightness of her throat. "I wanted to tell her, but . . . I left it too long."

"These past months, I have seen no sign of madness in you, other than the madness all true artists share. Perhaps you simply have a greater portion of it. But there is something I must know. You speak of talismans and spirits—but do you also pray to God, and to our Savior Jesus Christ?"

"I do, Maestro. I don't worship demons or spirits. I turned to magic once, but I will never do so again."

"Swear it."

"I swear it. On my soul, I swear."

"Well, then." Ferraldi sighed. "Once before I let you talk me into taking you on against my better judgment, for the sake of your gift and for Humilità's memory. It appears that I intend to do so again."

The relief was so overwhelming that Giulia could not speak.

"Before you thank me—as I am sure you mean to do—I must tell you that I can teach you only as a private pupil. You cannot be my apprentice. If I'm to keep my membership in the artists' guild, I can't test convention so far. Agreeing to teach the girl who spoiled Archimedeo Contarini's competition will be stretching it quite uncomfortably enough. Is that acceptable?"

"More than acceptable, Maestro. Thank you. Thank you!"

"You will come to me three times a week—let us say Tuesday, Thursday, and Saturday, at four o'clock of the afternoon. You'll supply your own materials, though I may supplement them from time to time. And"—he paused, his brilliant eyes holding hers—"you will tell me the truth. Always. About everything. Do you understand?"

"Yes, Maestro."

"I don't know what may come of this. Perhaps nothing. The world will change, but not, as Giovanni said, today. We will simply go forward and see where that takes us."

"I could ask for nothing more, Maestro."

"We're agreed, then."

He rose from his chair and extended his hand across his desk. She took it, looking into his familiar, almost-ugly face, which she'd long ago stopped seeing as anything but pleasing, especially when, as now, it was warmed by his smile.

"Thank you, Maestro. I'll try to make sure you don't regret it."

The smile widened. "I think I already may. But those are often the best decisions."

—

Alvise was lurking in the storeroom when Giulia returned downstairs. She opened the door but then, on impulse, turned back.

"I wanted to thank you, Alvise," she said. "For telling the truth about Stefano."

"Didn't do it for you," he muttered.

"Well, I'm still grateful."

"What were you talking to my uncle about?"

"I asked him to teach me."

"What did he say?"

"He agreed."

"So you'll still be here." He swiped his hand under his perpetually running nose.

"Yes, but as a private pupil, not an apprentice. So you needn't fear I'll take your place."

"But now you'll be his special pet," Alvise said bitterly. "I'd like to know what it's like to be the favored one. Just once, I'd like to know."

Giulia felt a surge of compassion for this ill-favored, ill-treated boy. "I can help you, if you like. I can show you how to draw better."

"You?" He practically spat the word. "Why would I let you show me anything?"

"Because you have some talent, if someone would only take an interest. Think about it."

She stepped out into the Calle del Fruttariol, closing the door softly behind her.

The San Lio church was open, and she paused there to say a prayer of thanks and to kneel before the priest and have her forehead marked with Lenten ash. Then she hurried homeward through the busy streets. *Homeward*—the word sang in her mind, for she knew now that she did not have to go away, that Sofia's house could truly be her home.

There was one more thing she had to do.

In her room again, she knelt before one of the wall chests, on whose lid a second sheet of writing lay waiting, identical to the one she'd given Ferraldi. Beside it was a blank sheet, a quill, and an ink pot. Nearby, the Muse leaned against the wall. Between last night and today, the crystal singing of her blue had fallen silent.

Giulia thought of Humilità, of the secret her teacher had guarded for so long—the secret that, even as it was revealed, became another secret, different for each person who possessed it. She thought of the oath she had sworn and had not been able to keep—should never have been tasked to keep. She thought of Sofia's words: *One must be strong to keep a secret. But stronger still, sometimes, to let it go.* She understood that now. In the understanding lay forgiveness, both for her teacher and herself.

And for another also.

She smoothed the paper, dipped the quill, and began to write.

To Maestra Domenica Arcello, greetings:

When I left Santa Marta five months ago, I took with me the recipe for Passion blue. Though it was bequeathed to me by Maestra Humilità of her own will, I believe now that it should not have been left to me alone. Accordingly, I am returning it, to you and to the workshop, exactly as she wrote it.

You should know that it will not only exist at Santa Marta. Matteo Moretti possesses it now, as does the painter who has consented to be my teacher. As do I. We will give it to the world, each of us in our own way, and Maestra Humilità will breathe again every time we do.

Giulia Borromeo

Giulia folded the letter and the recipe together, wrote Domenica's name and the name of the convent on the outside, and got to her feet. She'd ask Sofia to seal the letter and send it, along with one she'd written to Angela, letting her friend know, at last, that she was safe.

She went to the window, where the grayness of the day was brightening as the sun burned through the clouds. The window looked out onto the side of the house next door, but if she leaned close to the glass she could just see the canal, its waters sparkling in the rising light.

Beauty should not be allowed to die. Humilità had told her that, five months and a lifetime ago. But Giulia knew now that beauty must also be shared. It had no value if it was hoarded, closed up inside a secret like a miser's gold inside his counting room.

And suddenly she could feel it: all the beauty she would create in the years to come, all the splendor that would issue from her hand, burning in her like the light of a thousand torches, so intense that for an instant it seemed she must be consumed. Then the heat was gone, leaving behind only a tingling in the fingers of her right hand, which had closed as if to hold a brush. But the flame was still there. It would always be there.

The dull weeks of Lent lay ahead. But after them came Easter, with its promise of rebirth. She too had been reborn: no longer a bastard, an orphan, a servant, a novice, a runaway, a boy, but someone new. Someone she did not yet know, and would discover in the time to come.

Giulia breathed deeply. Then she turned to go in search of Sofia and Bernardo and tell them that she would not have to disguise herself again, would not have to call herself by any name but her own. That with her own true face, she would stand against the world.

Part VI

Epilogue

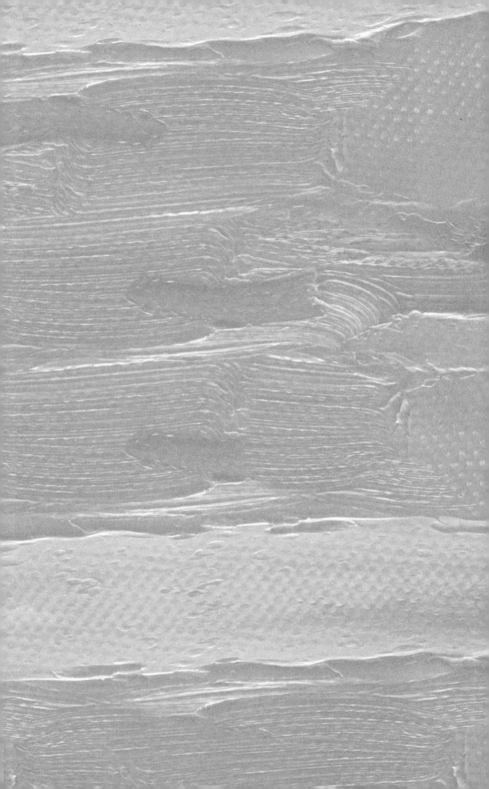

Rediscovering the Gamma Master:
The Art Sensation of the Decade

March 15 (New York)—One of the most talked-about exhibits of the past decade opened today at the Metropolitan Museum of Art.

Gathering together all twenty-four known paintings by the sixteenth-century artist known only as the Gamma Master— so-called for his habit of signing his paintings with the Greek letter gamma—the exhibit is the most comprehensive ever mounted of the work of this mysterious Renaissance artist.

Celebrated as a genius of color, especially the brilliant, glowing blue that is unique to his work, the Gamma Master is considered by many experts to be the equal of his more famous and much more prolific contemporary Titian. However, beyond the fact that the Master lived and worked in Venice during the first part of the sixteenth century, almost nothing has been discovered about his life, not even his true name.

Until four years ago, that is, when a Venetian estate sale yielded an astonishing find: a hitherto unknown work by the Master. Rolled up with several canvases by minor painters of the same period, the work's true provenance might never have been recognized had it not been for the sharp eye of art appraiser Fernando Foscari. Struck by similarities to the Master's style, Foscari bought the painting himself and subjected it to close analysis. In the process, the Master's signature was uncovered.

Far more sensational than the discovery of an unknown work by a significant Renaissance artist, however, is the work's subject: the Gamma Master himself—or, revising centuries of speculation about the Master's identity, the Master *herself*. For this work, a self-portrait, reveals that the Gamma Master was, in fact, a woman.

Only a handful of female painters of the Renaissance and Baroque period are known. While there has been reassessment of their work in recent years, most are regarded as minor artists. Whether their limitations sprang more from limited talent or from the restrictions placed on female painters of the time, is a matter of debate among scholars of art history. What's not in doubt is that no female artist of the period ever achieved the celebrity of the Gamma Master.

Now completely cleaned and restored, the portrait depicts a handsome, dark-haired woman of middle years seated before windows that open on a Venetian cityscape. She wears an elaborate gown in the luminous, intense shade of blue for which the Master is known, and in her hands she holds a book, turned toward the viewer. On the left page is written *Ego sum* (Latin for "I am"), and on the right page is the Greek letter gamma, the Master's famous signature. That signature is repeated in the painting's upper right-hand corner, along with the date, 1510.

"It's as if she's saying, 'Here I am; make of me what you will,'" says art expert Elizabeth Pratt, author of the book

Hidden Workshops: Female Painters of the Renaissance. "She wanted us to know her; everything in this painting is a clue. The objects on the table in the foreground—the horoscope, the necklace with the blue stone, the faces in the portrait sketches, the brushes and other painter's tools—all represent people and things that were significant to her. The well-appointed room suggests she had wealth. The white cloth beneath her foot may be a nun's veil, signifying that she left Holy Orders or was forced to take them against her will. It's also interesting to see that she wears no wedding ring. All that's lacking is her name. We know her face now, but we still don't know her name."

Asked why the Master might have wanted to conceal her name, Pratt speculates: "Perhaps to be taken seriously. Some female artists of the time did win recognition for their work, but many were forgotten soon after their deaths, and rediscovered only recently. The Master surely wanted her paintings to live after her; perhaps she knew that wouldn't happen if she was remembered as a woman. Though if that's so, the self-portrait suggests that she might have had second thoughts."

While a reassessment of the Master's work is already under way, it's to be hoped, in today's changed cultural context, that her reputation will only be enhanced by the revelation of her self-portrait.

The exhibit remains in New York until July, after which it travels on to Washington, Houston, and Los Angeles.

❖ Author's Note ❖

Every character in this book is a product of my imagination (including art expert Elizabeth Pratt). The one exception is Giovanni Bellini. Bellini was one of the greatest painters of early Renaissance Venice; over the course of his long career, he produced many wonderful paintings and altarpieces, including the famous altarpiece that Giulia visits in the church of San Giobbe (the altarpiece now resides in the Accademia in Venice). While I hope I haven't done him a disservice by making him skeptical of Giulia's artistry, that attitude would have been far more typical of the time than Ferraldi's.

Most of the locations in the book are real, including the great market square in Padua; and in Venice, the Campo and Salizzada San Lio, the Calle del Fruttariol, and the Rio dei

Miracoli. I've invented Ferraldi's and Sofia's houses, however; and the Convent of Santa Marta is also my own creation.

I visited Venice years ago, and it made an indelible impression on me. Much of what Giulia sees and feels reflects my own memories: the maze of canals and streets and squares, the breathtaking palazzi, the incredible vista of the Piazza San Marco, the sense of a city that exists in defiance of nature. And, of course, how easy it is to get lost if you go about on foot.

Venice is one of the most photographed and written-about cities in the world, and I found many books to assist me in my research. Two of the most helpful were the English edition of Umberto Franzoi's *The Grand Canal*, a photographic and historic journey down the entire length of the Grand Canal— much of which still looks as it did in Giulia's day—and Patricia Fortini Brown's *Private Lives in Renaissance Venice*, which gave me many fascinating details of the lives and lifestyles of wealthy Venetians.

I also relied heavily on the amazing map of the city created by painter and printmaker Jacopo de' Barbari. Published in 1500, it shows every street, canal, campo, and piazza in fifteenth-century Venice, and is so detailed that you can actually count the windows and the chimney pots of the houses. It helped me—and Giulia—find our way around the city, which in 1489 was both very similar to and quite different from Venice today. Barbari's map can be seen online at http://www.mcah.columbia.edu/venice/barbari_full_zoom.html, with a handy feature that lets you zoom in close and move around.

The recipe for Passion blue is based on instructions for making ultramarine pigment in Cennino Cennini's *Il libro del'arte*, a "how-to" book on the painter's craft written in the fourteenth century. Made from lapis lazuli—which was quite literally more valuable than gold—ultramarine was the costliest and rarest of all the paints in a painter's palette. I've added a few ingredients to Cennini's formula to help explain Passion blue's transparency and luster, including ground glass, which recent research has shown was indeed used by Venetian painters to increase their paints' light-reflecting qualities.

Last but not least, I hope Giulia's story will help give a voice to the handful of female painters of the Renaissance who stood against the prejudices and conventions of their time to follow their gifts, including Sofonisba Anguissola, who became a painter at the Spanish court; Lavinia Fontana, who received the patronage of two popes; and Artemisia Gentileschi, the first woman to be admitted as a member to the Academy of Fine Arts in Florence. Their work was nearly forgotten in the centuries after their deaths, but thanks to twentieth-century research, these long-disregarded artists are finally receiving the attention they deserve.

❖ Acknowledgments ❖

As usual, thanks are due to many people:

My wonderful editor, Melanie Kroupa, whose insight, skill, and meticulous attention to detail has helped this book become the best it could be. I've loved working with you, Melanie.

Everyone at Skyscape, for sending the book out into the world in style.

My former and current agents, Jessica Regel and Jennifer Weltz, who do so much on my behalf.

The Jean V. Naggar Literary Agency, the most savvy and supportive bunch of people a writer could hope to have on her side.

My mother, whose editorial eye has guided me through all my books.

And my husband, of course, who puts up with my writing-related crises and mood swings, and never fails to remind me, when I'm positive I'll never get it right, that I *always* say that. And then I carry on.

❖ About the Author ❖

 Victoria Strauss is the author of *Passion Blue*, praised in a starred review as "a rare, rewarding, sumptuous exploration of artistic passion" by *Kirkus Reviews* and selected a *Kirkus Reviews* Best Teen Book of 2012. Her fiction for adults and young adults includes *Worldstone* and *Guardian of the Hills*. She is also the cofounder of Writer Beware, a unique antifraud resource that provides warnings about literary schemes and scams. Victoria Strauss lives in Amherst, Massachusetts. Visit her at www.victoriastrauss.com.